AF324758

Captain Coranto

Captain Coranto

Julian Spilsbury

Hodder & Stoughton
LONDON SYDNEY AUCKLAND TORONTO

British Library Cataloguing in Publication Data
Spilsbury, Julian
    Captain Coranto.
    I. Title
    823'.914[F]   PR6069.P49/

    ISBN 0 340 40299 7

Hodder and Stoughton Editorial Office: 47 Bedford Square, London WC1B 3DP.

1

Captain John Shipton would have stood out in any circumstances from the group of four with whom he rode that morning on Hounslow Heath. He was half a head taller than any of his fellows, and with his lean face, blue eyes and the light brown curls that hung about his shoulders, had already that morning drawn one willing smile from the maid who had served them their morning ale. He had shown no interest in her, but had remained as though deep in thought. Indeed, what chiefly distinguished him from his companions as they rode slowly westwards was his manner. They seemed calm, almost totally indifferent to their surroundings, whereas he was distinctly ill-at-ease. Presently one of their number reined in and waited by the roadside; the remainder continued over a small rise to where, thanks to a neglectful parish, the bushes encroached onto the road. Here they too halted and took cover amongst the foliage.

It was an hour after dawn on a June morning in 1661, over a year since the return from exile, amidst general rejoicing, of King Charles II, and nearly six months since the return, almost unnoticed, of that same Captain John Shipton, who was now having trouble with his horse. Somehow his nervousness had communicated itself to the beast, for all of a sudden it broke from the others and trotted the few feet to the mud track which was the main road to Reading. Another of the group, a short stout man with a lined and weatherbeaten face and shaggy grey brows like an old terrier, spurred forward to join him.

"Come now, Jack!" he said, "this is not the way. You've seen worse days than this!"

Shipton turned. "Aye Noll," he answered, "many worse. But . . ." and here he continued half under his breath, "I fear I never did worse."

The older man looked for a moment as though he were about to say more, but decided against it and instead offered his friend a silver drinking-flask.

Jack drank deep, handed the flask back, and then drawing his pistols from their holsters began checking them for the third time that morning. Neither man cared to break the silence. Although the birds were singing now and the horizon was brightening the moon still loitered in the sky, as though she felt her light better suited to what was about to take place. Jack huddled down into his heavy military cloak and considered what lay before him; what had seemed so simple and sensible in the Dog tavern in Southwark four hours earlier seemed a dreadful thing now.

Noll started to say, "You're surely not thinking of . . ." when Jack turned to him and he fell silent. Although the younger man's hands were still shaking, his expression left no room for doubt. All further conversation was prevented by the return of the fifth member of the party, who appeared over the rise and trotted down to where they stood.

"One man on his own," he said, "about two minutes away. Looks half asleep."

Both now looked questioningly at Jack, who by way of an answer slipped a pebble into his mouth and adjusted his scarf until only his eyes were showing. Then, pulling down the brim of his hat, he turned his horse and rode back into cover with the other two close behind him.

Martin Wilkins, travelling to Reading, did not see his attacker until it was too late. He had made an early start and had high hopes of reaching Reading well before nightfall. Normally he would have avoided this stretch of the road but it had been a long night as well as a good one, and he was on the point of dozing, lulled by his horse's motion, when the man struck. The first he knew was of a thumping of hooves from just behind him, a hand grabbing his bridle, and a pistol clapped to his breast.

"Stand!" bellowed a voice in his left ear, and as he almost fell from his saddle in shock, he found himself staring into the face of a masked man, whose scarf revealed only his eyes. "Off the horse if you please!" said the man in a deep and garbled voice. Wilkins dismounted and swore under his breath. He should have known better; things had gone too well last night and he had grown careless. The masked man walked him back into the trees until he was pinned against one of them, and proceeded to search his pockets, keeping the pistol against his breast. Wilkins thought quickly; fighting was foolhardy even though he had a small pistol in his pocket – it was not worth the risk, especially as he could hear the sound of other horses, as well as muffled laughter from the bushes. Flight was impossible; his horse was probably faster than the highwayman's, but he would be shot down before he reached it. No doubt the man would have that too, as well as his watch and his twenty pounds. He cursed himself once more for a fool, but being a practical man wasted little time on this, and began instead to mutter to himself in piteous tones.

"This is it, then, this is the end. Martin Wilkins you are undone. What's to become of you?"

The highwayman, who had removed Wilkins' watch and pistol and was now assessing the weight of his purse, stopped and said, "Hush, Sir. Such a fuss! And over so trifling an amount. No more than twenty pounds I'm sure."

"Twenty pounds!" wailed the other. "Did you never read in the Gospel of the woman who gave more to the poor than any other, because she gave all she had? To take my twenty pounds, Sir, would be the most grievous of thefts since it is all I have. I am but a poor farmer. I am to be married in three weeks' time. What sort of figure do you think I'll cut in these clothes? My house is falling down about my ears, my cattle are blighted, my bride is but a poor girl."

The highwayman was frog-marching him back towards the horses now. "I implore you, Sir, have pity, if not on me, upon my poor wife." To his astonishment the masked man set him on his own horse and, fumbling in his purse, gave him ten pounds out of it before slapping the horse's rump and sending him on his way at a gallop. "God bless you, Sir, God bless you!" shouted Wilkins over his shoulder as he careered off down the hill, scarcely able to believe his luck. His previous night's winnings were halved of course, but if one had to be robbed it were better to be robbed by a fool.

Back on the hill the muffled laughter Wilkins had heard was muffled no more as Jack's companions crashed out of the undergrowth. Jack removed his scarf and spat out the pebble he had used to disguise his voice. His pleasure in the haul and the successful conclusion of what had been his initiation was diminished by the mockery of his comrades as they crowded around him. First to reach him, and laughing loudest was Tom Ratcliffe, closest in age and appearance to Jack and already his friend. He leapt from his saddle and still laughing, clapped Jack on the shoulder. It was nearly a minute before he could stop laughing long enough to blurt out, "The horse . . ." then subsiding once more. His laughter was infectious and even Jack smiled as he went on, "You should have taken the horse. It was better by far than your own, and in any case why let him race down to the nearest village and raise the hue and cry?"

"Not that he will," said Noll grinning down at them both, "since you saw fit to give him half his money back. He'll probably cut his losses and keep moving. God knows where he got the money."

"The cock pit probably or a game of cards," answered Tom.

"I'm but a poor farmer!" this was Dyer, dark and wiry like a Welshman, "how many poor farmers are there?"

Close behind him came Cole, round and red-faced but with the eyes of a sneak-thief; these two were never far apart. "If he was using the money to buy a suit of clothes," he sneered, "why was he carrying it *out* of London?" As the absurdity of the man's story dawned on him, it was Jack's turn to curse himself. Noll chuckled, "He gulled you Jack!"

"But I have ten pounds of his money!" protested Jack showing the purse. Noll smiled sympathetically, and patted Jack's arm, "Say rather, he has ten pounds of yours! Never mind. You'll soon learn to turn a deaf ear to that sort of tale, and better to learn sooner than later. The important thing is that you're one of our number now for better or worse. Now then, let's be gone."

In the Dog tavern in Southwark, from which the gang had set out for their morning's expedition, Jonathan Frost, the host, had been at work for some time. He sat behind a small inlaid table of virginia walnut, and entered figures into a book of accounts. Only honoured guests and business associates were admitted into these private rooms which formed such a contrast with the public part of the tavern. The Dog stood, or rather leaned, in Crooked Lane in the parish of St George's in the district known as the Mint. Like Whitefriars and the Savoy, the Mint offered its inhabitants shelter from the law and its agents. Sanctuaries under the long-departed monastic houses, they remained, by an anomaly in the law, outside the jurisdiction of any justice or magistrate and as such were a haven for debtors, card-sharpers, high-pads, low-pads, pimps and prostitutes. In the narrow streets outside various of these were already abroad. Soon some would come into the tavern's main room calling for their morning draught. None of this greatly concerned him however: he left most of the running of the tavern to his wife and daughter. Nevertheless he had a busy day ahead of him with several visitors to see and one small matter of business to clear up. Although he continued to work at his figures his mind was occupied with the five men up on Hounslow Heath.

Down in the kitchen Frost's daughter Jane and John Simmons the pot-boy were going quietly about their work. They were busier than usual; the new girl, Ann, had asked leave to make arrangements for her father's burial. Without consulting Frost Jane had sent her off and willingly taken her place for the morning. Now, stirring the mulled ale she looked over at John from time to time and smiled. Although it was cold at this hour before the fires had taken, they always loved these quiet times together, safe from her father's uncertain temper. He was kind enough to her, it was true, but her love for John, a love which was returned tenfold, incensed her father, who now lost no opportunity to persecute the boy. He had come in late last night having lost heavily at cards; no doubt he would be in a foul mood and would take it out, as usual on John. She decided that she would take her father his breakfast that morning.

In fact by the time his daughter brought him his anchovies and morning ale Jonathan Frost was in the best of moods; he smiled at her and sent her on her way with kind words. His breakfast finished, he returned to his books until the arrival of his first visitors of the day. This was his friend Mr Samuel Richardson accompanied by Captain William Harper, Master of the *Repentance*. They stayed for nearly an hour, discussing Richardson's plantations and Frost's investments in the West

Indies, to which Harper was bound in two days' time. After they had gone Ned Wicks and his two cronies (surly ox-like men known locally as Gog and Magog) had called in for instructions. No one knew in what capacity they were employed by Frost and few cared to ask. These three did not leave but lurked on the staircase outside when Frost's sixth visitor of the morning arrived. This was Tim Willis, leader of a gang of pickpockets who worked out of Southwark. He was a bright, engaging youth and he chattered gaily as he unloaded his impressive haul onto Frost's table: assorted rings and jewellery, silk handkerchiefs and gloves bordered with lace and gold and silver braid, four jewelled snuff-boxes and two gold watches.

Frost chuckled delightedly at the boy's chatter and seemed well pleased. "You go from strength to strength Tim," he remarked.

Willis thrived on flattery, as Frost well knew. "Nimblest fingers in the trade Mr Frost," he grinned, "and the sharpest wits too, saving your own of course."

He glanced cautiously across the table as he said this noticing how Frost seemed to dwarf the table between them with his deep chest and powerful frame. Normally even Tim's celebrated good humour quailed a little before Frost's dark intimidating presence, his pale grey eyes and pock-marked face. Today however, he seemed in the best of humours and when he chose, no man could be more charming than Jonathan Frost.

Emboldened by his warm reception Tim launched into a description of some of his more spectacular recent successes, illustrated where necessary with appropriate gestures from his slim elegant hands. In his excitement, and encouraged by Frost's smiles, he failed to notice the door behind him open on oiled hinges, and Wicks and his companions move up slowly behind him. His account was suddenly interrupted by Frost, who without changing his smile asked, "And what about the Jew in Hatton Garden?"

Willis gaped. "What?"

Frost's smiled remained fixed, "I said what about the Jew in Hatton Garden?"

"I don't know any . . ." began Willis, but Frost cut him short.

"Don't lie to me Tim. You've been cheating me. Thinking

you can get a better price from him. Trying to play us off against each other." Tim paled, but then Frost continued, "I'm not angry Tim. In fact I admire your enterprise."

Gradually Willis' confidence returned. He even managed a weak smile as he replied, "Well you have to play the market, Mr Frost. As a man of affairs I'm sure you understand that."

Frost smiled once more, "Of course I do Tim," he said, "but there are other things which are important too, such as keeping good faith." His face took on a sorrowful expression, then he shrugged and held up the purse for which Tim had been waiting. Tim reached forward, but before he could grasp the purse two massive arms reached over from behind and clamped his arm to the table. As he turned in shock, Wicks wrapped the folds of his cloak around the lad's head, laughing as he did so. Unable now to see or cry out the pickpocket was helpless as his other arm was held across the table in an iron grip.

Frost was on his feet now, all trace of a smile gone as he reached behind him for his black, silver-topped walking-stick. Loaded with lead it could shatter a brick if properly used, and Frost had used it before. It was all over in seconds; with four swift blows the nimblest fingers in Southwark were reduced to pulp. The boy swooned dead away.

"Earn your bread with those if you can!" hissed Frost as the others dragged the limp body across the floor. "Take him down the back stairs!" He threw the stick onto the floor where it landed with a heavy thud, and crossed the room to stand by the fire. After pouring himself a cup of sack from a bottle on a small table at the fireside, he stood for a long while staring into the flames with a smile of satisfaction.

His reveries were interrupted some twenty minutes later by a faint knock at the door, followed by the entry of John Simmons who stood awaiting his master's attention. Frost's face clouded. Here before him was a circumstance less pleasing. It would have to be that milk-sop boy of all people who disturbed his thoughts.

"Well, what is it?" he barked.

"M . . . M . . . Mrs Stanway," the boy stuttered. "She's downstairs and says you sent for her."

"Well show her up then," snapped Frost and the boy darted down the stairs. Frost scowled after him. No sooner, it seeemed, did he remove one thorn in his flesh than another made itself felt. That boy and Jane! That whey-faced wretch and his daughter! And when he had plans for an alliance with someone who had good connections in the city! Richardson had a boy, a horrid youth who took after his mother, but none the less Richardson's heir for that. Or there was Gilbert Hope's boy, set fair to become an attorney. No – something must be done now before it was too late.

Then an idea struck him. It was so simple and obvious that it was a wonder he had not thought of it before. As soon as he had finished with the Stanway woman he would hurry round and see Richardson and his sea captain; there was one last little piece of business in the West Indies that he wished to discuss.

Minutes later, Simmons reappeared and announced Mrs Stanway. Frost beamed and, brushing past Simmons, ushered his latest guest into the room. "Brandy for Mrs Stanway!" he shouted, and John Simmons flew from the room like a startled bird. The new arrival was a large woman in her fifties dressed in a scarlet gown laced as tightly as she could bear, and dripping with jewellery. A large diaphanous shawl barely covered a bust that had once been the toast of Whitefriars. She smelled of drink. As Frost drew her up a chair by the fire she simpered at him; her chins wobbled.

"How nice to be in your house once again, Mr Frost," she said. "Such a beautiful home you have." She settled into the chair. "I've always admired these chairs; so soft, so comfortable. Why, when I was a young girl, it was all benches and hard wood. I could have done with a bit of padding then. Mind you I've plenty of my own now!" She slapped one of her massive thighs and laughed coarsely. "No," she went on, "I was thin then, skinny as a whippet I was. Had to be, or I'd have starved. That's why I always say to my girls, 'You get fat, my girl, and you'll be out.' I always say . . ."

This monologue which Frost had borne with patience was interrupted by the entrance of Simmons with a tray which he set on the table. Not taking his eyes off Frost for a moment he backed towards the door. "Well, serve Mrs Stanway then!" snapped Frost. Simmons lurched forward again, poured a glass of brandy for Mrs Stanway, and once more attempted to back towards the door. He missed and bumped into the doorpost before fleeing downstairs.

Mrs Stanway smiled at the door. "Such a pretty boy; such gentle eyes. When I was a young girl I'd have fallen for him in a moment," she began, then stopped for a deep draught. Frost smiled to himself now at the thought of the boy, and allowed the woman to prattle on. Mrs Stanway continued with her reminiscences, content to enjoy the fire, the brandy and the sound of her own voice; no doubt whatever Frost wanted would emerge in due course. In fact Frost was thinking once more of the five men who were out on Hounslow Heath, and in particular of their new recruit. Which brought him back with a jolt to his present purpose. "Dear Mrs Stanway," he smiled, "how is Lucy these days?"

The sun had reached its height when the gang halted in a small copse to rest the horses. It had been a quiet day on the road, but none of them seemed greatly concerned, being content to lie around in the shade as old Noll continued Jack's education. What the old man already knew of the newcomer's past had created an instant sympathy between them, and as the others dozed or attended to their mounts Noll grew expansive. He told Jack of his own past: how he had started life as a herdsman in the north country, and had run away to join the Earl of Newcastle's forces after his master's cattle had been driven off by soldiers. Following the execution of the King and the collapse of the royal cause he had taken to robbery on the highway, at first confining his attentions to Roundhead officers and Puritans but later, as he put it, "casting my net a little wider". He had ridden with the famous Captain Hind (who had once tried to rob Cromwell, and had been turned off the cart at Worcester crying "Vive le Roi!"). Although he had never abandoned his life of crime he had always, he claimed, remained loyal to the Crown. In that cause he had shed and lost blood, as well as suffered the mockery that had inevitably attached itself to a Royalist who had had the misfortune to be christened Oliver.

The rest of the gang, who had so far punctuated Noll's tale with humorous asides of their own, fell silent as soon as he turned once more to the tricks of their trade. Jack had already noticed that, mock him as they may and frequently did, his word was law on all practical matters.

"Never pay a bit of notice to their tales of woe," repeated Noll. "If you do you'll starve. In my time in the profession I've become as flinty-hearted as a Scotch attorney, and the first time you feel the pinch of hunger in your belly, so will you."

Jack nodded as the man went on. "And another thing: forget all that 'If you please' and 'Dear Sir' nonsense. You won't impress yourself on the travellers that way. These are dangerous people you're dealing with; unless you put the fear of God into them they'll like as not stick you, or blow your brains out. Foul oaths, swearing and blasphemy, that's the way; let them think they're dealing with a desperate, God-forsaken fellow. Falsehood's at the bottom of our profession, Jack. We put it on like a cloak in the morning. How else can a runaway apprentice style himself 'Captain' and convince a man whom he has no intention of harming that he will shoot him dead for two pins?" Just then a large party of travellers passed by, strung out on the road for upwards of two hundred yards.

"You see Jack," Noll gestured towards them with his drinking-flask. "Experienced travellers. Moving in a large party and keeping well spaced out. If we attack either group the other will ride to their aid or, if we are too many, down to the nearest village for help. Why, even three or four men, if well spaced out, may pass as safely as a squadron. Remember also with people like that, that they have any number of hiding places. Look out for quilted doublets and waistbands, and search under the saddle and in their shoes and stockings." The travellers passed on unconcerned by the small party in the copse.

"Now as to giving back a portion of the money," said Noll. "It can be a good investment. It's well known in our trade that the very severity of the law often works against it. For though people resent you taking their money, many are reluctant to see you hanged for it, especially if you leave them a little to continue their journey. I've had friends of mine walk free from the county sessions because their victims refused to identify them, all for the return of a few shillings. Remember that if a traveller is robbed between sunrise and sunset it is the responsibility of the hundred to reimburse him at least half of what he lost – it makes little difference to him whether you are caught and hanged. Some will take time raising the hue and cry so as not to have your death on their conscience; others will cut their losses and move on. Which brings me to my last point for the moment – horses. Don't forget to look the horses over. Often they're a man's most valuable possession, and a fast horse may save your neck one day. You need a change of horses anyway from time to time as it's one of the few things you can be identified by. Never set a victim back on his horse. That's asking for trouble. Take the horse with you if you can't bear to shoot it (and many I've known who would slit a sleeping man's throat wouldn't shoot a horse) but whatever you do, slow your victim down if only for a while." In the course of this commentary Jack learnt a number of things which seemed obvious once he had heard them, and which quickly became second nature, but which he would never otherwise have thought of. It was clear that he was learning from a master at his trade.

The day was hurrying on and little progress had been made apart from the education of their new recruit, when Cole, who had been scouting the road to London, spurred back the hundred yards or so from the next rise and announced breathlessly "A coach, two coachmen, no postillion, coming towards us." Noll weighed the alternatives. A coach was always bound to be a risk for so small a band as theirs, but a coach meant wealthy travellers, and the sum total of the day's gains being Jack's ten pounds, he gave orders that they would attempt it.

Evidently the gang had worked together often, as each man knew his alloted place, and scarcely a word was needed from Noll to adjust their positions. Concealing themselves just below the rise they waited for the coach to appear, in the meantime slipping pebbles into their mouths and adjusting their scarves. As the coach breasted the rise they struck, coming from three sides at once. The coachman could see, as the coach rolled into the hollow, that it was hopeless to attempt flight, yet his eyes swept the horizon searching for an avenue of escape. With drawn pistols the gang slowly circled the coach like sharks around a foundering ship. As he drew near the coach Jack could see that the only occupants were an elderly gentleman and his slightly younger wife; Noll's gamble had paid off.

What occurred next, however, took them all by surprise. From inside the coach came the unmistakable sound of a flageolet playing a popular dance tune as the coach finally rolled to a halt in front of Dyer's levelled pistols. Noll, Jack and Tom drew closer to the side of the coach; what they saw inside filled them with admiration, for there sat the lady engrossed in her music, and the gentleman tapping out the time with his walking stick, both as seemingly unconcerned as if they were at their fireside. Jack glanced over to Tom in wonder at this display of lordly indifference; his friend's eyes betrayed the smile beneath his mask as he reached into the pocket of his riding-coat and produced a small flute. As the lady paused in her playing to glance out of the window, Tom took up the tune where she had left off.

It was their turn to be astonished now as, before Noll could say a word, Jack dropped from his saddle, strode up to the coach and pulled the door open. A look of fear crossed the lady's face for the merest instant, and vanished as swiftly as it came when, instead of a pistol Jack produced an open, gloved hand and asked, "Madam, will you dance?"

She hesitated for only a second before smiling slightly, inclining her head, taking his hand and stepping down from the coach.

What followed was like something from a dream as, surrounded by armed men, a lady and a masked man danced a 'Coranto' on the cropped grass of a hollow on Hounslow Heath. She danced well. So, despite his riding-boots and jingling spurs, did he, and the gang beat the time with their hands while Tom played, and even the lady's husband in the shadows of the coach smiled to himself. The dance over, all applauded as Jack escorted his partner back to the coach. Dyer stepped forward and reached out to grasp the pearls from around the lady's neck; she turned at once to Jack who caught Dyer's hand in a firm grip.

"My dear fellow . . ." he said, though in a tone that brooked no argument. Then turning to the lady, "A shame, I think, to prise such jewels from so fine a setting." She smiled at him, and the eyes flashed the same fire that had caused more than one duel some years earlier. Jack handed her back into the coach, and turning to her husband addressed him politely. "I fear, Sir, you have forgotten to pay the musician."

The man's voice bespoke cheerful resignation, "Not a bit of it!" he replied and leaning from the coach he threw Tom a weighty purse, which Tom quickly opened and examined before nodding in satisfaction to his comrades. "In which case, Sir," said Jack bowing low, as Dyer unhitched the coach horses and led them off, "we must bid you farewell." And mounting once more he led the gang over the rise and away, waving his hat with a flourish at the coach as he did so.

"Nicely done!" shouted Noll, laughing and shaking his head at the same time. "It seems there is room for manners in our trade after all."

"Surely the most elegant robbery there ever was," laughed Tom, and the others, even Dyer, joined in. "By the time they get home we'll have grown to twice our numbers and you'll have become the handsomest rogue that ever walked the earth."

It was already growing dark as they left the Heath, returning by a different route laughing and chattering like any group of weary, travel-stained gentlemen nearing their destination. Jack was in high spirits. His first day had gone well, he had put money in his purse, and earned the regard of his new comrades, a regard that was already starting to show itself in their changed manner towards him. The bantering of earlier in the day had given way to a new, more respectful tone. Noll was at the front of the group, reminiscing out loud about the Wars, when he became aware that Jack, who had been at his side, had stopped. He looked in the direction of the younger man's gaze then nodded in understanding.

At the top of a small hill beside the road stood a gibbet. The body, covered in pitch and bound in an iron frame, was swinging slightly in the breeze. A crow stood on top of the cross-bar preening itself contentedly; it looked sleek and fat. It was by no means an uncommon sight and Jack, like anyone else, had seen hundreds but this one he saw through new eyes.

"Government Signpost!" said Noll breaking the spell as they rode up to the summit of the hill. "Their way of telling us the law is working, but who's going to believe them? No need to worry about this one," and he stood in his stirrups to give the body a playful swing. "He's just one unlucky one out of thousands."

"And *we*," cried Tom, spurring his horse, "shall prosper!" and they galloped off together down the hill laughing and cheering like dragoons on a pursuit. The crow watched them until they were well out of sight then flew home unhurriedly.

2

It was quite late the following morning before Jack was up and about in his temporary lodgings at the Dog. The drinking bout that had concluded his first day at his new profession had lasted well into the night and left him with a throbbing head. Shortly after he had called for his breakfast there was a quiet knock at the door, and the serving-girl Ann entered with a tray. Jack merely grunted in reply to her greeting, and watched her as she crossed the room. She was aware of his eyes on her as she laid out the toasted bread, salted herrings and jug of ale on the table; Jack had taken an interest in her from the moment she had arrived at the Dog only the day after he had himself taken up lodgings there. With her slender body, dark brown curls and delicate features she had already turned a number of heads at the tavern, but what interested Jack most of all was her speech. Neither her accent nor her manner of speaking were of Southwark or anywhere like it, and she seemed strangely out of place there. It was this more than anything else that had attracted him to her, but his first attempts at familiarity had been but coldly received, and he was in no mood that morning for a further rebuff. Taking up her tray she turned to leave, but glanced at him briefly as though expecting him to say something. Instead he simply nodded at her, strode across the room and threw himself into a chair beside the fire.

She seemed to shrug and left without a word, passing Frost in the doorway as she did so. He, in contrast to his guest, seemed cheerful this morning. As he stepped into the room he smiled over his shoulder in the direction of the girl and then at Jack. Getting no response he advanced to the table, and at Jack's invitation poured two cups of ale, handed one to Jack and took a seat beside him.

"You've caused quite a commotion in the town," he said.

"Indeed! How?" said Jack without looking up.

"With your activities yesterday," said Frost. "The whole town seems to have heard of it. Everyone wants to know what kind of highwayman it is that dances with his victims. Do you know what they're calling you?" Jack looked at him and raised his eyebrows questioningly. "Captain Coranto!" said Frost, and Jack smiled reluctantly.

There followed a silence of some minutes. Frost endured this patiently – he was a patient man – and then began again. "They are wondering why such a fellow as this should take up such a trade and in such company."

"And so, no doubt, are you," continued Jack. Frost smiled and shrugged but did not deny it. Jack continued to gaze into the fire for some time, and then, just as Frost was about to give up and leave, began to talk.

"I *was* born into a gentle family," he said, "but all that remains of that family or its estate is what you see before you. We lost everything in the Wars." Seeing Frost begin to smile he turned on him sharply. "No doubt you've heard the same from any number of runaway apprentices or discharged troopers, but my story is true." He took a deep draught and continued. "My father's lands were in Yorkshire. He rode off to join the King at York in 1642 – I was just a boy at the time – and he was killed at Hessay Moor." He saw Frost frown. "Marston Moor you may have called it two years later. Of course the local Parliament men made it hot for us, my mother and I, after that. Timber-felling on our land; requisitions for their army. They spared us nothing, but we made shift as best we could. When the King came down with his Scots in '51 I took my chance and slipped away to join them. I thought I should be home again in a matter of months – it is nearly ten years now."

"You were at Worcester then?" asked Frost.

"Yes I was there. Sat my horse for most of the day, took part in one charge and then fled with the rest of them. I came away safe enough; the Ironsides were mostly looking for Scots and the King of course, and I looked too young to be a soldier. Since then it has been Holland, France, Spain and now the Dog tavern in Southwark."

"And your lands?"

"Bracewell has them now."

"Bracewell?"

"Martin Bracewell, one of our local parliamentary commissioners. He assessed the fines to be paid by local Royalists and made himself a good deal richer by buying up the lands of those who were ruined. My mother went that way and quite a few of our neighbours. She died five years ago I heard – living with her sister in the East Riding."

"So you never went back?"

Jack shrugged, "Bracewell would set his dogs on me, and that's one pleasure I mean to deny him."

Frost leaned forward and replenished Jack's cup, "But surely you have a case at law?"

Jack shook his head, "None at all. The sales were all voluntary as far as the law is concerned; they were confirmed by an Act of this Parliament. Oh, the King would no doubt like to help all his friends, but he won't risk throwing the whole kingdom into turmoil by evicting people from land they have held for years. He's here on sufferance as far as many are concerned, and he's in no hurry to go on his travels again. He'll leave well alone where he can. Which is why my return to England has been less triumphant than his."

Frost smiled once more. "But now at least you'll thrive, judging by your start yesterday. Two hundred pounds will keep you all well enough for a good while." Jack wondered how he knew that, but then, as he had just found out, there was something about Frost that encouraged confidences.

Frost stood and drained his cup. "Well," he said, "I have much to attend to. I'd almost forgotten my purpose in calling, which was to invite you to dine with me today."

Jack raised his cup and smiled in answer.

"Good," said Frost. "There will be one or two of my friends there, who you might like to meet. About one o'clock then." With that he left. Jack noticed how silently he moved for a big man.

For some minutes after this Jack sat and stared into the fire, lost in thought. This unburdening of himself to Frost far from relieving his mind had added to his unease. The previous day's events and the break they represented with all that had gone before still preyed on his mind. During his years in exile, however degraded his state, he had always had the comfort of knowing that he had acted in accordance with his father's principles and his own. There had always too been the prospect of reward when the King enjoyed his own again; within the last six months both these comforts had been denied him. He knew in his heart that if his parents had been alive now they would have utterly disowned him; and his only reward had been poverty and humiliation. The remembrance of this, only five days previously, was still strong. Having lost the last of his money to a card-sharp, he had been arrested by the Watch in the act of trying to kill him and carried off to Poultry Compter. Penniless in prison his fortunes reached their lowest ebb; he would have considered self-murder had not several of his cell-mates seemed likely to do the job for him, for the sake of the lace on his clothes. It was then that he had met Tom Ratcliffe. Tom had been picked up by the Watch on the same night. They had suspected him of being up to no good – in fact he was making his third illicit visit to the constable's wife in as many days. Respected and feared by the other inmates he had been blithely unconcerned by his predicament and straightway informed Jack that he had sent to a friend for money, and that he would have them both out of there in time for breakfast. Within the hour, having paid the appropriate amounts to the turnkey and the constable, they had started out for Tom's lodgings at the Dog, and by the time they arrived they had become firm friends.

It had been then that Jack had resolved never again to be dependant on another man's goodwill. He had finished with playing the suppliant, petitioning ministers, writing letters to former commanders and loitering at Whitehall and St Paul's. He determined that from that day forth he would do whatever he must to prosper. Hence his drunken decision on meeting Tom's friends two nights later to join them in their venture on Hounslow Heath. Jack looked over to the table on which lay his sword; ten years earlier he had drawn it in the King's cause – from now on he would draw it only in his own. His eyes lit on the full purse beside it and he smiled. It was not a happy smile, but the smile of a man grimly determined to follow the path he had chosen to wherever it might lead.

Further thought was prevented by the arrival of Tom, who burst into the room in a flurry of green silk, lace, ribbons and clicking spurs. He crossed the room without a word, and without waiting to be invited or bothering with a cup, drained the contents of the jug and wiped his mouth on his sleeve. He beamed at Jack. "Come on, stir yourself," he laughed. "We have a lot to do this morning. That purse of yours is full and you look like a scarecrow. I mean to put both right. We've the tailor, the barber and the wig-maker to see before dinner so get dressed."

Jack smiled as he rose and reached for his doublet. "I'm afraid I shall be dining with Frost today."

"You are honoured." Tom sat on the edge of the table resting an elegantly booted leg on the chair. "I don't think any of us has ever received such an invitation. I'll say this for Jonathan, mind. He can mark quality a mile off." He did not seem to mind in the least that he had never been invited to Frost's private rooms. He had started life as a Cooper's apprentice before running away to London, which had promised and provided better opportunities for good looks and an agile mind, and he was fully satisfied with how well he had done. Intended for a life of barrel-making, he lived instead in the style of a gentleman. He strode the town decked in the latest fashion, drank deeply, gambled heavily, and distributed largesse with a liberal hand. Unsurprisingly, he was welcome amongst those who were called ladies, and those who were not, and sported freely with both. This uncomplicated, generous soul revelled in his own good fortune and resented no other man's.

As Jack buckled on his sword-belt and reached for his hat Tom chuckled to himself. "So Frost's taken an interest in you?"

"So it seems," said Jack. "Before I knew it I was telling him the history of my life."

Tom laughed again, "You might as well do. He'll find out soon enough. Information's one of his most precious commodities; it's our lifeblood. That's why we all live close by. There's scarcely a thing happens in this city but he knows about it in an hour. He has business acquaintances and informants all over the town. If a wealthy citizen is about to make a journey Frost knows where he is going, when, what route he intends to take, and how much he'll be carrying. He knows the hostler of every inn from Ludgate to Posterngate, and no traveller with a heavy

portmanteau or carrier with a valuable cargo passes out of the
city but we know of it. If you want rid of gold watches or
jewellery he'll give you a good price for them, and if you should
want anything – anything Jack – he can provide.''

"A man worth the knowing," mused Jack.

"Well worth knowing," continued Tom with his accustomed
enthusiasm, "and this is a good place to live, as you'll soon
discover. The outside is rather shabby of course, but that's just
to throw strangers off the scent. Frost does well for himself and
for his friends and Margaret's cooking . . .''

"Margaret?"

"Yes that's Frost's wife. You haven't seen her? That's hardly
surprising. She spends most of her life in his kitchen. She's
Frost's second wife. The first – that was Jane's mother – was the
original owner of the Dog, but she's long dead.''

By this time Jack had thrown a light cloak over his shoulders.
Tom looked him over and grimaced. "Your case is more urgent
than I thought. Come on, there's no time to lose. We'll start in
Cheapside.''

After a morning spent amongst tailors and hatters, glovers and
bootmakers the two made their way through Ludgate in the
direction of Whitefriars, or more popularly 'Alsatia'. Tom had
taken it upon himself to familiarise Jack with those parts of the
city which might be useful to him in his new career. Like that
part of Southwark in which the Dog lay these seething
tenements were a fortress safe from the attention of the law,
whose occupants sallied forth by day and night to prey on the
pride, greed, gullibility, or plain weakness of the world outside.
By no means the only such Liberty it was the most populous
and provided Jack with a close look at this world which was
rapidly becoming his element.

To Jack the place looked like a town which was permanently
being sacked. Ragged children sprawled and bickered around
their slatternly mothers, patched and painted whores beckoned
from windows or lurked, affecting shyness, in doorways.
Toughs plotted in groups on street corners or in the seedy
alehouses drank the proceeds of their latest foray. There
was quality here too: tired, sad-looking gentlemen and their
wives and children, whole families thrown into debt by

fraud or misfortune, suffering with dignity and dreaming of the past or the future like exiled princes. Merchants flitted furtively, unloading or obtaining goods of dubious origin. Lawyers, scholars, and apprentices all went about their various businesses or negotiated with the dandified 'apple-squires' for the services of the women they lived off. Others like Tom with velvet cloaks and ostrich plumes, booted and spurred, swaggered in the middle of the street making way for no man – the aristocracy of this hellish little town within a town.

It was not long before Tom, declaring that he was "dry as a dog", stopped at a doorway in a side-street. He led Jack into a dingy alehouse, one of six in that street alone. Inside, once his eyes had grown accustomed to the gloom, Jack saw a sight which as a soldier for ten years was by no means unfamiliar to him. The small room was mostly taken up by a carousing group of whores and soldiers, who would occasionally send one of their number lurching over to the fire, where sat an old crone sucking at a clay pipe and doling out mulled ale from a copper vessel at her side. At the table in the far corner near a doorway which led deeper into the house stood the alehouse keeper.

As Tom and Jack took their seats at a table close by he was haggling with a couple of shifty youths about some silk scarves they were keen to be rid of and a quack doctor who was trying to pawn his watch. He was clearly a man who prided himself on his wit, and was displaying it now for the benefit of a claque of his friends who were seated at at table beside him. Unconcerned with all this Tom and Jack ordered a jug of ale and drank and talked for some time until all of a sudden Jack's attention was distracted by a burst of raucous laughter from behind him. The youths and the doctor had gone now, and the latest object of the innkeeper's wit was a young woman who was trying to pawn the contents of a wooden box on the table in front of her.

The girl who was the involuntary object of all this attention was facing the innkeeper across his table, and so had her back to the rest of the room. Jack could see that she was slender and of slightly less than medium height. The sunlight streaming in through the open door behind revealed her dark brown hair to be touched with red, and the blue dress she wore to be of fine quality but approaching its last days. Even so she had brought brightness into that murky room. When she turned for an instant to glance nervously at the jeering drunkards beside her Jack glimpsed a face pale and pretty with dark, arched eyebrows and green eyes beneath long lashes. It was Ann from the Dog. She did not notice Jack or Tom, however, but turned once more to the innkeeper. Unused to ribaldry such as this she blushed slightly as she spoke again, but neither this nor the note of entreaty in her voice seemed to affect the innkeeper who smirked back at her. Her voice when she spoke was so soft as to be almost inaudible.

"I had somehow thought that they would be worth more than that . . ." she faltered. "My father paid . . ."

"Well you *somehow* thought wrong my lady!" interrupted the innkeeper, and the fat pot-boy at his side sniggered at the way his master had aped Ann's accent and stressed the words 'my lady'. "One pound's all you'll get anywhere in the city," the innkeeper continued, suddenly growing weary of the sport. "And that's only if you throw the watch in." As he said this he indicated the watch the girl was holding in her left hand, obviously reluctant to part with it.

For a few moments the scene being enacted before Jack's eyes faded to be replaced by one from the past which he had trained himself to forget. He was standing next to his mother at the front of the house – his father had been dead for two years – he heard again the sound of timber being cut down in the valley, saw again Bracewell and his minions glaring down at them both from horseback, noticed how Bracewell's eyes wandered over the property in appraisal. He heard once more their voices and the phrases they mouthed – "That man of blood Charles Stuart . . . the wages of Malignancy" and worst of all he could hear again their mocking laughter as his mother pleaded for more time. The laughter in the room brought him back to the present.

Rising from his seat he crossed the room unnoticed by anyone save Tom, who followed him without a word. Ann was about to speak again when she noticed Jack, who by now stood beside her facing the innkeeper. Jack glanced down. On the table in front of him was a box which he now saw contained a set of surgeon's implements: forceps, a saw, spatulas and sharp-bladed knives. When Jack looked up again the innkeeper was regarding him with an expression which mixed hostility with a vague unease. Without taking his eyes off the other man's for an instant Jack reached down into the box and took out one of the knives. He held it up before the innkeeper's face, its point six inches from the man's cheek; the sunlight glinted on the blade. Jack's voice was level when he spoke, but the innkeeper had heard that tone of voice before and all his former confidence drained away like ale dregs.

"I think you are mistaken, my friend," Jack almost whispered. "Take a closer look at this blade: such craftmanship, observe its keeness. It could slice a man open like a peach."

There was silence in the tavern now. Some of the soldiers glanced over and then returned to their drink: it was someone else's fight. The innkeeper looked over to his friends' table for support and found none; under Tom's watchful eye they had developed a sudden interest in their ale and cheese. Beside the innkeeper the pot-boy stood as rigid as a sentry though his aspect was anything but martial. Jack's voice maintained its reasonable tone as he continued, "Perhaps you'd like to change your opinion." The man nodded, his eyes on the blade. "Three pounds seems a reasonable sum," said Jack. The innkeeper winced, but nodded once more, and with the careful movements of a man confronted with a venomous snake, indicated to the pot-boy to go and fetch the money. The boy scurried off just as Jack finished his sentence, "without the watch."

Within seconds the boy had returned and breathlessly spilled the coins onto the counter. Jack turned to Ann and nodded and she, after hesitating for a few moments, scooped up the coins and emptied them into her purse. Before Jack could say another word she muttered, "I am most grateful to you, Sir," and fled the scene, slamming the outside door behind her as she left. Jack just had time to see her glance over her shoulder at him as she did so. If he was surprised at this sudden departure he gave no sign of it to the others in the room, who remained as still as statues. Beckoning to Tom to follow, he too left after sticking the knife point first into the table-top in front of him, where its vibrations made the only noise to be heard in that room for several minutes. After they had gone the innkeeper stood leaning on the table for some time, his eyes closed, breathing hard. Then with a foul oath he swept the box and its contents onto the floor.

Outside in the street Jack was dismayed to find that the young woman had been almost immediately swallowed up in the crowd and that although he dashed from street to street for some time with Tom in hot pursuit, she was nowhere to be found. He had half expected to find her waiting for him in the street. Having thus come to her assistance Jack felt that he was at least entitled to more than the cold politeness he had so far encountered. He was anxious too to hear the story behind the pathetic little scene he had just witnessed. Clearly, however, she was as keen as ever to avoid him. Sensing his friend's frustration, Tom remained silent as they made their way back to Southwark, in the hope that Jack's mood would brighten, which presently it did. The sun was shining, he had a full purse, and the girl could wait; whatever her feelings towards him, she was now in his debt. He was smiling once more by the time they reached the Dog.

The clothes that Jack had ordered would not be ready for two or three days so it was in a suit of borrowed clothes that he arrived at the appointed hour outside Frost's chambers. Just as he approached the studded oak door it opened and through it rushed Ann clutching an empty tray. She was looking over her shoulder back into the room from which came the sounds of laughter and conversation, and in her haste she almost sent Jack sprawling to the foot of the stairs. Seeing him, she stood for a moment as though on the verge of flight, then realising that it was too late, greeted him civilly.

"What? Still in a hurry?" Jack smiled at her, "I thought you might have been about to take ship for the Americas, you left us in such haste the last time."

She seemed confused for a moment, then, obviously feeling that some explanation was necessary, she said, "It's not that I'm not grateful for your help this morning . . . the instruments were my father's. I needed the money to pay off what remained of his debts, and save his body from a pauper's grave. The best part of his fortune was spent on my mother during her final illness. By the time she died we were deeply in debt. He had nearly paid them all off, but the effort took its toll . . . he died himself a week ago."

Jack was about to offer some words of sympathy, but before he could she continued, "That's why, as I say, I am grateful . . . for my father's sake . . . But I cannot approve of the way it was done. Watching you with that innkeeper, I almost believed you would have cut him."

Jack was aghast. "I would have done and serve him right. What else do his type understand?" he almost shouted.

She shook her head sadly. "I suppose I have seen too much of that sort of thing. The last few years we have spent in Whitefriars, out of reach of my father's creditors. Many a night I watched him vainly trying to stitch together some young man such as yourself, cut to ribbons in a fight, the cause of which he would have forgotten if only he had lived long enough to sober up."

Jack was philosophical, "These times force hard measures upon us," he said.

The girl glanced down the stairs to the doorway of the main room where Frost stood chatting with his customers. "And bad company too it seems," she muttered.

This stung Jack to reply, "Mr Frost has already proved a better friend to me than many another." Instantly he regretted his pompous tone.

"Well, I wish you much joy of your friends!" she retorted.

Jack was angry now. "I should have thought you had reason enough to be grateful to him."

"Forgive me, Sir!" There was anger in her eyes now. "I forget my place. It ill becomes me to discuss my master's failings with those fortunate enough to be his friends!"

Jack was about to attempt some conciliatory reply, when the silence was broken by Frost at the foot of the stairs. He smiled up at them, "Ah, the Guest of Honour!" he said to Jack, and in the same breath, "You're wanted in the kitchen, girl, run along." Without another word to Jack, Ann swept down the stairs past Frost and away to the kitchen.

Frost followed her with his eyes and then turned once more to look up at Jack. "Dinner will be ready in about a quarter of an hour," he said. "I think the rest of my guests have already arrived so go on in. I have a small matter to attend to in the kitchen. I'll join you in a few minutes."

Jack stepped up to the door and tapped lightly on it. It was opened by John Simmons, who was himself dressed up for the occasion in a suit of borrowed clothes of which he seemed immensely proud. He ushered Jack into the room where Frost's guests were assembled and then rushed off to help Jane with the preparations for dinner. It soon became clear that this was to be no ordinary occasion; Jack had heard whispers of the style in which Frost lived behind the grubby facade of the Dog but had dismissed them as mere idle gossip. He now knew he had been wrong. Before Jack could do more than glance round the room and admire the hangings and furnishings Frost had arrived. He greeted Jack once more, and with great cordiality took him forward to join his guests. He looked for Simmons, did not find him, and so served Jack himself with hot punch from a silver bowl.

Jack thanked his host and exchanged a silent nod with Wicks, the only other guest he recognised. Wicks looked ill at ease; he found himself in unfamiliar surroundings, uncertain why he had been invited, and knowing no one except Jack, whom he did not like anyway. The other guests were an improvement on Wicks. Jack was introduced first to Mr Samuel Richardson and his wife. Richardson was a fat, florid man who wore his clothes with an aldermanic dignity though Jack noticed that his long silk waistcoat was well powdered with snuff. On being introduced he inclined his head and smiled as graciously as he could manage. Mrs Richardson, as fat as her husband, could have been taken for his sister. She was gaudily overdressed in a silk gown that did little for her; well into her third cup of punch she already seemed a little tipsy. The last two guests were two exceedingly handsome young women. The first was a pale red-haired girl by the name of Alice, who then and at all other times, Jack noticed, stayed close to Frost. Her companion, who in truth had caught Jack's eye the moment he entered the room, was a striking woman with jet-black hair and eyes of bright blue. She was dressed in a gown of blue silk with a white satin stomacher and her black hair was clustered about her ears in those small curls known as 'confidants'. She smiled as Frost led

Jack towards her. "And this," said Frost as she curtsied and smiled even more beguilingly up at him, "is Miss Lucy Luscombe. Lucy, this is the Captain Shipton I've been telling you about."

"Ah Captain," she said, her eyes widening. "I've heard so much about you. Jonathan tells me you were at Worcester. You must tell me all about it. Did you see the King there? And how did you escape?" Jack was no more susceptible to this kind of approach than any other young man in his situation, which is to say, he fell immediately. From that moment he had eyes for none but her and was gratified to find that she returned the compliment. His delight was unfeigned when he discovered on entering the dining-room, that she was to be seated on his right, he having the place of honour at Frost's right hand.

It was the dining-room that really confirmed the whispers that Jack had heard before. The room, warmed by a large log fire, was protected from draughts by brilliant and richly-woven hangings of wool and silk, decorated with hunting scenes, kings and queens from real and mythical history and flowers, birds and beasts of every description. A long dark wood table with beautifully carved spiralled legs stood in the centre of the room, covered with a tablecloth of Turkey work. The chairs were of a similar pattern and behind them against the walls were small inlaid tables covered with silver, Venetian glass, bottles of French and Spanish wine, and, far from the fire, bottles of Rhenish in silver bowls full of ice. The guests filed in with gasps of astonishment, and Frost received with pleasure the unspoken compliments.

On the heels of the guests came a small, dark, smiling fellow with a harp who, as the guests sat down, placed himself at the bottom end of the room and began to play. The music of the harp was clear, bright and fluid, and the whole scene seemed to Jack, as he watched the golden wine splash into his glass, like something out of some long-forgotten dream. The unlovely company at the bottom of the table faded in his mind to join the beasts and grotesques on the wall hangings, and his world became filled for the moment with Lucy to his right, Alice opposite and his fascinating host.

Frost was in his element as course followed course: dishes of oysters, stewed prawns and lobster, buttered eggs with anchovies, steak pie and herring pie, mutton and venison, and claret and Burgundy of the finest quality. Laughing, jesting and encouraging his guests to eat heartily, he seemed to be enjoying himself hugely. For Jack, to whom the memory of poverty and desperation was still sharp, the dinner was something of a celebratory feast. The beautiful woman at his side listened spellbound to his tales of adventure and reacted to his ill-treatment by the world with expressions of sympathy and outrage; the food and wine were exquisite and the music divine. The past and future melted away and he immersed himself in the moment.

Frost, a man of many surprises, had a few more up his sleeve. Instead of the vulgarity Jack had expected from a man of his type, he displayed a wide range of knowledge and interests. When Jack praised the quality of the wine he talked knowledgeably on the subject for some time, and Jack gathered from certain remarks that he had travelled in Europe. He showed a keen understanding of the politics of the day and was able to recount for Jack's benefit much that had taken place in the past ten years, though he was careful not to express any opinion. Nor had the intrigues of the Court escaped his notice, and he entertained Jack for some time with the goings-on there. He also proved a gifted mimic and took off both Tom and Noll to perfection. In short he proved the perfect host, cheerfully urging his guests on to further self-indulgence, enjoying the feast himself and willing and able to discuss any subject under the sun. The only subject he carefully avoided was himself, and Jack realised a few days later that he had skilfully and politely turned any question which might have forced him to reveal anything about his past life, or his plans for the future. No one ever knew more about Frost than he wanted them to.

The meal over, their palates were refreshed by tea, a new drink from China. It was served in the small red pots that had been sent over with it, and Richardson pointed out in awe that it cost two pounds a pound; Frost smiled and shrugged. Too polite to mention it himself, he was by no means averse to having it known. As the table was cleared and spiced Levantine wine was circulated, the harpist produced a flageolet and accompanied the guests in a number of catches and rounds.

By this time, Jack was, like everyone else in the room, gloriously drunk. Frost, after expressing the warmest regard for him, had turned his attentions to Alice, to whom such attentions were obviously neither unfamiliar nor unwelcome. At the end of the table Wicks was looking half asleep. Mr Richardson was in a world of his own, singing softly, and his wife was sound asleep, snoring loudly. Watching Frost and Alice, Jack wondered in his drunken state why it had not occurred to him earlier exactly what these two women were. Any doubts he might have had were dispelled moments later when Lucy leaned drunkenly over and whispered in his ear. It seemed that her lodgings were close by. Jack, no saint at the best of times, felt that it ill became him to point the finger at this young woman, who after all had to live, when he had lately taken to robbing folk at gunpoint. Taking Lucy by the hand, he made his excuses to Frost who, by now lewdly engrossed in Alice, waved his hand in farewell without turning his head. In a few moments he and Lucy were hurrying through the streets to her lodgings arm in arm.

Downstairs in the Dog in the spitting hell of her kitchen Margaret Frost heard the sounds of carousal from her husband's rooms with no regret. At least he was occupied and she was safe from his tyranny. The new girl, Ann, seemed virtually to have taken over the running of the kitchen, leaving her, for the first time in years, with little to do. Since she had married, her life had seemed to be one long round of drudgery, and she found it bewildering now, suddenly, to have time on her hands. Still, she would remain in the kitchen, keeping, as it were, an eye on things. John and Jane looked at her from time to time in sympathy; they too were glad of the respite. Although the work seemed endless, at least they were together. Here under Margaret's benign ineffectual rule they could talk together and even hold hands without fear of retribution.

By midnight, by which time only John Simmons was working, the sounds of revelry had died away. It had been a good day for John too; the dinner had gone well, he had made no mistakes, and had been allowed to wear that suit of clothes – the finest he had ever worn. If he had dared he would have whistled as he went about the few last tasks left to him. Apart from Wicks and his side-kicks in the downstairs room, everyone in the tavern was asleep. The master had gone out – his absence was always a cause for rejoicing on John's part – but it was the master who was responsible for his lightness of mood. It was all to do with his unaccountable change of attitude since yesterday. From never having a good word for him, the master had changed to smiling at him occasionally and even calling him 'John'. Instead of kicks and curses, which he had come to expect though never grown used to, he now received the odd nod of recognition or even a word or two of praise.

As to what could have been the cause of this sudden change of heart, he had no idea. Jane had tried in vain to intercede with her father on his behalf; perhaps Margaret had more influence with her husband than they had realised. John had arrived at the conclusion that he would never understand his master's sudden conversion, but was content to remain in ignorance and accept it with gratitude. Frost was to him like idols were to a painted Indian: arbitrary and terrifying beings whose mercy was to be hoped for, but whom it was impossible to fathom and pointless to resist. If Frost was better inclined to him now, it was the answer to the prayers of years, and he would show his gratitude by working harder and more cheerfully than ever. For the first time in his life the future did not seem as bleak as the past had been. Born in Bridewell of a whore and a sailor, both long dead, he had found at the Dog a home at least, and now perhaps a future. Perhaps the master's harshness had simply been intended to train him up properly, perhaps he *had* been idle in the past; if so all that would change. In a few years, it was even conceivable that he and Jane should, with the master's blessing . . . His thoughts were interrupted by Wicks, who lurched into the room.

"Mr Frost wants you out in the back yard." He stumbled out the words as he swayed in the doorway. "I'd cut along, lad, he looks mighty angry to me!" John rushed past Wicks without a word. As soon as he was past, Wicks turned and followed him out. In the yard, as his eyes adjusted to the dark, John could see the tall frame of his master standing by one of the outhouses with his back to him. John approached cautiously, wondering what he could have done wrong when he had tried so hard to please. His master turned, but it was not his master, though it was a face he recognised. From behind his arms were pinioned and a filthy rag was stuffed into his mouth; he tried to scream, but merely gagged and choked instead. A blanket was thrown over his head, but he continued to struggle; a desperate kick connected with a shin-bone. There was a yell and then something hit him across the side of his head and he fell limp. In the darkness three figures carried the bundle to a waiting hand-cart.

Quietly before dawn on the morning tide the brigantine *Repentance*, Master William Harper, slipped out of port headed for the Straits of Dover, bound for Barbados.

The time that followed seemed to Jack in retrospect to have been the happiest he had ever passed. The proceeds from the coach robbery had amounted to two hundred pounds, enough to enable them to live well for the next few months. At last it seemed, he was reaping the just reward of all his former sufferings. The all-pervading influence of Frost was on hand to open doors and smooth his way, and through his good offices Jack was able to obtain lodgings on the other side of the street from the Dog. Like the tavern the house was unprepossessing from the outside, but inside was as comfortable and well furnished as any gentleman could wish, and Jack rented it from a merchant on very reasonable terms.

Tom, who lived at the Dog with his mistress Eliza, viewed these arrangements with approval, for a firm friendship had grown between the two men. As soon as the money was shared out the remainder of the gang disappeared, Noll into the country, and Cole and Dyer deeper into the city. It was at Tom's urging that Jack encouraged Lucy to join him.

"As I've said before," Tom had said, "keeping a mistress accords with the spirit of the times; if we condemn it, we disparage the modes of the Court!" Lucy needed little persuasion to move in with Jack from her own modest apartments, and once they had settled they, in company with Tom and Eliza, set out to sample the pleasures of the town.

London was at that time newly released from the stifling rule of the republic, and with the return of the King had put on its joyous raiment. For a young man with money at his disposal and leisure to enjoy it, it was indeed the 'flower of cities'. The craftsmen of the city thrived on these four as they spared themselves no extravagance, be it velvet cloaks in the French style trimmed with lace, lace collars and boot tops, riding boots of Cordovan leather, and silver, star-shaped spurs, or for the girls, gowns of silk, fur muffs and masks of velvet to protect the complexion, hats and jewels and perfumes galore.

At the theatres, mingling in jostling crowds of toughs, jades and gentlemen, they ate, drank and wrangled whilst the actors tried to make themselves heard. As discerning as any, they hissed or cheered the action, applauded the dances and laughed and jested amongst themselves if the play grew dull. Sometimes they would see the King in the company of Barbara Palmer, whose husband had recently been created Earl of Castelmaine (and not for any services *he* had rendered) and Jack would reflect without bitterness that he too had met with better fortune now that his travels were ended.

Wherever they went they demanded music: fiddles, lutes, bagpipes and flageolets, and they sometimes danced whole nights away, going from stately galliards and corantos to 'Flaunting Two' and 'Petticoat Wag'. They were known and welcomed at the best taverns and ordinaries, and feasted nightly on princely foods and the finest wines. In the bowling alleys, cock fights and card games, they cheerfully gambled sums that would once have been the stuff of dreams without a thought for the past or a fear for the future.

Day in, day out, life was carefree and leisurely and devoted to acquiring new tastes and new experiences. One day they found a waterman willing to take them under London Bridge. Even after several months in London this was still a source of wonder to Jack. Above its twenty arches stood a street, poised above the roaring waters. Apart from the occasional glimpse of the river between the houses and the fact that the rooftops met overhead, one could have been in any street in the city. Travellers by river would get off at the Bridge, walk round, and catch another boat on the other side rather than risk the turbulent waters that rushed between its piers. Only a few daring souls and fewer watermen would risk 'shooting the Bridge'.

Full of Dutch courage they cheered and shrieked as the boat bucked and walls of white water rose around them, and the Bridge blotted out the sun as the piers shot past.

Then it was over and soaked and laughing they reached the steps below the Bridge. The waterman had argued about the fare and struck Tom and was kicked into the icy water for his impudence.

Later at the fair they had witnessed miracles: dancing dogs, a bull with five legs and a calf with two heads. They had watched the fire-eater devour hot coals and molten glass, and the rope-dancers from Italy use only their toes to climb almost vertical ropes and dance high above the heads of the crowd. Then during a laughable, bumpkin production of *Hero and Leander* they had watched with great delight a pickpocket relieve a goggling citizen of his watch.

Once they had gone to the Bear Garden and seen the dogs attack a tethered bull. They had cheered with the crowd as the bull tossed the mastiffs high in the air, and the butchers ran forward to catch the dogs and break their fall. Lucy had cried for the poor dogs and had been laughed at for it. Next day Jack bought her a spaniel, which he soon had reason to curse as it chewed his best gloves, but she loved it extravagantly and took it with her everywhere.

All their days, in short, were taken up with the pursuit of pleasure. The only dark cloud on this bright horizon as far as Jack was concerned was the continuing coldness, almost amounting to hostility, of Ann. This disturbed Jack for he felt somehow linked to her in misfortune; for all his present prosperity, this world was not the world into which he had been born and he found it possible to sympathise with her. Yet an early, painful attempt at reconciliation on his part was coldly received. It was plain she felt keenly her present degraded state, and she made even clearer her disapproval of Jack and the company he kept. However, Jack was not a man given to brooding, and the enchantments of Lucy eventually proving strong enough to turn his head once and for all, he resolved to leave Ann to her own devices.

After a while Noll reappeared, and Cole and Dyer began once more to hang around the Dog. Jack soon found that the money he had so quickly acquired and which had seemed set to last forever was rapidly dwindling under the dual pressure of his manner of living and Lucy's insatiable desire for furs and jewels. He had also discovered what the others already knew, that the highwayman pays dearly for his pleasures wherever he is known. Every tradesman from the tailor to the tavern-keeper was eager for his custom, but their prices were the higher for what they knew. It was hard to haggle over prices when the man facing you could hang you with a word.

3

It was Noll who first raised the matter that was on all their minds. "Soon be time for a little expedition, lads," he remarked one afternoon as they sat drinking by the fire in the down-stairs room of the Dog. The others nodded in agreement and waited respectfully for Noll to continue. He puffed at his pipe and kept them waiting. "We're all short of funds now, and some of you – " he gestured with his pipe at Tom and Jack – "look as if you need some country air."

The two grinned then Tom asked, "Where did you have in mind, Noll?"

Noll narrowed his eyes and watched the smoke of his pipe for a while before continuing, "Well, considering all things – that is the state of the roads, the time of the year and so on – my experience tells me that if we were to take the road to . . ."

"Reading!" interrupted Tom and all except Jack, who understood none of this, laughed.

"Yes, Reading," snapped Noll, reddening. "It's a well-travelled road in good condition much of the way; we know the routes . . ."

"And of course, a safe haven at the other end!" laughed Tom.

"Fresh air, country ale," added Cole.

"Watkin's ale, more like," said Dyer.

Noll scowled at this last remark, a reference to an obscene ballad of which Dyer was particularly fond. Dyer smiled unpleasantly; Jack felt that everything Dyer did seemed unpleasant. Dyer could have rocked a babe in a cradle and made it seem unpleasant. Noll had by now assumed his more familiar scowl, that remained even after the others had agreed on Reading and began discussing arrangements.

It was agreed that they should depart in two days time, and

39

as they began to prepare Jack quizzed Tom about the mirth with which Noll's suggestion had been greeted.

"Oh, he's got a woman in Reading. You must surely have heard of her, 'The Fat Woman of Reading'; we're always ribbing him about her. She's a farmer's widow with two grown sons. They run the farm and she runs an alehouse in the back room of the house. That's where he disappears off to. Actually he's quite right about Reading; it's a reasonable road and there's lots of profit to be made on it. After we've finished we can lie up at Joyce's (that's her name) until it all quietens down. We've done it a few times before. It's quite merry if you're fond of rustic pleasures!"

Later Noll had stopped by to view their preparations. He examined with approval Jack's new riding-coat and pistols and was particularly taken with one of his innovations. A few days earlier he and Tom had had their hair cut and had bought a variety of periwigs. As well as conforming with the very latest fashion it afforded them an instant change of appearance whenever it was needed. Noll seemed impressed and talked to Jack at some length of the forthcoming expedition.

"I think it is very important that you take notice of what goes on, Jack," he said, tapping Jack's chest with his finger. "This is one of the safest methods I know, but it requires you to keep your wits about you. No doubt you'll find it interesting as well as profitable and we usually meet with some merriment on the way."

The following morning they set off. Lucy bewailed Jack's departure until he was well out of sight, then paid a call on Mr Frost and, remembering that an officer of the Duke of York's Guards had smiled at her in the Park the day before, set off there immediately. The gang travelled in two parties, Tom and Jack forming one, Noll, Cole and Dyer the other. It was important that they were not seen together on the way out. At about six that evening Tom and Jack arrived at the Star Inn at Reading as 'Mr Walton and Mr Simpson on their way to Bristol'. The host had nodded and smiled at Tom in such a way as made it clear that they had met before. As the hostler led the horses round to the stables, Tom taking Jack by the arm said, "Come on, I like to see to the stabling of the horses myself."

The hostler was busy unloading their portmanteaux as they

stepped into the stable yard. He smiled a gap-toothed smile at Tom as he approached. "Well?" said Tom. The hostler smiled shyly and shrugged. Tom reached into his purse and produced two shillings which the man pocketed quickly and after looking round him leaned forward. "A tall man with grey hair. Wearing a red doublet and a beaver hat. On his way to London. His portmanteau was right heavy and it clinked, like. On his way to London . . ." he mused, but by this time Tom and Jack were on their way into the tavern. "Like to go to London myself one day." Indeed, he was to get his wish some twenty years later, having left his wife and children and the Star far behind him. One night, lured over a hedge by a whore in Spittlefields he was kicked to death and robbed by her and two grenadiers who were lying in wait.

Inside the inn, having been shown to their rooms by a smiling chamberlain who of course had been paid well, they were conducted by their host to a corner table in the downstairs room, where Tom ordered a shoulder of brawn and some hot claret with sugar and cinnamon. The remainder of the company in the room had already eaten and were about their private concerns. A recruiting officer snored drunkenly in the fireplace, slowly spilling ale onto his breeches. Two huddled farmers conversed in low tones; an elderly Puritan peered through his spectacles at a commentary on St Luke, and near the door a quack and a peddlar were arguing noisily about some point of astrology. It was not difficult to spot the man the hostler had been talking about: he was sitting near the fire drinking and staring into the flames, seemingly in want of company.

Tom leaned across the table and whispered, "The host tells me he is an attorney on his way to London from Bristol. As soon as we've finished we'll move near the fire and try to engage him in conversation. Remember, act as though you suspect him."

It was nearly three-quarters of an hour later that the two rose from the table, called for another jug of wine, and moved their chairs near the fire. They nodded a greeting to the man and then proceeded to talk between themselves quietly. Tom speculated on the state of the road and the time of their arrival in Bristol. At the mention of this city the attorney stirred and said, "Excuse me, gentlemen, I could not help but overhear that you are on your way to Bristol. I've just come from there myself. It's a fine town, is it not?'' He spoke with evident pride. Tom was hesitant, almost rude, but replied, ''Yes, so we have heard. This will be our first visit.''

The other spoke lovingly of the city, its fine walls, splendid merchants' houses and thriving commerce, and sensing the suspicions of the two travellers was keen to introduce himself. ''My name is William Sanford, attorney. I am a Bristolian by birth, but I practise in London. I have been visiting my brother in Bristol on some business over our late father's estate.''

It was Jack's turn now to take a hand in things. He appeared to warm to the attorney and introduced himself and Tom, claiming that they had business with a merchant in Bristol. They were understandably vague about the nature of their business, an attitude that served to reinforce the attorney's view that they suspected him of being a highwayman. He was eager to prove his good faith and so offered some advice. ''If you're going to Bristol, avoid Marlborough Down; it's a great favourite with highwaymen.''

''Indeed, Sir,'' said Tom. ''You seem to be well acquainted with the ways of that brotherhood!''

''Only by the nature of my profession, Sir,'' replied the exasperated attorney, ''And because I have travelled that road before.'' Tom, however, continued to look at him strangely, which led him to further confidences.

''I've as much to fear from the likes of them as you have,'' he whispered confidentially, looking carefully round the room as he spoke. ''I'm carrying fifty guineas. Only twenty in the portmanteau, though; the rest about my person and under my saddle. I always rearrange it just before I arrive at an inn though, because you can't trust these hostlers.''

''You surely don't mean . . .'' began Jack.

''Take my word for it,'' smiled the attorney. ''Biggest set of rogues alive. In league with all thieves for miles around. Take it from one who knows!''

''Well, we shall certainly follow your advice in that case, Sir,'' said Tom.

''It's certainly worth your while,'' replied the other, gratified. ''Most of these highwaymen are neither very thorough nor possessed of any great deal of wits. So if you are robbed they'll like as not take what's in your portmanteau and miss the rest.''

The two expressed their gratitude and asked the attorney to join them in more wine, an offer he cheerfully accepted. They talked for two hours or more, the attorney amusing his companions greatly with his tales of the criminal world of London, before they all retired to their several beds. Minutes later, Tom and Jack crept back down the stairs and crossed the room to the main door. The room was empty now, except for the recruiter who was still sleeping in the fireplace. Half an hour later on the stroke of midnight at a prearranged site near the town square, they met up with the other three who were staying at another inn on the other side of town. Despite the cold weather they were all looking flushed and from their stumbling speech it was clear they had drunk deep.

"God, he took some plying," said Noll. "We posed as discharged soldiers on our way home and invited him to drink with us. He's no mean drinker. Anyway, he's on his way to Marlborough; he'll be taking the Newbury road and he's leaving at six. You couldn't mistake him; he's about thirty, six feet tall and riding a grey. He's dressed in black, wearing a low-crowned castor hat with a gold hat band. He should be good for about twenty according to the chamberlain. What have you got for us?''

Tom described their attorney in as much detail as he could, adding that he was taking the southerly route via Bracknell to avoid Maidenhead thicket, and not omitting to mention the hidden thirty guineas. "Well," said Noll, "it's no night for standing around, and we've all got an early start to make. See you both tomorrow night at Joyce's.''

By five thirty the next morning three of the guests at the Star inn were astir, and having breakfasted on egg possets, went out into the stables to collect their horses. The two gentlemen bound for Bristol thanked the attorney for his company and advice the previous night and wished him good luck on his journey. Then with fond farewells on both sides, they set off in opposite directions. As good as his word, the attorney headed south to avoid the notorious Maidenhead thicket; if he knew one man who had been robbed there he knew a thousand. He chuckled as he rode along at the thought that those two travellers had suspected him of being a highwayman himself; he was quite flattered in a funny sort of way that they should think him capable of such a thing. He was rehearsing in his mind the story he would tell his wife about that comical pair and their absurd suspicions, when there occurred the incident which actually did form the basis of his talk that night and many another besides. They never gave him a second in which to resist or run. There were three of them, heavily cloaked and masked and they knew their business well. As well as taking his portmanteau they removed his saddle and subjected him to a hurried and undignified search before making off with every penny he possessed and his watch and snuff-box, not even leaving him his horse. As he splashed down the wet track, towards Bracknell, cursing his ill-luck, he remembered with irony the advice he had given that pair at the inn the night before. He hoped they had had better luck.

They had. Their man had been the first along the Newbury road and reached the copse where they had taken their stand at about six thirty. He was exactly as Noll had described him and, a tribute to the strong heads of their companions, he was still quite befuddled as they bundled him off his horse and frog-marched him into the bushes. A thorough search revealed twenty-two guineas, the most part concealed in the quilting of his doublet, for which they damned him for a rogue, and a gold watch, which they left him.

Having put a good deal of distance between themselves and their latest client, they slowed down to a walk; nothing could appear so suspicious as two men galloping across country. Tom suggested they made for Marlborough and then returned towards Reading by a different route. "The Watches are mostly decrepit old men in these parts," he said, "but there's no point in pushing our luck. Still, since we have most of the day before us, it would be silly not to do a little business as we go along."

"If the others meet up with our attorney," said Jack, "we should have quite a nice little haul at the end of the day."

Joyce's alehouse was typical of hundreds the length and breadth of England, though renowned locally for the quality of the ale she brewed in her own brew-house at the back of the farmyard. The sight that greeted Tom and Jack as they passed through the yard may not have been much to Tom's taste, but to Jack, born and brought up in the country, it was a sight to gladden the heart, a vision of a vanished Arcadia. The floor of the room was flagged and covered with fresh rushes, and in a large fireplace well hung with pewter, highly-polished copper vessels hissed and steamed and several unidentified birds sizzled on a spit. There were three tables and benches in the room, and several more out in the yard. At one of these two earnest graziers sat savouring their ale and saying little; at another sat Cole and Dyer already well drunk. Over in a corner two greyhounds were eating from a dish. Near the fire, sitting on an oak settle, was Noll with a pot of ale in his hand, talking to two youths and looking happier than Jack had ever seen him.

He welcomed them warmly to the alehouse as if it had been his own, and at a nod from him one of the lads rushed off to fetch two more tankards of ale. This ale when it arrived proved worthy of the reputation that had preceded it, and Jack could not remember having tasted any as good since the days of his childhood. The two lads, Mark and Peter, were Joyce's sons, but were introduced to Jack with such evident pride that he was tempted to wonder if they were Noll's as well. Certainly, they seemed to regard him as a father, laughing at all his jests, attending to his needs, and listening with unfeigned pleasure to his tales, however preposterous. They proved agreeable company, and Jack took great pleasure in talking with them of country affairs, of dogs and hunting. Nothing would suit them, on the other hand, but to hear of London, and of their adventures on the road, for the nature of Noll's profession was clearly no secret here. They continued talking and drinking for some time until a loud exclamation sounded from deep within the house and from its dark interior emerged a large, smiling matron with open arms who, bustling across the room with a swish of skirts, proceeded to greet Tom like a long-lost son.

Her entrance seemed to transform the whole room; suddenly everyone in it was smiling, and even the two dour graziers brightened a little and began to talk to one another. She was Jack noticed, as she continued to hug and kiss a slightly embarrassed Tom, very much as he had imagined her from Tom's description. Her round, plump face glowed red with health and mirth and she had a kindly look in her eye. It was clear that she had been a beauty in her youth and, despite her bulk, was not unattractive now. Having finished at last with Tom, she turned her attentions to Jack, though of course less effusively, to his great relief. "I've heard much of you, Jack," she said. "Noll tells me you have a wise head on your shoulders. You'll no doubt need it with this crew, most of whom have puddings for brains!" and so saying she dug Dyer, who was slumped over his pot, sharply in the ribs. For an instant Jack caught his breath; he had seen someone do this to Dyer once before in London with dire results. To his amazement Dyer simply grinned and took another pull at his ale. "I don't know why I bother with them, any of them," she went on as one of the dogs came up and nuzzled at her hand. "They're none of them worth it, least of all these two!" and she gave the boys a look that belied her words.

"Come on you two, attend to our guests," she said, cheerfully cuffing one of them. While one refilled the tankards, she and the other produced within minutes a meal that was simple but exquisite: pullets roasted on the spit, bread still warm from the oven and – a great luxury for a townsman – butter. All fell to greedily, even Tom, who prided himself on his delicate palate, and a sort of silence fell on the room.

Scarcely had they finished when a great clamour arose from out in the yard. It was compounded of the squeals of excited children, loud discordant singing and hoarse cheering, and turned all eyes in the room towards the door, where the two graziers had already stood up, about to leave. Joyce on the other hand did not even bother to look, but clapped her hand over her eyes and, chuckling in spite of herself, cried, "Oh no! I suppose they were bound to come here!" and rose to greet the new arrivals.

Outside were as ragged a collection of vagrants and vagabonds as Jack had ever seen. There were upwards of thirty of them, men, women, and children, and even babes in arms, and they seemed for the most part to be well drunk already. Despite the cold and the sparsity of their clothing, they seemed in the best of spirits. Joyce turned her head towards Noll and the others and said by way of explanation, "I have let the barn to them for a penny each; I should have guessed they would turn up here at some stage." Her sons immediately rushed off to get more cups, for it was clear that this assembly had come to drink. As they did so the company disposed themselves around the yard, inside the room, and even on the floor, and continued chattering and bickering amongst themselves like so many rooks in a rookery. From amongst their midst emerged a tall, one-eyed man in coarse clothes and a brown cloak, who bore himself with great dignity. As he approached her Joyce smiled. "You're welcome here," she said, "as long as you keep this rabble under control; if you don't, I'll have the Watch up here in minutes and have the lot of you whipped clean out of the parish!" It was an empty threat, and the man's smile showed that he knew it to be so. From under his cloak he produced a fat truncheon bound with brass. "This'll keep order here, mistress, never fear," he grinned. "Now, your finest ale if you please; we have cause to celebrate."

At this all the band began cheering as Mark and Peter dished out cups of ale. Joyce led the leader over to Noll's table; he followed her with a stately tread, as though he considered this no more than his due.

"This parcel of rogues have been ravaging the country for miles around," she said, "and this is their . . ."

"Upright man!" interrupted the other, grinning.

Joyce shoved him with her elbow, a thing few others would have dared or got away with for, beggar or no, this was a dangerous man. "Away with you!" she cried. "Spare us your peddlar's French! I'll thank you to speak plain English while you're under my roof!"

The man sat down at the table without waiting to be invited, and accepted the ale which Joyce gave him with a nod and a smile. "As the good lady has told you," he began, "I am the colonel of this ragged regiment. I am called Jacob. I direct their foraging, making their dispositions, appoint their officers, decide when we make camp and where . . ."

"And plunder them as they plunder us!" said Joyce. "Whatever of theirs he wants, anything at all mind you, he takes."

He smiled. "It is my privilege. But look around you, see the dreadful case of these poor unfortunates, blind, lame, crippled, orphans, some thrown into destitution and beggary through no fault of their own. They stand in need of a king to direct their affairs."

Joyce interrupted him. "No fault of their own be damned! There's not one of them ever done an honest day's work or ever tried. And as for being lame, crippled and the like, why most of them are as sound as my two boys and will like as not outlive the lot of us. Save your tales of woe for fine ladies and tender-hearted kitchen maids, Sir; your band are nothing more or less than a band of thieves!"

Jacob smiled slyly then said, "In which case, mistress, we be in good company!" This drew general laughter, and Noll to call for more ale for this fellow, whose wit was much to his taste.

"Is it true," asked Dyer, "that the womenfolk are all yours for the asking?"

"Why, certainly!" replied Jacob, unabashed by a question that the others may have wondered about but would not have asked. "My court is no different from any court in Europe, with this exception – that all its members live like kings."

"How so?" asked Dyer.

"Well, consider," said Jacob. "Are we not, on our progress around the country, received at all the best houses? Our food is prepared in the rich man's kitchen, our money is kept in the rich man's coffers, he directs his servants to attend to our needs when we wait at his door, and is proud of himself for having done so."

"But are you not ashamed to beg?" asked Tom, who had listened to all this in silence.

"Beggary or robbery, why is one more shameful than the other?" countered Jacob, casting a look around the members of the gang which brought a few wry smiles.

"But there *is* a difference," said Tom. "No man who calls himself a gentleman would . . ."

"Ah, but *I* never did!" said Jacob, and gave Tom a curious sideways glance that brought a blush to Tom's cheeks and eventually a reluctant smile. Jack leaned over to whisper something in Noll's ear, but before he could, Jacob interrupted him. "You are wondering perhaps, my friend, how I come to know so much about you all?" Jack nodded. "It's not difficult," he explained. "When my band of scavengers scatter over the countryside they act as my eyes and ears, and then like birds they fly back to their master and whisper in his ear. There's not much goes on anywhere that I don't get to hear about sooner or later."

Jacob half turned in his seat and began to point out certain members of his band. "They're quite an accomplished crew," he said proudly. "Whatever your little weakness, they can play on it. Moll there could tell you a tale of how her house caught fire and her husband and two children and every worldly possession were consumed. She could bring tears to the eyes of the most heartless among you. If a madman's antics are more to your taste, Tom o' Bedlam there – " and he indicated a near-naked fellow with a garland of roses about his neck " – will dance and caper for a whole half hour before telling you piteously of the cruel treatment he received in the madhouse before he ran away. Or if you're not at home, he'll come to your door and act dangerous, till your wife or maids give him money to be rid of him. Martin over there knows the name of every local commander in the late wars, on both sides, and can quickly convince any man that he served under him, or his brother, or his cousin, or tell some widow of the wounds he received at the side of her late husband. Will there can raise hideous sores on his body with crowfoot, spearwort and salt, and could make the soundest among you seem at death's door. And while all this is going on at your front door, there'll be others at the back, hooking any linen you've put out to dry, or slipping one of the little ones in through a narrow window to see what he can filch. Is it any wonder that we thrive?"

"Or any wonder that you're chased out of some parishes as soon as you appear?" said Joyce.

"Well, at least *you* have nothing to fear from us, mistress," Jacob replied. "As I have said, today is a day for celebration, and – " he looked around at his companions who had by now been carousing for some time " – I think it's about time we started." At this he stood up and walking into the centre of the room, bellowed for silence, which fell immediately.

"My friends," he began. "Let us prepare ourselves to welcome a newcomer into our midst!" and at once the entire company began to cheer, and with much back-slapping, one of their number – a young man in the clothes of a farm-worker – was led out into the yard. Joyce and her sons, Noll and the gang followed them out, fascinated. The beggars had by this time formed a sort of hollow square in the yard, and stood awaiting Jacob. He, before gracing them with his presence, politely explained to his hostess and her friends that what they were about to witness was the acceptance of one John Fletcher, a former ploughboy, into their company, to whom as a token of his favour he was going to give one of his women in marriage. As Jacob stalked majestically into the centre of the yard, a rather drunken, but nonetheless extremely embarrassed young man was thrust out towards him accompanied by much ribaldry. Jacob held up his hands for silence, which again fell at once. He held out his hand to receive the brimming tankard of ale which was proffered and holding it above the young man's head, pronounced as follows: "I, Jacob Colvin, by virtue of this sovereign liquor, do stall thee, John Fletcher, to the rogue. Henceforth it shall be legal for thee to beg for thy living in all places!" A great cheer arose from the assembled multitude as he poured the contents of the tankard over the head of Fletcher. Scarcely had the cheering stopped, however, than a young dark girl, pretty but dirty, and by no means unwilling, was pushed into the centre of the square. Jacob took her and Fletcher by the hand, and for the first time smiled at them both. As he did so a dead fox was brought out into the open area in the middle of the crowd, and laid at the feet of the couple. Everywhere the beggars were recharging their cups to toast the pair as Jacob led them forward and placed them each side of the dead animal. They held hands over its body as Jacob asked them, "Do you both solemnly swear to be loyal and true to each other and this company until death carries one or the other of you away?" They both replied, "We do!"

"Then I, Jacob Colvin, do pronounce you to be husband and wife!" He had hardly time to finish the sentence before the whole crowd with a great cheer closed in on the couple and raising them shoulder high, carried them into the house once more.

As they all filed back into the room, Joyce complaining about the stench of the dead animal and sending Mark to dispose of it, Jacob approached them. "Well, my friends," he declared, "now you have been privileged to see what few who are not of our fraternity have seen. Do any of you fancy joining our number? You've seen how easy it is, all you need is my blessing,

and I think our life may suit some of you." He was looking at
Dyer, who was greedily eyeing some of the beggar-women.

"I think we can do well enough in our own way," said Noll,
to which Jacob nodded and shrugged. Now various members of
the group had produced fiddles and flageolets and were
dancing, and within a short time the whole of the room and the
yard outside were filled with the most motley collection of
dancers ever. A passer-by could have been forgiven for thinking
that the citizens of hell had broken out and were making
holiday here above. For here were beggars and cripples,
madmen and urchins, several gentlemen in silks and fine lace,
and eventually even the alehouse keeper and her two sons
jigging and leaping, kicking and hand-clapping to a series of
country tunes scratched out by a vagrant orchestra. Somebody
did pass by, it seems, and alerted the Watch who arrived
shortly after and, after a few words with Joyce, leaned their
staves against the wall and joined in. Thus, as it were, granted
the sanction of the law, this extraordinary gathering continued
well into the night lit by a bonfire which was quickly built by
Mark and Peter as soon as darkness fell. As the music and the
dancing tailed off people snored where they fell or lurched into
the house to find a space amongst the bodies that by now
littered the floor and the tables and benches. A few could still be
heard as dawn broke, stumbling through the words of a song.

> Of all the brave birds that ever I see
> The owl is the fairest in her degree.
> For all the day long she sits in a tree,
> And when the night comes away flies she.
> T'wit t'woo to whom drinkst thou? 'Sir knave
> to thee!'
> This song is well sung I make you a vow
> And here is a knave that drinketh now!
> Nose, nose, nose, nose, and who gave thee that
> jolly red nose?
> Cinnamon and ginger, nutmeg and cloves,
> And that gave me this jolly red nose!

4

The next day the army of beggars moved on, and shortly afterwards Tom, Cole and Dyer made their farewells and headed back to London. To Tom's surprise, Jack elected to stay on in the country for a little while longer. In truth he had found this place much to his taste and wished to enjoy its pleasures as well as the company of Noll and the two boys for a few days more. "Tell Lucy I shall be back soon," he said to Tom as he left. "I don't imagine she's too lonely there without me!"

For the next few days Jack threw himself into a manner of living which he had not known for many years, and rediscovered delights he had utterly forgotten. In company with Mark and Peter he hunted the hare following the baying, deep-mouthed hounds over frosted fields and through tangled copses thick with bracken. They shot rabbits and birds and Jack found to his surprise that he had not lost his boyhood skill with bow and arrow. One day he set up a mark in the field behind the house and he, Noll and the boys took turns to shoot at it with pistols. Jack was always careful, however, in what he encouraged the youths to do, for Noll watched over them carefully, as though afraid that they would be tempted to follow him. Indeed, if he had given them any encouragement, they would in all likelihood have done so, but although his profession was no secret at the farm, there would often come a moment when Noll's storytelling was in full flood, that Joyce would say "Enough!" and Noll would nod in understanding.

However much Jack might have enjoyed his brief idyll in the country, the city and the delights it offered to a man with money exercised a stronger influence. So after promising Joyce, who had grown quite fond of him, that he would pay them another visit soon, he too returned to London. Noll stated his intention of returning to the Dog in a few weeks. "The better weather's coming on, Jack," he said as Jack mounted his horse. "People will be taking to the roads in greater numbers soon, and we would be foolish to lie idle at such a time."

On his return to London, life continued much as before. Lucy sulked a good deal on his first arriving back at their lodgings. Tom had been back for nearly a week, she said, why had he delayed and left her all alone here? In fact, as Jack had suspected, she had been far from lonely in his absence but her sulks and pouting were enough to drive him to further acts of extravagant generosity, which had been precisely their purpose. In no time, decked in new gowns of silk and sweetened with a necklace or two, she was her old self again. Jack did not resent her infidelity or the money he was required to spend to keep her. He was by nature a tolerant and easy-going man, and reasoned that he had little right to begrudge her money which he had obtained so easily, and which she could, ultimately, be said to have got from him in a manner more honest than that by which he had acquired it. If it was a sad and demeaning thing that he was forced to earn his living by robbery, was not her fate equally unhappy? Although each professed undying love for the other, both were fully aware of the truth of their situation, and, like many another, made the best of it.

As good as his word, Noll returned after about three weeks; Frost was bringing news of increased traffic on the roads and of the movements of various wealthy citizens. He had proved as useful as ever in the disposal of goods acquired on the Reading expedition, about which he seemed to know a great deal more than any of the gang could remember telling him. Despite his usefulness, they had all learned to hold their tongues in his presence; he had been a good friend to them in the past in so far as a highwayman could be said to have any true friends, but he remained an unknown quantity. Eventually, when the wine had circulated the table once too often one of them was bound to talk a little too much, and wherever that was, Frost heard it.

Be this as it may, his information service was faultless, and if his prices were high his clients lived well. It was while they were enjoying a particularly fine old hock at the Dog that Frost dropped in to inform them that a ship of the line had put in at Chatham and that a number of sailors was due to be discharged. It was immediately agreed that such a body of men could offer rich pickings as they could be expected to be carrying as much as two or three years' wages.

The following day upon Shooter's Hill had proved most fruitful. Whilst waiting for the expected sailors they had stopped a parson, who in ringing tones had called the wrath of the prophets on their heads and called down upon them every curse the Old Testament had to offer, and had been warmly applauded by the whole gang for his efforts. Next they had waylaid an ingrosser of corn who, despite his pleadings of poverty and lamentations over the imagined fate of his wife and children, had proved to be worth one hundred pounds. A stout, grey-haired gentleman whom they had seized just before midday had bemoaned the fact that he was not twenty years younger, and upon being quizzed by Noll, proved to be an old Cavalier. He was immediately set once more upon his horse, restored to his money, and offered a drink to His Majesty's health from Noll's flask, which he accepted. Then with cries of "Vive le Roi!" he was sent on his way unmolested.

Despite the fact that the day had gone well enough so far, there was nonetheless no sign of the sailors. It was already turning darker when over the horizon from the direction of Chatham there appeared a solitary rider who, from his garb and peculiar style of horsemanship, could only be a sailor. To say he rode awkwardly would be grossly to understate the case; his horse, presumably hired that day at Chatham, was a good deal too small for him, but even so he appeared to be having difficulty controlling it. It seemed unlikely therefore that this was the lead scout of a larger group, as however bad his companions might have been, they would surely have caught up with him. In Jack's experience though, as he was quick to remind the others, sailors were a commodity best handled with care. They let him cross a good stretch of open ground so as to be sure he was alone before accosting him. He was too surprised to resist, and flight was clearly out of the question. Cole searched him, producing sixty-five pounds from a purse at the sailor's belt. To everyone's surprise he came out with no sailor's oaths nor dire threats of revenge, but remained calm and reasonable throughout.

"Gentlemen!" he began, and the gang, seeing that the coast was clear and having decided that this would be their last robbery that day, sat back in their saddles to listen to his story. "The money you have just taken from me is all I possess in the world. I have a wife and children who are awaiting my return; that sixty-five pounds is three years' wages for me. I am a proud man and scorn to beg, but I implore you, spare an honest sailor who has earned his pitiful wages in the service of the King."

After appropriate expressions of sympathy and regret, Tom asked the sailor to dismount from his horse so as to avoid the necessity of shooting it under him. "Not the horse as well!" he exclaimed. "Then I am truly ruined! What is to become of me? I can't go back to sea, nor do I care to go back . . ."

"The horse, if you please!" interrupted Tom with a wave of his pistol. The downcast sailor stepped from his horse and seemed for a moment to consider his next words carefully. "If I am a ruined man with nothing to lose, why, may I not join you? I must confess myself greatly in love with a profession where I can earn as much in five minutes as I have in three years at sea. Gentlemen, I don't begrudge you my money; take it as an earnest expression of my good intentions, but take me with you wherever you are going. I may not yet be the best of horsemen – " and at this the whole gang laughed, " – but I am courageous and resourceful and a quick learner. You'll find me a good comrade, a man who'll stand by his friends. Accept me, I beseech you, as one of your number, and I promise you you'll have cause to bless the day you took Francis Blacker into your midst."

By now this garrulous young man had caught the interest of Noll as well as amusing the others by his turn of phrase and comical manner. After all, they were always on the lookout for new recruits; this fellow seemed sincere enough in his intentions and it might be worth trying him out. Jack was in favour, so was Tom, as they huddled together on horseback and discussed the strange business that had suddenly arisen. After all, Tom reminded the others, what had they known of Jack when they first took him into their number, except what he himself had told them? Noll had heard of such a thing happening before, when a gang's number had been augmented by one of its victims who had turned out to be one of the best of them. Cole and Dyer had not the wit to decide one way or the other, nor were either of their opinions much regarded by the others, so it was agreed that this Blacker should be accepted into their number.

They turned and approached the sailor who had been anxiously awaiting the result of their deliberations. It was Noll who spoke, as was the custom on matters concerning the running of the gang. "It has been agreed that you shall be accepted into our number. We are making for London this evening, and tomorrow you shall begin your apprenticeship in the noble profession of a scoutmaster of the road!" Then with a great deal of hand-shaking and clapping of backs the newest member of the gang was welcomed by his comrades. As it was growing late it was agreed that they should split up into groups and return to the Dog by separate routes. Noll and Jack, would form one group, Cole and Dyer as usual another, and Tom would bring Francis along, "and no doubt regale him all the way with accounts of his doings on the road," said Noll, as they moved off.

As they approached London, Noll's spirits seemed to rise and he became expansive, which he seldom did with anyone but Jack. "Well, we may not have met up with many well-laden sailors, Jack, but today's takings have been good enough, and we have got something more valuable in the long term than the money we took: a new recruit. We need greater numbers; that coach we took on your first day was a risk, and anything that size always will be as long as we remain so small. To tell the truth, neither Cole nor Dyer are much use and I wouldn't trust either of them if things went wrong. This new fellow seems to be the sort we need; he's a bright lad, could mix well with the travellers, gain their confidence; that's the way to succeed at this game. If we could get a few more like him, and get out of Frost's way . . ."

"Surely Frost's invaluable to us all, Noll," said Jack. "Without his eyes and ears we'd . . ."

"We'd have to find things out for ourselves, or simply take our chance on the road," continued Noll. "It would be perfectly easy to do. We've become lazy, that's all, too dependent on the likes of him. And the likes of him have a way of not letting go. Of course he and I are friends, but I don't trust him an inch, and he knows it. Even you, with your free-spending ways, must have noticed how much we pay for everything at the Dog."

"Well, we have to pay him somehow for the information he gives us," offered Jack. Noll smiled. "If you think that's what we're paying for, my friend, you're sadly mistaken."

It was intended that supper at the Dog that evening should be a festive meal to celebrate the arrival of a newcomer. Frost of course showed a great deal of interest in this matter and immediately began plying Noll and Jack with questions about Blacker.

"You'll see for yourself when he gets here, Jonathan; I presume you'll be able to join us at the table?" said Noll. So it was that about half an hour later those three, with Cole and Dyer who had just arrived, were sitting around the fire in that same small room in which Jack had first met them, when the sounds of footsteps on the stairs announced the arrival of Tom and Francis. All rose to greet the latest arrivals when the door flew open and in stormed Tom. Mud-spattered and swearing he stumped over to the fire, grabbed Jack's cup, drained it at a draught and immediately refilled it before throwing himself into one of the chairs and staring into the flames. "Where's Francis, and how did you get into such a state?" asked Jack, leaving aside for a moment his friend's ill-mannered behaviour.

"If I knew where he was, I would already have killed him!" growled Tom, by way of answer, and continued to glower into the fire.

"You mean he . . ." began Noll.

"Yes he did!" shouted Tom. "And he took my horse, sword and pistols to boot and, before any of you laugh too loudly, he ran off with all our takings for the day!" Tom's exhortation was futile however, for despite the loss of the money all his companions had begun to snigger.

"Tell us what happened," said Jack.

"About half an hour after we set off, Blacker began asking me all sorts of questions about the life he was about to enter. I, thinking this as good a time as any to begin his education, started to tell him some of the tricks of the trade, as well as recounting for him some of our adventures on the road. I painted for his imagination the easeful life he would lead and the excellent provision he would be able to make for his wife and family if he still had a mind for such things.

"'When shall I start?' he asked me. 'Why, first thing in the morning,' says I, suspecting nothing. 'We'll need to get you a horse more suitable of course, but you can borrow one of mine until you can afford one of your own, which I promise you won't be long.'

"Well, I wasn't to know, which you would Cole you muttonhead, if you had searched him properly, that he had a small gun about his person, which, as soon as I had finished speaking, he produced and stuck into my ribs. 'I thank you,' says he, 'for the offer of the loan of a horse tomorrow, but I fear I cannot wait till then. If I am to embark on a life of thievery I might as well begin right away.'

"What was I to do? There was no doubt but he intended to kill me if I offered any resistance so, in short, in a matter of minutes he had possessed himself of all I had as well as one hundred and fifty pounds. Of course I appealed to his sense of honour, and reminded him of his promise to stick by his friends. 'And so I shall,' he says, 'those I count as friends, but I should sooner stick by the devil as by the likes of you. Now on your way, and think yourself lucky I haven't marched you into town to be hanged, which is no better than you deserve. And take care I don't see you again or I shall shoot you like the dog you are!' So I had to walk all the way to the nearest village and try and borrow a horse. The parson there could see I had been robbed and was all for raising a hue and cry; I had the devil of a job persuading him not to. How could I explain to them that I had been robbed by a man I had robbed myself not an hour earlier?"

He stared gloomily into the fire once more and in the silence that followed his tale the others looked from one to another before bursting into helpless laughter, as much at Tom's telling of it as at the content of the story. Only Tom was not laughing; his anger welled within him before exploding, and before anyone could prevent him he had launched himself at Cole, whose negligence he considered to be the cause of his misfortune and humiliation, and clutching him by the throat, wrestled him to the floor. Dyer had drawn his sword and Jack had pinned him to the wall with the point of his own before the others had managed to separate the two on the floor. They stood up, Cole spitting out a tooth as he did so. Thus a day which had begun so promisingly ended in discord and bitter recriminations, as Cole and Dyer stalked off into the night not to be seen again for several days, and Tom retired to his rooms to sulk.

It was some days before Tom could be induced to see the funny side of the affair. The loss of the money was not so much of importance to him as the damage to his self-esteem, but it was pointed out to him by Jack and Noll that they had all been taken in by the sailor's protestations of goodwill, and that he had just been unfortunate in being the one who had gone with him. Cole and Dyer returned after a few days and an uneasy truce was patched up, based more on mutual need than upon any real amity. It was Frost who provided a postscript to the whole incident which after a while made even Tom laugh. It came in the form of a leaflet that he dropped without comment on the table where they were drinking one morning. It read:

Any gentlemen who were robbed on
Shooter's Hill
on
the fourth day of April
may come to the Red Lion at Watton
where, upon satisfying MR FRANCIS BLACKER
that their case is genuine, they may retrieve
whatever of their goods and money remain.

"Perhaps you ought to go, Tom!" said Noll.

The gang lay low for some weeks after that particular little debacle; but as money was short they were severely tempted when, one afternoon after he had been out visiting friends, Frost came to see Noll with a tasty piece of news. "I've just come from Richardson's house," he said, "and ran into a friend of mine who has heard that Sir William Beamish is going the rounds of his friends in town today. It seems he is leaving for Devon tomorrow. This friend of mine knows that I am fond of such morsels as this, so he passed it on to me. He's a wealthy man, this Beamish, but he's liable to have a few servants in tow. I merely mention it," and with that he moved on and went to see how Margaret was doing in his kitchen. Noll took Jack aside and together they pondered the matter. He had taken of late to consulting Jack in everything the gang did, not only because a friendship had grown between them, but because he had a great regard for this young man's judgement.

"What do you think, Jack? It's a tempting proposition though the risks are high." Jack thought the thing over carefully before saying, "I think we should leave it. We can do well enough without taking risks. Let's wait until we can increase our numbers. We got off lightly with the business of Blacker. He saw all our faces; we could have ended up on the gallows. Let's not tempt fortune."

Noll was still uncertain. "But a chance like that does not come our way every day. With the money we stand to grab from such a prize we could last for months. If we take them quickly we should get away with it; we've done so a dozen times before. I think we should attempt it."

Jack nodded. "You're the leader. You're the one with the experience; if you are satisfied that we can get away with it, that's good enough for me." The decision was announced to the others, and preparations began immediately. It was agreed that they should start out early the following morning; Noll told each member of the gang their dispositions and that he would assess the situation as the coach came by. The signal to attack was to be the discharge of a pistol in the air. If there was no shot they were to remain in their places and let it go by.

The western end of Hounslow Heath had been selected by Noll as the place affording the most cover, and by seven the next morning they were all in position. They were to use the same formula as usual: Tom would cover the two coachmen, Cole and Dyer would deal with any mounted servants, and Noll and Jack would get the passengers out of the coach. An hour passed in fretful waiting; everyone was on edge and even the horses seemed nervous this morning. Several travellers went on their way unaware of the danger that lurked either side of the track, before the expected coach appeared.

There were two mounted servants following the coach and two coachmen up top. In many ways it was simpler than their last coach because of the lack of a postillion. The coach was moving rather faster than Noll would have wished; the coachman being an old hand was keen to get clear of this bushy area as quickly as possible, but nevertheless Noll pointed his pistol at the sky and fired. No sooner had he and Jack broken cover than the coach was wreathed in smoke and a split second later they heard the report of the passengers' pistols. There was little danger of their fire being accurate, thrown around like that in the back of the coach, but the very fact that it was so unexpected served well enough. Tom's horse shied and both Noll and Jack reined sharply as they saw the two mounted servants deploy to the right and one of the coachmen drop to the ground, levelling at them. Way over to the right they could see Cole and Dyer making off in the direction of London as fast as their horses would carry them. Noll wasted no time. "Leave it!" he yelled. "Get out!"

Jack turned his horse's head and galloped off, swallowing the pebble in his mouth as he did so; to his right he could see Tom plunging down a steep bank at breakneck speed as he himself crashed through the undergrowth in blind panic. For a few moments he was back at Worcester; the smoke, the panic, the sound of pistol balls buzzing past his ear like wasps, and then the confusion and the fear of pursuit. Then he realised that there was no pursuit and, steadying his horse down to a trot, he looked around for Noll. There was no sign of him. From the direction of the coach he could hear excited shouting and the awful realisation swept over him.

Without thinking he turned again and gained the edge of the covert. What he saw there made his blood seethe. Noll's horse was lying kicking out its last agony, and the two mounted servants were dragging Noll between them over to the coach where the passengers, two men and two women, were waiting. All were laughing in relief and triumph, and one of the mounted men, laughing still, struck Noll across the face with the barrel of a pistol. At that moment Jack stopped thinking and instinct took over. Shouting he knew not what, he emerged from the covert at the gallop, firing his pistols as he came. The passengers, taken completely by surprise at this new assault, scattered and dived for cover around the coach; the mounted servants who were dragging Noll just had time to turn open-mouthed when Jack was upon them. Turning his empty pistols in his hand he clubbed the nearer of the two from his horse and threw a pistol into the face of the other, who was attempting to draw his sword. As Noll tried to pull himself into

the vacant saddle, Jack closed with the second servant who had
now got his sword clear and, before he had time to use it, Jack
served him as he had served his companion. Noll, stunned from
his fall, was still hanging suspended between the horse and the
ground. The coachmen and the two male passengers had by
this time recovered from their initial surprise and were running
towards them. Jack leaned over and grabbing Noll by the belt
heaved him into the saddle and the pair of them galloped once
more to the safety of the trees.

It was fortunate that the travellers, flushed with their
victory, had not bothered to reload their pistols; the two were
able to make their escape unmolested and galloped away hell
for leather across the rough country to the south. They put a
good ten miles between themselves and the scene of their defeat
before stopping to rest in a small wood where Noll bathed his
wounds in a stream. Apart from being shaken by his fall, and
having a cut on his forehead where the servant had struck him,
he was unhurt, and he gasped out his thanks amidst a torrent of
curses and self-reproach.

"You were right, Jack; I should have known it was too risky.
Everything was against us, what with the servants being armed
to the teeth, and Cole and Dyer scuttling off like that as soon as
they saw the way things were going. God! When I catch up with
them, I'll . . . I'll . . ."

"Calm yourself!" said Jack, removing his pistol ball from his
coat tail.

"These things happen from time to time."

"I'd be on my way to Tyburn now if it wasn't for you, Jack.
I'll never forget that," Noll went on, quieter now.

"I didn't think," replied the other. "If I had thought I
wouldn't have done it."

Noll smiled at his friend. "That's not true. You came back;
none of the others would have done, not even Tom." He paused
for a moment before saying, "I think you should take over as
leader. I'm getting old and sloppy. You could see it was a bad
risk and not worth it; I should have done, would have done
once. It's time I moved over."

Jack waved his remarks away. "You're just annoyed because
it went wrong for once. There's no one on the road today with
your experience."

"We need more than just experience. We need a proper leader, aye, and some better men too. If we're to survive and prosper we need new recruits and proper leadership. Men will follow you, Jack, where they wouldn't follow me. You take over; I'll be your right-hand man and then see how much better things'll be. I was only leader in the past by default, Tom being too young and the other two too witless. It's not just today; it's been on my mind for some time, almost from the day you first arrived."

"Let's talk about it some other time," said Jack, and with that they mounted and continued on their way to London. As they rode off, Noll was still muttering to himself and shaking his head. "You wouldn't have had to do that twenty years ago, Jack," he said. "You wouldn't have had to heave me into the saddle either." Jack shook his head. "You only got caught because you stopped to fire your pistols to cover our retreat while Tom and I just ran for it!" But Noll would not be consoled. "Twenty years ago you wouldn't have had to run for it."

They rode on in silence for some time before Noll said, "I hope Sir William Beamish pays his servants well."

5

It was in the tavern several days later that the issue was raised again, this time in the presence of Tom. He had returned a couple of days after the event, relieved to find that his comrades were safe, but horrified to hear that it had been necessary for Jack to rescue Noll. As soon as Noll had finished his account of the affair Tom had launched into a bitter bout of self-recrimination. He felt he had abandoned his friends and was determined to punish himself severely for the crime, despite the assurances of the others that they bore him no ill-will. "I gave the order to run," said Noll. "There is no need for you to reproach yourself."

"I didn't know you had been taken, Noll," replied Tom. "If I had I'd have come back too, as God is my witness."

"We both know that," Jack reassured him. "Forget the whole thing ever happened. What is important now is not the past but the future. Obviously things cannot go on as before. We need to make changes; we need new men, and we're going to have to rely on you as never before, Tom. Cole and Dyer finally proved as useless as we all knew them to be, and we need better men than that. I want you to start thinking of men you know who might be suitable. Noll here scarcely knows anyone in London, and I am still a comparative stranger, so it's amongst your friends and contacts that we must look. And when the new gang is formed I want you to continue as treasurer."

Tom gaped for a moment; he looked from Jack to Noll and back again before saying, "Forgive me, but *you* want me to . . ."

"That's right," Jack interrupted him. "It was Noll's idea. He wants me to take over the running of the band, and I have agreed to do so."

Tom looked once more to Noll who nodded in such a way as

to indicate that he did not wish to discuss the matter further. It never took Tom long to make up his mind. "Well, it suits me well enough, Jack. And if Noll is happy about it, that's good enough for me."

"I've had it in mind for some time," said Noll. "Almost from the day Jack joined up with us, and nothing I've seen since that day has changed my mind. I'll be at his side to give advice of course, but from now on he makes the final decision, and his word is law."

Tom raised his cup to Jack in salute. "Here's to our new leader!" The other two smiled; it had been easier than they had anticipated. They raised their cups in acknowledgement and the decision was confirmed, like every other in the gang's history, with drink. Jane, who had been attending to the other occupants of the room, namely Wicks and his ever-present cronies Gog and Magog, was called over and a bottle of her father's finest Rhenish wine was ordered to seal the agreement. As she bustled off, Jack followed her with his eyes; since the sudden disappearance of John Simmons she hardly ever seemed to smile. She was unrecognisable now as the bright chatty creature who had been so popular with the customers at the Dog when he had first arrived there. By the time she had returned with the wine, Tom had begun to consider the matter of new recruits.

"There are one or two I can think of who might prove reliable though not all are in the business at the moment." The others shook their heads to indicate that this did not matter. "Then there's Hugh Jeffrey; he's always worked alone up to now as far as I know, but we've been sort of friends for a couple of years now. He might be agreeable to the idea of joining us if it were put to him in the right way."

"You bring him to us and I'll deal with him," said Jack. "But only if you're satisfied that he is suitable." Tom was in truth greatly pleased with this display of confidence in him by his friends, which was precisely what Jack intended, and soon became his old self again, putting behind him his earlier self-condemnation. Within half an hour he was sufficiently recovered to offer, "What about Blacker? He's an accomplished thief. Why, I can vouch for him personally!"

Upstairs in the room which served as his office, Frost, who

had been working on his account books, heard their laughter and laid down his pen with a smile. He had already heard from Lucy that Shipton was to take over control of the gang. He had received the news with extreme satisfaction; his judgement had been proved correct yet again, and he had paid Lucy particularly well for the news. Shipton had been worth cultivating, and as for Lucy, she had been a good investment too. He looked over to the space near the fire which had formerly been occupied by the chair that Mrs Stanway had admired so much. It had been given to her along with several pieces of jewellery as part of Lucy's price. Lucy, dear Lucy; he wouldn't mind dabbling with Lucy himself. Alice was becoming a bore to him. Still, there might be time for that when Shipton grew sick of her or was hanged. The important thing was to keep her talkative and Shipton happy. She should present no problem; her greed was boundless and should that fail there was always that matter with the Life Guards officer while Shipton had been in Reading. Shipton did not seem the violently jealous type, but he was sure Lucy would rather not have it put to the test. As for Shipton becoming leader of the gang, he felt sure that this was an improvement. He had made considerable efforts to befriend the man, and could confidently expect to extend his influence in that quarter. In any case, no doubt Shipton would need information as much as Noll had. The prospect for that side of the business looked much better now. With new members, and Shipton in charge, he could expect richer pickings; they would be spending more in the tavern, passing more and better goods on to him for disposal, and – who knows? – in time they might even have a price on their heads. All in all things were progressing well, and Frost smiled to himself as he crossed the room to stand and stare into the fire.

The whole of the week that followed was spent by the gang in seeking to increase their number, an endeavour which met with better success than they had met with in any other field lately. Delighted at the confidence placed in him by his new leader, Tom threw himself into the task with vigour and disappeared for several days in search of old friends, while Jack and Noll waited at the Dog and discussed plans for the future.

Hugh Jeffrey, when he finally came in the company of Tom,

proved to be as wary as Tom had said he might. Jack was not to be put off, however, regarding the man's caution as a good sign, and went to great pains to convince him that his interests lay in joining with them. Jeffrey was a dour, almost sullen man, whose stature and bearing, as well as the scar which ran down the whole of his jaw on the right side of his face, confirmed him to be the ex-trooper he claimed to be. "I prefer to work alone," had been his first, sulky answer to Jack's proposal. "That way I don't have to trust anyone else, or share my takings."

"And that way," replied Jack, "you cannot attempt anything other than a solitary traveller; you have no access to sources of information other than your own; you cannot rely on the support and protection of friends, or make use of their safe houses, spare horses, aliases or contacts in the country. Such things as coaches, waggons, large parties of travellers will be forever forbidden to you."

"I value my independence. I like to be free to go where I please and do what I please," said the other.

"So you shall be; so shall we all be whenever the gang is not working together," replied Jack, who went on to explain in greater detail the plans he had. When it came to the beauties of Frost's information system, one thing he did not mention was his intention of distancing the gang and its activities as far as possible from Frost without losing the benefits he could offer. He was anxious to paint as fair a picture as possible for the potential recruit, and so avoided any reference to anything that might reflect uncertainty about the future. He lacked the persuasive powers which Tom had, but something about Jack's manner seemed to have impressed Hugh Jeffrey, for he finally agreed to join up with them and accept Jack as his captain. From that moment on, fortune smiled on them, for within a few days, two more recruits – friends of Hugh's who were both known to Tom – came of their own accord and asked to be included.

The first, Robert Warren, was a short, dark, wiry man with a country accent which nobody could quite place. He was reticent about his past, but it was a commonplace of criminal etiquette not to ask too many questions, and in his growing mistrust of Frost, Jack was beginning to prize reticence.

The other, William Reynolds, was built like an oak door and possessed with as much sense. He was nonetheless known, according to Tom, whose judgement in such matters Jack respected, for a true friend and a dangerous enemy, and had been at the trade for some years.

Satisfied that they now had at least enough to begin with, and furnished with a list of names of those who might be called upon if need arose for greater numbers, Jack called a meeting one week hence at the Hole in the Wall tavern in Whitefriars, where the whole gang would be sworn in, and the commencement of their operations together would be celebrated in suitable style. Jack was pleased with his week's work; three new members, by all accounts good men, had come to replace the two worthless poltroons who had fled and of whom there was still no news. He felt sure that under his leadership the gang would thrive and soon be in a position to attempt things more ambitious than parsons and farmers and even Sir William Beamish and his doughty servants. Predictably, Lucy was all curiosity about the new arrangements and Jack, who already had a pretty fair suspicion of what lay behind this concern, saw no harm in telling her what in any case would become common knowledge soon enough. Although he felt the hand of Frost lay too firmly on the shoulder (or it may be the collar) of the gang, he was also aware how useful he could be as an ally and how unwise it would be to make an enemy of him. He had deliberately chosen the Hole in the Wall as the venue for their first meeting so as to hold it out of Frost's reach, in so far as anything ever was. Apart from this, things were to go on as much as possible as before; he would continue to live near the Dog and gain his information and pass on any valuables there; other sources of news and outlets could come later.

A week later, at the appointed time in a private room of the Hole in the Wall, Jack, Noll, Tom, Hugh Jeffrey, Robert Warren and William Reynolds gathered to drink before getting down to the serious business of the evening. Tom brought news of Cole and Dyer. Cole had been seen stalking Paul's Walk in company with a couple of frayed swordsmen, putting on airs but looking down at heel; he had fled at Tom's approach.

Dyer, it seemed, had left the city once and for all, and had joined a group of wandering beggars. "Just what I expected!" spat Noll in a rage, "After seeing him ogle those poxy beggar-women in Reading. They will suit him right down to the ground, they will. Just the life for him too; rather be whipped from parish to parish like a dog than earn his living on the road like a man. I never thought I'd side with them on anything, but I hope the constables lay his backbone bare in every town and village between here and Bristol."

After this and sundry other curses had been brought down on the heads of the traitors, Jack called them to order and began to speak. He was a little hesitant at first, but as he saw how the others, taking their example from Noll and Tom, listened respectfully, he grew in confidence. After stressing that he was sure such reminders were unnecessary, he proceeded to remind all present of the solemn nature of the oath they were about to take which was binding unto death; that from this day on they were to regard themselves as soldiers in a common cause, and were bound in loyalty to one another and in obedience to him for the good of all. That said, he then went on to remind them of the prosperity they could soon all hope to enjoy together and concluded by calling the first of them forward to take the oath. Noll came first as Jack's right-hand man, followed by Tom who, as the only one known to all, was to be treasurer, and then in turn the others. The oath that they swore was as follows:

1 I, —————————, swear by the head and soul of our captain to be obedient to all his commands.
2 To be faithful to my companions in all their designs and attempts.
3 To always be present at such meetings as the captain shall appoint, here or in any other place, except his leave to the contrary.
4 To be ready at all hours, by day and by night, upon call or notice.
5 Never to desert my companions in any danger, or otherwise, to the last breath.
6 Never to fly from an equal number of oppressors, but rather die, courageously fighting on the place.
7 To help one another, whether taken, imprisoned, in sickness, or in any other distress.
8 Never to leave, if possible I can bring it off any of my companions' bodies wounded or dead behind me to fall into the enemies' hands.

9 To confess to nothing, if taken, or ever to discover the
abodes and residences of my accomplices, though put to
the punishment of death itself. And this oath when I break,
in the least tittle, may the greatest plagues and damnation
seize me here and hereafter.

The whole company swore this oath, after Jack had sworn a
suitably amended version, with all the solemnity such an
occasion demanded. Even for a band of thieves, an oath was an
awesome undertaking, the breaking of which would not be
contemplated lightly. Then, their mood lightened by further
draughts, supper was called for, and, had they not been making
so much noise themselves the revellers of the Hole in the Wall
would have heard the sound of merry-making coming from the
upstairs room well into the night.

Over the year that followed the meeting in the Hole in the Wall
there grew up a legend which in the manner of the times spread
across the country like a flood tide. It was Sir William Beamish
who almost inadvertently set the ball rolling. On his return
from Devon, he repeated wherever he went the stirring tale of
how he and his son with the help of his servants (who, to do that
gentleman justice, had been well rewarded) had beaten off an
attack by upwards of seven highwaymen on Hounslow Heath.
The story, much embroidered so as to reflect most credit upon
himself, was told all over the city, as this was a popular
gentleman. Nor did Sir William, who was nothing if not a
sportsman, fail to pay tribute to one of their number who had
dashed out of the smoke and confusion and snatched one of his
comrades from under their noses, in spite of their hot fire and
slashing swords. It suited Sir William's purpose very well to
have his opponents painted as the blackest and most desperate
villains out of hell, and so by advancing his own reputation he
did the same, by degrees, for Jack.
It was not long before the public's imagination was fired
by the tale, and linking it with the oft-repeated story of
the gentleman high-pad who danced with his lady victims,
concluded in a rare moment of accuracy that the heroes of
these stories were one and the same man. Then Frost took a
hand. Having noticed almost immediately how under Jack's

leadership the gang had become less dependent upon him, and even begun to distance themselves from him, he started to prepare against the day when it might become necessary to discard them. Whatever the future held it could only be in his interests for the gang to grow notorious, so he set out to encourage rumour. Thus, it soon became a commonplace in the City that although travel was always a risky business, a man could consider himself fortunate come what may if he managed to avoid one Captain Coranto and his confederates. Before long reports were coming in from all quarters of the deeds of this intrepid little band. Jack was by no means averse to the public notice that had somehow mysteriously attached itself to their operations. He reasoned that the terror their name might now inspire was worth another two men, and if somehow his name had become common knowledge, this was a small price to pay for such an advantage. With rumour and folklore tending only to confuse such matters as his appearance, his origins and his whereabouts, the risk of detection and discovery remained small.

The gang prospered exactly as Jack had said it would, and the scope of their operations grew until they were the subject of Justice's reports from London to Exeter, and Bristol to Nottingham.

Sir, on the fourteenth of June, in the Parish of Y———, a party of four travellers on their way to Bristol were approached on the road by a man calling himself Mr Simpson who asked if he might join them as he was exceeding fearful of encountering highwaymen on that particular stretch of road. On their approaching a certain wood he became very agitated and, professing that he was sure he had heard some noise, urged his companions to take a different route. This they agreed to do, whereupon entering a small copse, the whole party was set upon by five masked men. As soon as they had struggled free from their bonds, Mr Simpson, notwithstanding the curses of his fellow travellers, offered to lead them to the nearest village where the Watch might be alerted and a hue and cry raised. This he did, and new horses being procured for the chase, he declared that he was certain he knew which direction the robbers must have taken. Accordingly he led the party and the Watch a merry and fruitless dance before vanishing into the night on his borrowed horse never to be seen again. I am of the opinion that this fellow was in league with the robbers from the start, and remained with the victims only to divert the pursuers and allow his fellows time to escape. Furthermore, it is my opinion that this man was none other than the felon who calls himself Captain Coranto.

Sir, on the thirty-first of June in the Parish of H———, a party of six on their way to Leicester were joined with by a couple of men calling themselves Dean and Fletcher, who appeared very well-dressed and polite. The whole party, with the exception of the one woman amongst them, was well armed, and travelled well spaced out so as to prevent ambuscade. However, on reaching the crest of a hill, the two newcomers who had fallen back slightly, produced two pistols each, and with the advantage of surprise, quickly overpowered the three men nearest them, as a further group of masked men emerged from some trees nearby. After all had been thoroughly searched and money and goods of great value had been taken, the entire party, including the woman (to whom no consideration was shown for the delicacy of her sex) was tied to a tree. I am in no doubt but that this gang was that of the notorious Captain Coranto. The travellers were able to furnish a description of the two who joined them, but I have my doubts as to its value. The smaller man's face was much patched and the other was wearing a periwig. This is the third robbery in this hundred in as many months, despite the efforts of the constable and myself, and the cost to the parish is becoming insupportable. Unless more money is forthcoming . . .

Sir, concerning the holding up of the army's pay-waggon by Captain Coranto and his men on S——— Hill on the fifth of August, I have this to say. Firstly, it is surely no business of the parish concerned to guard the army's baggage, which was attended on this occasion by a sergeant and ten men who would seem to have put up but little resistance once the sergeant was wounded. Secondly, once the crime was discovered every effort was made to apprehend the felons, but these efforts have met with no better fortune than the efforts of many another justice. Everything necessary was done to attend to the sergeant and the two wounded men, at considerable inconvenience to my wife and cost to myself (the doctor's fees were paid by myself, Sir, for which I am not yet reimbursed). That the loss occasioned by this raid should be borne by the hundred is, I am sure you will agree, a monstrous imposition, since the chief fault lies with the army itself for its neglect of providing an adequate guard. I must add, Sir, that both my wife and I were wounded by your comments of the seventh July, you who have so often been a guest in my house . . .

Sir, on the twenty-third of July, I was myself robbed not half a mile from my house whilst riding to answer a summons from the constable at H———, he having sent a message to the effect that two travellers were robbed up on H——— Hill. Of the three men who surprised me and my servant, I have no doubt that one was Captain Coranto, and that they had lain in wait in the sure knowledge that I would respond with alacrity to the first robbery, which was no doubt the work of their companions. As well as depriving me of five pounds and my watch they were extremely impudent and subjected me to much insult and this in front of my servant, whom it has since been necessary to dismiss. On my swearing that I should see them ride backwards up Holborn Hill, they set me backwards upon my own horse and sent me off in the direction of my house, where I arrived ten minutes later, much bruised and torn, to the consternation of my wife and servants. Sir, it is essential that this villain be caught and hanged at the earliest opportunity, for every moment he is at large threatens the very stability of the nation. If such a crime can be carried out under the very nose of the law, and upon one of its instruments . . .

These reports gained popular currency, and stories grew in the telling until they formed a picture (composed in equal measure of truth, falsehood and exaggeration) of a band of freebooters who travelled where they pleased, set the law and its agents at defiance and robbed with impunity.

As the legend grew and spread, it changed shape to fit the needs and prejudices of its propagators. Captain Coranto was a Northerner, a Welshman, a Frenchman or Irish. He was the son of a Cavalier, and involved in a plot to kill Fairfax; he was one of the King's bastards, which explained his impunity; he was a former Roundhead officer, a serving officer in the Life Guards, a Jesuit priest. He had been seen in York, in Carlisle, in Exeter. The story of how he had rescued a fallen comrade from a dozen armed men was well known, though this feat seemed to have taken place in a dozen different locations. One week he was dead, shot outside Pontefract by two brothers under the name of Wilson; the next week he was very much alive and had robbed the Duchess of Albermarle in broad daylight not three miles from the centre of London. In short, for every robbery that could be laid at the door of the gang, another ten were attributed, and those robbed considered themselves ill-robbed if it were not by Captain Coranto.

Meanwhile at the Dog life continued much as normal. Jack and Tom kept up the relentless pressure of their career in debauchery, Noll disappeared for weeks at a time, and the others came and went as they pleased, except that all were obliged upon oath to muster on their leader's word. Jane worked ceaselessly as ever, but spared little time for banter now, and would often appear red-eyed from weeping. The sudden disappearance of John had shaken her, and as day after day passed by without word of him, she became more and more convinced that something terrible had befallen him. She had gone to her father and begged him on bended knee to try and find him. He had been unusually sympathetic, saying that he had always known Simmons to be no good, and that his sudden defection had come as no surprise to him, but that as she was so obviously concerned he would do what he could, though he could not hold out much hope. What little hope she had was not strengthened by her father's words, and late in the night, she would often confess her worst fears to Ann from whom, alone of all the occupants of the Dog, she could be sure of a sympathetic hearing.

For his part Frost was well pleased overall with the way his affairs were progressing. Ann, who had proved her worth in the kitchen, had attracted his interest for her other qualities too, and he felt she had distinct possibilities. She seemed a little shy in his presence at the moment, it was true, but he could overcome that in time, play on her greed or vanity (whose existence he never for a moment doubted); what was more she seemed to have gained Jane's confidence, and might in future be instrumental in furthering his plans for his daughter. As for the gang they were going from strength to strength; if Shipton had not proved as pliable a leader as he had hoped, at least their takings were continuing to increase, and if at any stage they seemed to be slipping out of his grasp, there was always a substantial reward to be counted on. That this was the case was confirmed by a poster which he had handed to Shipton one morning as he drank his breakfast draught downstairs.

> Whereas Captain Coranto alias Simpson, alias Fletcher, and his known associates have grown so bold and reckless in the prosecution of their base and murderous designs, any person whatsoever who shall make discovery of the said offenders to any Justice of the Peace shall receive the sum of two hundred pounds, which is deposited in the hands of Mr Blanchard, goldsmith, next door to Temple Bar for the said purpose.

"Murderous!" spluttered Noll after he had read it, "It says 'Murderous'! We've never yet murdered anyone. And in my whole life I never killed anyone that wasn't trying to do the same to me. Mark my words, Jack, we're taking the blame for every robbery committed between here and Derby, and dozens of gangs are taking shelter under the cloak of our reputation. Are you listening to me Jack?"

Jack was staring across the room to where Ann was supervising the setting of places at the table. They seldom spoke these days, but sometimes as she went about her work she would look across at him with the same expression as on the first day he had seen her, darting out of the tavern in Whitefriars; which always, in spite of himself, disturbed him. Noll's voice intruded into his thoughts, ". . . I was saying that a dozen gangs are sheltering under our . . ."

"I know, I heard you," Jack lied, and looked at the poster. "I suppose this is the price of success in our trade. I think it might be better if we lay low for a while — avoided attracting any undue attention. We can still go out individually if we need to; not that any of us should after what we've made these past few months."

Accustomed now to obeying their leader's every word, and having grown to respect his judgement, the others readily agreed. Suddenly eager, for some reason he did not fully understand, to get away from London, Jack announced his intention of travelling up to Leicester to scout the roads in that county; Noll was off to Reading, Tom going deeper into the city, and the others to bolt-holes of their own. The following morning, therefore, after agreeing to reassemble in three months' time at the Dog, the gang dispersed.

6

When Jack entered the village of Cadeby one evening several weeks later, it was not with any high hopes. His excursion to Leicestershire was intended as much as a reconnaissance for future ventures as to make a profit, which was as well since no opportunities for the latter had arisen. Having avoided Leicester Jack had resolved to visit the Star in Cadeby, which he had been assured by Hugh Jeffrey was a likely base for operations in that area, as the chamberlain and, he suspected, the hostler were amenable.

Now, as he turned into the one street that was the village, he saw before him a scene of great confusion and excitement. The whole street was blocked by a large crowd; at that distance it was difficult to see what the cause of all the excitement was, but as he spurred his horse forward, it became clear that some sort of procession was in progress, and was being followed by the people of the village. From the midst of the crowd there floated the sound of flute music as well as a man's voice trying to make some sort of declaration.

By now Jack had caught up with the rear part of the gathering, and from the saddle could see over the heads of the people to where a mixed group of men and women in assorted forms of dress were gathered round a tall, stately individual, who was competing with the noise as best he could. The men were for the most part dressed in furs and outrageous plumed helmets and all carried somewhat battered blunt swords; the women were in an assortment of cheap but gaudy stuffs, the young ones well decked with diaphanous veils and scarves. On the fringe of the party were a number of drummers and flautists, as well as a bear-ward with a brown bear on a chain who danced clumsily to the music.

It was clear that the arrival of this group had been eagerly

77

awaited by the locals, and the mood of the crowd was good-natured as they pushed and shoved to get a better view. Jack was just able to hear the last line of the tall man's speech, "the affecting tragedy of *The Scythian King* at Beck's Barn tomorrow night!" before his horse grew restive and he was forced to withdraw from the crowd and make for the Star, which was at the top end of the street.

Having casually inspected the place, he decided to stay the night since the food had been recommended to him by Hugh. It did not seem an opportune moment to attempt to gauge the hostler, although the chamberlain did look a promisingly shifty fellow. For the moment he was more interested in the leader of the players whom he saw as he entered the room. Here was a man likely to be worth a penny or two. As it happens, the same thought had occurred to him as Jack had entered the room, and they were immediately drawn to each other. "Good day, Sir," said the actor, eyeing Jack's fine riding-coat and boots of Spanish leather.

"Good day to you," replied Jack. "Your arrival seems to have created quite a stir."

The actor smiled complacently and nodded slightly, "It's the same wherever we go. Our reputation precedes us. We are particularly popular in this district, operating as we do under the protection of Sir Ralph Wardby himself," and here he puffed out his chest with pride. "In fact as soon as we are finished here," and he waved his hand almost dismissively, "we will be giving a private performance of our tragedy at Wardby Manor, where no doubt we shall be well rewarded. You know it I suppose – Wardby Manor, that is?"

"I have heard of it, of course," answered Jack, "but I am a stranger here myself. I come from London."

"London!" The actor's eyes lit up, and then he remembered himself, and went on, "ah yes, London," with the air of a man who knew it well, although he had in fact been there only once in his life. "My dear Sir, I wonder, would you do me the pleasure of taking some refreshment with me in my rooms? A gentleman like yourself I am sure will have a lot to tell of the state of the theatre there, and I should love to hear it, for I must confess – I miss it terribly." Never one to refuse such an invitation and sensing a possible opportunity to separate this man from the weighty purse that hung at his belt, Jack readily agreed, and within a matter of minutes the two were seated by a healthy fire in an upstairs room drinking wine and waiting for the tray of custards that the actor had ordered. He introduced himself as Mr Robert Bancroft and seemed keen to hear all there was to hear about the playhouses of London, of which Jack, although by no means a regular playgoer like Tom, was able to give him a spirited account. From time to time he would nod his head and sigh, "Ah yes!" as though in reminiscence.

When Jack had finished, the actor said, "There was a time, my friend, when my name was as commonly on the lips of the London playgoer as those you have mentioned. Of course, all that was a long time ago before the wars and the Puritans. Now you see me reduced to this, and to subterfuge." Here he leaned forward confidentially. "We are not really under the protection of Sir Ralph, you know, nor of anyone else. We simply make it up as we go along – it is unfortunate, but it keeps the constables off our backs.

"Not that it was always this way; oh no, in my father's day, if you had the support of a wealthy noble or gentleman you could be sure you would thrive, whereas these days we live from hand to mouth. I can remember when my father's company was under the warranty of Sir Anthony Appleton. I was a mere child at the time; they performed *Dido, Queen of Carthage* at his home in front of the assembled gentry of the whole county. Oh, that was a glittering occasion, Sir, a glittering occasion, marred only by the leading flautist being caught making off with three silver spoons. But I'm afraid those days are over." He paused and sipped his wine meditatively, staring into the fire before going on, "Not that I don't have my plans, mind you. Oh, the people in the country may not be the most discerning of audiences, but they know quality when they see it. We've performed for the best and the worst the length and breadth of the country, and all of them with streaming eyes, for in truth Sir, it is a most affecting tale. Are you familiar with it yourself, Sir?" Jack shook his head. "Well, perhaps you'll get a chance to see it tomorrow evening?" said Bancroft, and Jack made some non-committal noise and buried his nose in his wine glass.

Bancroft scarcely bothered to wait for his answer, but carried
on with his monologue, "What we really need is a wealthy
sponsor," and he looked significantly across at Jack. "A man
of quality, a man of discernment, a man of weight in the
community, who seeks to add lustre to his name by becoming a
patron of the arts. With such a backer there's no telling what we
might achieve, or what return such a man might receive for his
investment." All the time he was saying this he stared intently
at Jack so as to reinforce his meaning. "For," he went on,
"there's no doubt that we are on our way to becoming one of the
foremost companies in the land. Indeed, Sir, to employ a
military metaphor such as a gentleman like yourself might use,
having brought my little army to its peak of training, it is my
intention soon to march on London! We'll start at one of the
fairs, and then as our fame spreads, who knows? I may be able
to find some person who might put us in the way of setting up
permanently in the city."

Throughout this, Jack had confined himself to nodding
sympathetically or tut-tutting where appropriate, and it gradually dawned upon him that this man had cast him in the role
of benefactor. It suited him to gain the man's confidence, so he
tried to look thoughtful, as though mulling something over in
his mind. Encouraged by the seeming success of his speech,
Bancroft pressed Jack further as to his plans for the following
day, and when Jack stressed that he must move on, and would
therefore be forced to miss the performance, he leapt to his feet.
"My friend!" he began, with a note of urgency in his voice,
"fear not! You shall have at least a taste of this noble tragedy; it
would be a shame for a man of taste such as yourself to miss it. I
shall perform a speech or two from the dramatic climax of the
play."

So saying he pushed back the chair on which he had been
sitting so as to clear a space in the centre of the room, and taking
up a position in the open he threw back his head. Swinging his
arm across his chest, he was about to begin when he stopped
again and looking at Jack said by way of explanation, "You are
to imagine that the Scythian king is flying through the woods
with his queen (having been defeated in battle) when they are
confronted by a ferocious bear." Once more he adopted the
dramatic pose and looking beyond the confines of the room to

some imaginary forest far beyond the Danube, he began in a
voice both loud and racked with anguish,

> Oh fly my Queen from this devouring bear,
> Let it suffice, he me alone doth tear . . .

It so happened that at this very moment on the stairs outside,
one of the serving girls, Nancy Trant, was about to enter the
room with the tray of custards, when she heard these words
which, to do the actor justice, were delivered with such a wealth
of feeling as to convince at least her that they were genuine.
With a shriek she dropped the tray, and stepped back only to
hear from inside the room,

> Oh save thyself! The bloody bear's jaws fly,
> Why shouldst thou, whilst thou may escape him, die?
> Oh haste, be gone, or thy death too is nigh!

These exclamations from inside the room were quite sufficient
to convince her that the creature she had seen earlier in the
street had somehow broken loose and found its way into the
actor's room, where no doubt it was wreaking a terrible revenge
for years of exploitation. Not bothering for a moment to ponder
the matter of whether even an actor would, in such a situation,
cry out in verse, she fled down the stairs screaming at the top of
her voice, "The bear! The bear is loose! It's in the upstairs room
and is tearing them to pieces!"

The effect of this alarm on the occupants of the downstairs
room, whose imaginations had already been fired by the
excitement of the earlier parade, can readily be imagined. The
host of the Star was unfortunately away at a card game or the
ensuing panic might have been nipped in the bud. As it was, his
wife, a lady a good deal less hard-headed than her husband,
straightway had one of her fainting fits and had to be revived by
her two daughters; the chamberlain was so shaken by the news
that he had to take recourse to his master's brandy, and the
hostler and a group of farm workers who had been drinking by
the fire rushed out into the street crying the news abroad, and
hurried to their homes to arm themselves. The village blacksmith, who also happened to be the constable, gathered a band

of stalwarts around him and, after sending one to fetch Tom Robinson and his mastiffs, marched towards the inn. Meanwhile upstairs Mr Bancroft was in full flight, eagerly demonstrating his full range before an increasingly embarrassed Jack, and in the stable of a Mr Beck, who had rented out his barn to the company, the brown bear who had capered in the street that morning and was now causing such alarm in the village was sound asleep, dreaming his innocent dreams.

With the arrival of Tom Robinson and his mastiffs, the constable and his men felt they were as ready as they would ever be to tackle the beast. From upstairs there was nothing now but an ominous silence, so releasing the dogs, they charged as one man up the stairs, broke down the door with clubs and staves, and fell in, weapons at the ready. There was no sign of the bear, only Mr Bancroft and his guest, apparently quite safe.

Undismayed, and without bothering to seek an explanation, they rushed past the astonished pair into the adjoining room. Hard on their heels came an assortment of servants and the host's daughters and their friends, apprehensive, but unwilling to miss the spectacle. By now the room was filled with people so that there was scarcely room to move, with the more dogged members of the constable's party searching under the bed and in ever-smaller hiding places for the escaped bear, others trying to restrain the mastiffs who had already bitten two people, and the great majority demanding angrily why Mr Bancroft had raised the alarm.

Nor was the situation improved when the host arrived, summoned from his cards by the noise, and began angrily remonstrating with the constable for the breaking down of a door which, presumably, bear or no bear, would have opened in the normal way. The clamour was such that Mr Bancroft could not make himself heard at all, nor could he appeal to his companion for support, since the latter was already edging towards the door tucking the actor's purse into his doublet as he went. In the mounting confusion which was now spilling onto the stairs and threatening to end in violence it was a simple matter for Jack to slip away past the prostrate landlady and the already drunken chamberlain out into the stable and saddle his horse.

It was an hour before the furore had died down, the host had been pacified, his wife revived, the blacksmith's guard dismissed, and the chamberlain kicked out into the yard to sober up with the intelligence that the cost of the brandy would be deducted from his pay. At the end of that hour Jack had put a good many miles between himself and the village of Cadeby and slowed his horse to a walk; at about the same time, Mr Bancroft slumped exhausted into a chair in the Star, threw his arm across the table and noticed for the first time that his purse was not where he had left it. Then the furore started all over again.

Although it was only ten o'clock in the morning, it had already proved to be a bad day for Doctor Jeremiah Winton, and there was no prospect that it was going to improve. He and his family had been expecting the arrival of the bailiffs for some days, but that did not lessen the shock when they did arrive. As he walked down the lane between the two burly men, gripped firmly on the arm by the man on his left, he could not forget the white faces of his wife and daughters at the door. They would not starve; his sister would see to that, but still it would not be easy for them, and God only knew when he would see them again.

The indignity of it! And that it should be at the hands of this man of all men! Allinson was clearly enjoying himself and was determined that this should be as humiliating as possible. To be committed for debt for the sum of six pounds, when he must be owed twice as much! The doctor was not a saint, more a gentle and tolerant man whose tolerance was particularly extended to the poorer families in the parish when it came to the payment of his fees. If certain tradesmen in the town of Reading had extended the same tolerance towards the doctor as he had shown to others, he would have been spared this ordeal at the hands of a man who for some unknown reason hated him; but it was not to be. Meanwhile, the poor of the parish continued to call him a saint, and comforted no doubt by the thought that saints don't need money like ordinary folk, made no effort to pay his fees.

This same day had been a long-awaited treat for the man on the doctor's left, Joseph Allinson the bailiff. He had known the doctor since they were boys and had always disliked him. In later years he had grown to hate him for his airs and graces and resent his learning as well as the respect he had earned from all who knew him. His marriage to Margaret Peck, on whom Allinson had had his own designs, was the last straw, and from then on he had awaited his opportunity. For all his learning, Winton was a fool, as Margaret was now learning to her cost, though he could have told her so years ago if she had been prepared to listen. Well, now she knew, and if she wanted help from Joseph Allinson it might be forthcoming, but on his own terms. As they walked Allinson cursed his decision not to hire a horse for the occasion. He was not to know that the doctor had sold his a week ago though of course he should have guessed. That would have been something, to lead the man through the village and into Reading like any common felon. As it was they had a long walk ahead of them, and of course they had to go through the village even though it was slightly out of their way. It would serve to remind all who saw it of just who was worthy of respect around here.

The doctor's customary patience was being strained to the limits. Did the man have to clutch onto his arm in that manner all the time as though he were a criminal and likely to run for it at any moment? Surely also he could have spared him the lecture on thrift, which had more than a hint of gloating in it. "You see, Jeremiah," he was saying, "all the learning in the world is no use to you unless you can exercise a little discrimination in the matter of business. And it's as I've always said about you, you're a clever man, but you haven't an ounce of common sense!" The doctor raised his eyes to heaven; the temptation to strike the man was almost overwhelming, but it would serve no purpose – perhaps that was what he wanted. They reached the cross-tracks which led down to the village and turned left; the doctor groaned inwardly. They were walking into the village even though it took them out of their way. Allinson was going to spare him nothing and broadcast his shame to the whole country. As they passed a small farmhouse set back from the track on the left, Allinson changed his grip on the doctor's arm so as to steer him into the yard.

"By God, I'm dry as a dog," he declared. "I think a drop of Joyce's ale is what we need. I'll treat you, Jeremiah. Enjoy it, mind – you'll not taste anything as good in gaol, not with an empty purse!" The three men walked into the back room and sat down. Allinson looked around him, clearly disappointed at the small number of people present to see his triumph. In the whole room there were only a couple of ploughboys, Joyce's two sons, and in one corner on an oak settle a small, grey-haired man, who showed but little interest as they entered. Presently Joyce herself bustled up to attend to the newcomers.

"Three cups of your finest ale, mistress; your very finest, mind – the good doctor here stands in need of it!" and he laughed. Joyce ignored him, and sensing something was amiss, turned to the doctor.

"I'm surprised to see you in here, doctor," she said. "Must be the first time you've honoured us, and in such fine company as well!" For the first time that morning the doctor smiled, as Allinson bristled at the calculated insult.

"Just fetch our ale if you please, mistress," snapped the bailiff.

"We're in a hurry. The doctor here has an appointment – in Reading Gaol." Joyce turned to indicate to one of the boys, who busied himself pouring the ale, and she turned again to the doctor.

"Who's ill in Reading Gaol that one of the doctors in town can't cure?"

Allinson grew increasingly exasperated. Fidgeting in his seat he almost shouted, "Nobody's sick there! He's off in because he can't pay his debts."

Without even glancing at the bailiff she continued, quietly now, "I'm surprised, doctor. I'd have thought there were enough people hereabouts who owed you, and not just money either." The doctor shrugged and smiled up at her wistfully. He couldn't bring himself to speak for fear he would let himself down by the break in his voice, or worse still, launch into a speech of self-recrimination which would delight his captor and provoke him to further excesses. The ale was brought, and Joyce walked away shaking her head and muttering to herself as Allinson, in between long pulls at his ale, continued his dissertation on learning, thrift and the true wisdom. So engrossed was he in this that he failed to notice that nobody, not even his assistant, was listening; he failed also to notice that the small, grey man in the corner had got up quietly and slipped away into the interior of the house.

It was half an hour and several cups of ale later that Allinson decided to move on into the village. "Come on, Jeremiah. I've put it off as long as possible for you, but it's time to be on our way," he said, then seeing that the doctor had not even finished his first cup, "Don't you want that? Well, waste not, want not," and he drained the cup before grasping the doctor by the arm and rising to leave, throwing some coins down on the table as he did so. Before he could reach the door, Joyce re-entered the room. "Before you go, Mr Allinson," she said, "there's something I would know. What is the sum of the doctor's debt?"

Allinson smiled; this was better. "Six pounds, mistress! A mere six pounds. A pitiful sight I'm sure you will agree, to see a man . . ."

"If you'll spare us a minute of your time," interrupted Joyce, "I am sure we can conclude this matter in a much more satisfactory way than it looks to be settled at present." Allinson, who could conceive of no more satisfactory conclusion than the one of which he was at this moment the instrument, gaped. Surely . . . His worst fears were confirmed; the woman was already producing a pen and paper. She was a large woman, and her two sons stood close at hand, so there was no resistance as she forced the doctor to sit once more at the table and write out a bond for the sum of six pounds. The doctor, scarcely daring to believe that deliverance could be at hand, but ready to grasp at the merest straw, readily complied. That done, Joyce reached into the folds of her gown and producing a purse, counted out six pounds and clapped them triumphantly into the hands of the stupefied bailiff. His eyes narrowed as she leaned forward and thrusting her face into his said, "There! Take that to whoever in Reading wants it!"

"There's also my fees to consider," said Allinson, who although his heart was sinking, was determined to make the best of the situation. Joyce counted out a few more coins, and poured them contemptuously into the man's upturned hand, taking care that at least two of them fell into the rushes at his feet.

"And now, Doctor," she said as Allinson, after hesitating for an instant, scrabbled at her feet for the coins, "Perhaps you'd care to join me in a glass or two before you go home, and we can discuss business." As if by magic one of the lads appeared at her shoulder with a tray on which were a bottle of Rhenish wine and two glasses, at which the doctor and tavern-keeper sat down and fell at once into the most pleasant conversation, neither of them giving Allinson so much as a glance until he turned in the doorway to look at them. "No doubt I'll see you again Jeremiah!" he said. The doctor smiled pleasantly up at him, "Doctor Winton to you!"

That was the beginning of a bad week for Mr Joseph Allinson, bailiff. Two days later, whilst carrying the sum of five pounds into Reading, he was waylaid on the road by a solitary masked man, who as well as relieving him of the five pounds and whatever of his own money he had about his person, took his watch and his boots before tying him hand and foot, gagging him with a filthy rag, and kicking him into a muddy ditch where he lay for four hours until his muffled groans alerted a passing peddlar. He was unable to furnish any description of his attacker, save that he was past middle age, small in stature and exceeding foul-mouthed.

7

As a watery sun shone on the puddles left by the morning's rain, Robert Canvey, gentleman, rode out of Rearsby in the county of Leicester, and began his homeward journey. He was in good spirits as he made his leisurely way down the deserted road. His cousin Peter had only recently been appointed high constable of the hundred, and had immediately called upon his kinsman, himself a high constable, for advice. Canvey had enjoyed the last few days; he was proud of his own record as high constable and the respect it had brought him, and cousin Peter had been most solicitous. Of course it was doubtful that Peter would be able to achieve the high standards that prevailed amongst the Watches in Canvey's own hundred, but at least he had set him upon the right road.

For nearly an hour he rode without meeting a single soul, but as he forded a small stream, he caught up with a solitary rider, who on Canvey's approach slowed down to await him. He was obviously a country fellow, being dressed in a tatty smock and a greasy black hat from which yellow curls cascaded. As Canvey rode up to him the man touched the brim of his hat and announced, "I'm glad to see you, Sir. I'm a stranger and moreover not used to travelling. I wonder . . . could I ride with you for the greater safety of us both?"

Mr Canvey readily assented and as they rode on the man continued in a confidential manner, "To tell the truth, I'm carrying a considerable sum of money – almost ten shillings – and I'm in mortal fear of running up against Captain Coranto or some such fellow."

Canvey reassured him. "My good man, I can assure you there is no need for alarm. Why, I myself am carrying a sum far in excess of that you mention, and do so regularly. In any case I can vouch for your safety here. My cousin is high constable; he

88

told me that this is a safe road." The man seemed impressed, and brightened considerably, "Then I suppose I am as safe as if I were travelling with the high constable himself." Mr Canvey smiled indulgently, "Well, in a sense you are. I too am a high constable . . . of a hundred about thirty miles from here." It was hard not to laugh at the way the man goggled.

They rode in silence for a while before the man, who had been musing for some time, spoke out, "Begging your pardon, Sir . . . but if you're a high constable, would I be right in assuming you had some knowledge of the law?" Canvey nodded wisely. "Then, Sir, I wonder if you could explain to me what Trover and Conversion is. My neighbour at home keeps on about it, and I am too ashamed to admit that I haven't any notion what it is."

Canvey thought for a moment. The problem was how to put it simply enough for this fellow to understand. "Well, let's see," he said. "Suppose I found something which belonged to you, and kept it for my own use though I knew it was yours, that would be Trover and Conversion."

The man frowned for a while as though grappling with the idea, and then nodded in satisfaction. They rode on a little further in silence. After a while the man said, "But suppose I were to find money about your person and put it to my own use?"

"Why, that would be robbery," smiled Mr Canvey.

"Then I fear I must commit one," replied the other, and Canvey's grin faded as he felt the muzzle of a pistol pushed into the pit of his stomach.

Two hours passed before Mr Robert Canvey managed to prise himself free from the bonds that held his wrists, shake some circulation back into his hands and set off on foot down the road back to Rearsby; his next meeting with his cousin was going to be embarrassing for both of them.

The gang had met with seemingly effortless success since it had been reorganised. Thus the illusion of invulnerability was always a likely danger in the mind of a man as young as Jack. If Noll after all his years in the trade could be guilty of carelessness, the danger was much more acute in his young protégé. This along with sundry other matters was shortly to be the subject of much reflection on Jack's part.

The day after the robbery of Mr Robert Canvey, having rid himself of his smock and black hat and changed his yellow wig for one made from his own hair, Jack, under the alias Simon Wells, was travelling south, fifteen miles from the scene of the previous day's events. Realising in the middle of the morning that his horse had a shoe loose, he rode into the nearest village, and having delivered his mount into the care of the local blacksmith, wandered over to the tavern to take a cup of ale. It should have occurred to him that the street was a little quieter than was usual for that time of day. He should have noticed also the cool reception he received from the tavern-keeper, and the appraising look the man gave him, and continued to give him as he drank. Blissfully unaware, however, that anything was amiss he took his time over the ale and was about to order another when a loud authoritative knocking at the door startled him. For a moment his instincts guided him, and he leapt to his feet searching with his eyes for an avenue of escape. The tavern-keeper continued to regard him coolly and there was no repetition of the knocking, but the door opened and in walked the parish constable and three watchmen with staffs. Before Jack could say a word, the constable had walked over to the tavern-keeper and simply said, "Well?" The man nodded in confirmation of something, so the constable turned to Jack who was already flanked by the watchmen and said, "I hope, Sir, you are in no hurry to be away from here, for I fear it will be necessary to detain you a little while." Jack's heart was pounding now but he determined to brazen it out.

"Damn you! How dare you lay your hands on me?" he shouted as the watchmen relieved him of his sword. "You'll answer to Sir William Saltley for this!" he spluttered, making up the name on the spot and hoping to overawe them. The others seemed unmoved. "You have no right to detain me!" he cried, knowing this to be untrue. "I've done nothing wrong!" he added as they began to wrestle him towards the door. The constable smiled.

"If you've done nothing wrong, why did you start to your feet like a felon when we came a-knocking?" To which the tavern-keeper at his shoulder added, "He did, Mr Goss; he did to be sure!" By now the watchmen had dragged him out into the street and, realising that it was getting him nowhere, Jack ceased to struggle and was spared the indignity of being frog-marched down the street to the constable's house.

"Into the front room with him, lads!" cried the constable as they entered the house, a dilapidated-looking cottage at the top end of the village. "I want a few words with him." Inside the house Jack just had time to catch a glimpse of a woman nursing a child by the fire in the kitchen with an older girl by her side, before he was bundled into a small room with a table and two chairs which evidently served the constable as office and lock-up. They sat in silence for a few minutes, the constable looking his prisoner over with obvious satisfaction, and Jack trying his best to assume the air of an honest man unfairly detained and too angry even to talk. He suspected that this pose was having little effect on this Mr Goss who was evidently a constable more than usually diligent. All was not lost, however; even if the man had a good idea who or what he was, he might be amenable to a small bribe. It would be foolish even to hint at such a thing yet, however, that being tantamount to an admission of guilt. After a few minutes another watchman entered bearing his portmanteau, which he dumped on the table as though it constituted final proof of guilt. "The horse fits the description," he declared, and the constable's smile broadened.

"Well now," he said. "There's a thing! Now let's see what our friend here carries with him on his journey." Jack's spirits sank as the constable produced and listed the contents of his portmanteau, pausing to look significantly when he found two periwigs, one fair and one black, and marvelling at the thirty pounds he found. "Two wigs, of different colour, plus the one he's wearing; that's three in all. Now what sort of person is it Tom, who has three wigs?" he asked the watch-man.

"It is by no means uncommon amongst persons of fashion," retorted Jack.

"Persons of fashion, is it?" laughed Goss. "Well, they must be persons of fashion I suppose, who regularly carry thirty pounds about with them. What trade do you suppose it is,

Tom, where a man might earn such sums?" The other grinned
and shrugged his shoulders.

"If you have a question I suggest you address it to me," said
Jack, still playing the outraged traveller. "And as for my
'trade', as you call it, I have none. I am a gentleman. The
money in my possession I won at cards from Sir William
Saltley, who is a gentleman not without some influence in these
parts, as you will shortly discover to your cost."

"And *you* may shortly discover," came the reply, "that
people that robs the high constable of the hundred when he's
out visiting his cousin would do well to avoid that hundred the
following day! Now where does this Sir William of yours live?"
Jack muttered the name of some village; it mattered little
which, for they would quickly find out that it was a fabrication.
He pondered his predicament. Of all the luck! To have robbed
a high constable one day and then be caught out by one of the
oldest tricks in the book the next day in the man's own hundred.
Noll had warned him about that ploy of knocking loudly at the
door to observe the reactions of a suspect. He should have been
able to carry it off.

"Put him in the kitchen with that other fellow; I must get a
note off to Mr Canvey right away," said the constable rising to
go. Jack restrained him with a hand. "Look," he began, "I'm
not the man you are looking for, but there are reasons why it
could be embarrassing for me to be found here. Couldn't we
settle this between ourselves?" and he glanced over to the table
where his thirty pounds lay.

"You're wasting your time my friend," said Goss after a
moment's hesitation. "If you're who I think you are, then no
doubt Mr Canvey will be generous enough, and with his money
in my purse I could sleep a-nights!" As he said this he was
pushing Jack before him into the kitchen where Jack now saw
the woman with the two children was eyeing another man who
was sitting opposite them by the fire.

"Tom, keep an eye on these two; I'll put Mark on the back
door," said the constable as he left. Jack crossed the room and
sat himself on the settle next to the stranger, whilst Tom took
up a position in the hallway from where he could observe them
both. The woman opposite Jack regarded him sourly as he sat
down and merely said, "That was a mistake, offering my

husband your money. He's not one of those! He's a good man, and a clever one." Jack was about to retort that he had seldom if ever met a man who was not 'one of those' as she called them, but reckoned that at this stage there was no point in making enemies. Instead he whispered to the man next to him, "Of all the constables in the kingdom I have to stumble on the one who is both good and clever!" The other smiled but did not answer. Jack looked his companion in misfortune over. He was an elderly, kindly-looking man dressed all in black with the exception of a narrow and not too clean collar. Jack guessed him to be a Puritan; no doubt this was something to do with his having been detained.

Jack's suspicions were confirmed when, after looking him over in return for a few moments, the man asked, "Are you saved?" Jack was about to answer that he was anything but, but remembering that they were not alone and that everything he said would be duly reported to the constable, merely shrugged. The Puritan continued to smile pleasantly and continued, "I am, through the grace of God, and though it has brought down upon my head the persecutions to which we are all subject, I would not exchange my lot with another's for all the wealth of the world."

"Why are you detained?" asked Jack.

"Oh, they stopped me yesterday evening, all in a panic because the high constable had been robbed. Then seeing what I am, they asked me had I a warrant to be more than five miles from home, though I live but four from here, as at least one of them well knows. When I could produce no warrant they held me here overnight. It's not the first time I have been so held, even this close to home. Periodically they decide to throw these obstacles in our way though to no effect."

"You are on the road a lot then?" asked Jack.

"Why, yes," replied the other, "visiting brethren, spreading the word, doing His work wherever He sees fit to send us. Last night they obviously decided that if I wasn't a highwayman, they might at least carry me before the justice on some other charge. I am afraid to say that your arrival might prove to my advantage. You seem to have caused something of a stir, and they may well let me go."

"They think I'm their highway robber!" said Jack nodding his head in the direction of the guard.

"And are you?" asked the other, seemingly amused.

"Of course not!" exclaimed Jack, but something in the Puritan's look suggested that he knew better.

"Well, no doubt you'll be able to prove it at some stage," he said, "though they're no doubt hoping you are their man. They were so keen to catch him last night they even convinced themselves for a while that I was he, until Mark Wooton, that knows me, came along. The idea of it, me a highwayman – my wife will laugh when I tell her."

Then his face clouded over and he went on, "Mind you, there was a time when those who knew me would not have been in the least surprised to hear such an accusation. Aye, and with good reason. You may not guess it to look at me now, but in the days of my youth I had no equal in the town for all manner of sin." Jack, his troubles for the moment forgotten, gaped at the man. "Oh yes," he continued. "I was the leader of the lads in my home town in every enterprise. Drinking, fighting, gambling, swearing, fornicating; so steeped was I in sin that decent folk despaired of me, and a loathsome spectacle I must have presented to all the world and to God.

"Even now I wonder at the miracle of His grace, that one as seemingly lost as I should have been among the chosen. For it was at the height of my career in debauchery that I began to feel within me the workings of His grace, which took at first the form of horrifying dreams of Hell. Later, an overwhelming sense of my own unworthiness overcame me so that I was like to have fallen into the sin of despair, had not the tailor I was apprenticed to taken an interest in my soul sufficient to lend me his Bible of an evening. I found such wonders therein as contrived in a very great measure to set me on the road to salvation. Then I was able to learn from others of the brethren of their own paths to grace, and was greatly encouraged thereby. This is why I travel the country so far as we are allowed, telling others, men such as yourself my friend, to examine your souls and search for signs of the workings of God's salvation. If you are of the elect it is there within you, even now."

At this point the Puritan's speech was interrupted by the

watchman who had been conversing with the constable who had re-entered the house. "Oy, you! On your feet. We don't want you now. You can lay off your canting and be on your way as soon as you've paid Mistress Goss for her hospitality."

The Puritan stood up and fumbled for his purse. "How much do I owe you, Mistress?" he said.

Before she could answer, the watchman had shouted, "Five shillings!"

The Puritan's jaw fell. "Five shillings? But all I've had is one cup of ale the whole time I've been here!" He looked to the woman for confirmation of the fact, but she continued to stare into the fire as the watchman advanced holding out his hand. Clearly it was futile to try and argue, so he handed over the entire contents of his purse before turning to Jack and saying in a low voice, "I will pray for you my friend. I will pray that you are as fortunate as I have been," and with that enigmatic message he walked out of the room followed by the watchman who sent him on his way with a volley of curses.

Jack remained in his seat and looked across at the constable's wife, who avoided his eyes, then up at the constable himself, who had just entered the room. "And you detained me on suspicion of highway robbery!" he said.

From: *Proceedings of Quarter Sessions for the County of Leicester. Epiphany 1663.*

The information of Robert Canvey, gentleman of the parish of Welford in the county of Leicester, in court this day on oath as followeth.

The informant saith that upon Monday the fourth of January about two of the clock in the afternoon, he being riding upon the roadway in His Majesty's highway leading between Rearsby and Gaddesby, there met with this deponent the person showed this day to this deponent in the common gaol at Leicester, who calls himself by the name of Simon Wells, who did there and then rob this deponent and took from him about five pounds. And also at the same time took from this deponent one gelding and saddle and bridle of the value of about four pounds ten shillings; which said gelding, saddle and bridle is since come into the hands of this deponent, being taken up at Leicester aforesaid.

Signed Robert Canvey.

Recognisance: the said Robert Canvey bound in twenty pounds for his appearance at the Lent Assizes in Leicester to prosecute the aforesaid for the felony and robbery. Done for the Assizes.

Thus committed for trial at the Assizes at Leicester in four weeks' time, the prisoner calling himself Simon Wells was conducted once more to Leicester Gaol.

Even after the depredations of the Watch at his arrest, and after the removal of the money believed to belong to Robert Canvey, Jack still had enough to pay for a cell of his own with cot, table and chair, and send out for food, wine and writing materials. He had made a point of hinting to the gaoler quite early on in their acquaintance that there was plenty more money which could be his if he proved accommodating, only for his hopes to be dashed by the man's reply. "While you're in here, Sir," he said, "you may purchase any little luxury that money can buy. All, that is, except one – liberty. I call it a luxury for such it is to a man in your situation. My predecessor was thrown out on suspicion of allowing a prisoner to escape, and I and mine are not about to follow him and his onto the parish, when there's money enough to be made legitimate. So use your money well until you can prove your innocence and if that, as I suspect, is impossible, at least spend your last few weeks in tolerable comfort."

Inwardly crying a pox on all honest men, but taking care not to upset the gaoler he had thrown himself on his cot and considered his predicament. There was a month to go before the Lent Assizes, a month in which he had either to bribe or break his way out of this place as there was no doubt that he would be found guilty and hanged if he let it come to trial. By no means a hero, but possessed of a strong instinct for survival and a capacity for clear thought in a crisis, he immediately set to work on the gaoler's assistant, a youth of some seventeen years. He scribbled a quick letter to Tom telling him where he was, under what name, and how much time he had. Then stressing

that there would be more for both of them if the letter was
delivered swiftly, he committed it to the care of the lad along
with a sum of money sufficient to hire a carrier to take it to the
Dog. Having done all he could for the time being, he called for
more wine, and for the next few days indulged himself in the
luxury of excessive drinking and even more excessive self-pity.

8

Both the gaoler and his wife, seemingly proud to have such a man in their custody, went out of their way to make him comfortable. However, Jack's thoughts in prison were far from happy ones. Firstly there was the reflection that even if the letter reached Tom and the others safely, there was little they could do to help him. In all likelihood they would be reduced to the role of helpless spectators at his hanging, and might, if he were lucky, be able to do him the last favour of pulling on his legs to shorten his death agony. Jack had seen several hangings in his time, and though they were not his favourite spectacle, he had always managed to watch them without batting an eyelid. This was because, even since he had taken to the road, he had never seriously believed it possible that such a thing could happen to him. The realisation that it could, and soon in all likelihood would, came as a severe shock to him. The choking death and that obscene kicking dance had always seemed a fate reserved for those less fortunate or of meaner condition than himself, and as the days passed with no word from his comrades the prospect loomed increasingly large on the horizon and seemed to occupy his every waking thought as well as intruding into his dreams.

When he was not thinking of this, his mind was troubled by the reflection that it was a good thing after all that his parents had not lived to see their son reach manhood, since fate had dealt him such cards as these. This led him to reflect on what his lot could have been. For the first time in two years he pondered the rewards that his and his father's service to the Crown had brought. In fairness to him, it should be added that his thoughts were not without an element of self-reproach, first of all for his carelessness in allowing himself to be caught so near to the scene of a robbery, and later for entering into this life of crime at all. When he considered what his fortunes would have been if he had not cast his lot in with those comrades who might yet contrive to save him, he became calmer, and determined that he would meet his fate with all the dignity he could muster.

He was in a considerably better frame of mind, then, by the time news arrived from Tom some days later. It came in the form of a letter brought by the gaoler's assistant without his master's knowledge. With the letter was a small cloth bag in which was a measure of white powder. The letter was infuriatingly cryptic and Jack cursed Tom and his love of mystery and subterfuge. All it said was, "Do not despair. Take this; it will make you feverish. Take to your bed and await my arrival. Tom." In such a situation, reasoned Jack, there was no alternative but to trust his companions as he had always urged the others to do. So that evening, having finished his supper, he poured the contents of the bag into his wine-cup and drained it at a draught before retiring early.

Tom proved as good as his word; in the middle of the night Jack was awakened by the unpleasant realisation that his sheets were soaked, and that for the past few hours he had hardly slept at all, but had been tossing and turning most of the time. When dawn showed itself through the small barred window high up on the wall of his cell, and the first birds had begun to sing, Jack felt more thoroughly miserable than he had done at any stage since his capture. He was incapable of tackling the ale and toasted bread that was brought to his cell as breakfast, and lay weak and miserable until halfway through the morning when the gaoler reappeared to announce that his brother was here to see him. When Tom walked in in a suit extravagant even by his standards, however, it was difficult for Jack even in his present state to restrain the expressions of joy and relief which almost overwhelmed him, and caused him to cry out weakly. Tom made no acknowledgement to his greeting, but turning to the gaoler demanded in a haughty voice as one most displeased, "How long has he been like this?"

The gaoler, on the defensive right away, replied falteringly, "Mr Wells has been in the best of health until this very morning, having received at my and my wife's hands the very best attention that . . ." and here he stopped, as much through a realisation of what he was about to say as from Tom's cold stare. Still mumbling to himself, he left, and Tom came closer to Jack's bed and smiled down at him.

"Well, you've certainly put our oath to the test," he said quietly. "Mind you, you may have cause to regret it in the next few days. We've a plan which should work. If it doesn't we'll have to try something more drastic. All it requires you to do is lie still and look ill, which you won't find difficult, I can assure you. Tomorrow you'll be visited by a doctor. Just do as he says and leave the rest to me. Now," he said, offering the toasted bread, "eat this. You'll need something inside you if you're to start vomiting," and with that he outlined the plan to Jack, and then, after a few words of encouragement, he left.

As soon as he had left the cell, Tom turned to the gaoler and in a confidential tone of voice asked, "Is there somewhere where we may talk privately?" The gaoler conducted him to a private room at the back of the building and begged the gentleman to excuse him for just a moment while he gave instructions to his assistant. On his return, he found the gentleman staring out of the window into the street below and could not help noticing his expression of grave concern. Almost afraid to interrupt the man's reveries he asked hesitantly, "What was it you wanted to talk to me about, Sir?"

"My brother of course!" snapped Tom, and then regaining his composure, he apologised and went on, "I don't like the way he looks. I have a feeling that I have seen something similar before. If you have no objections, I would like my physician to see him."

"We have our own doctor nearby, Sir," began the gaoler weakly.

"No, I think it's important that my man sees him, for reasons that I will explain later if it becomes necessary," said Tom, then added in an undertone just loud enough to be heard by the gaoler, "Pray God it is not so!"

"Well," said the gaoler, "it should really be our own doctor, but being as you've been so kind already, Sir, and Mr Wells himself a perfect . . ."

"I'll bring him first thing in the morning," interrupted Tom. Then leaning forward and touching the man lightly on the sleeve he said, "And until we've been, I would try and keep away from him if I were you. It's probably nothing, but if my worst fears are confirmed . . .'' He left the sentence hanging in the air as he walked out of the room, leaving the gaoler to ponder its meaning.

The next morning it was the gaoler's assistant rather than his wife who took Jack his breakfast, and who, minutes later interrupted the gaoler's own breakfast with the intelligence that Mr Wells had been mightily sick in the night. Tom and the doctor together with a nurse had no sooner arrived therefore than the doctor and nurse were hurried to the cell, and Tom to the gaoler's private room where he was subjected to a close questioning on his suspicions of the nature of Mr Wells' illness. Tom, however, refused to be drawn, preferring to wait for the doctor's report.

Meanwhile in Jack's cell the doctor and the nurse were shown in by the assistant who waited for only a moment or two before leaving them alone. Jack had no way of recognising the doctor who, calling himself Doctor Stamford, was in fact the same Doctor Winton who had been threatened with gaol himself near Reading some months earlier. He recognised the nurse immediately, however, and was hard put to hide his astonishment. It was Ann from the Dog. The two wasted little time on words but set immediately to work. From her bag Ann produced the makings of two evil-smelling poultices which the doctor with scarcely a word, and to Jack's considerable embarrassment, began to apply to his armpits and groin. As he worked he spoke to Jack in a whisper, ''I am told by Noll to tell you that he got these from an old friend of yours, a one-eyed vagabond called Jacob.''

''What will they do?'' asked Jack, recoiling from the stench.

''Well,'' said the doctor, ''with any luck they'll kill you. I am sorry about the smell, but it is necessary, as I am sure you realise.'' And with that they picked up their bags and left, the doctor saying over his shoulder, ''Don't disturb them, whatever happens,'' and Ann looking briefly at him as they left the cell and smiling slightly, a smile which in the circumstances brought Jack as close to tears as he had been for some years. That the gang, Noll, Tom and the others, should put themselves at risk for his sake was a thing moving enough in its own way, but that this young woman, who was still virtually a stranger to him, should have risked so much was beyond his comprehension. He assumed that the doctor, whoever he was, had been hired by Noll for the occasion; there was no shortage of such people in that profession after all.

These thoughts occupied his mind for most of the day that followed, which was as well, since the poultices began first to itch and then to burn in such a way that it was all he could do to refrain from ripping them off and abandoning the scheme altogether. Whenever he was most sorely tried however, he cast his mind back to the last hanging he had seen at Tyburn, or to that first day out with the gang, and the gibbeted man swinging there in the breeze with the crow waiting patiently for them to move on, so that it might resume its feast. If he closed his eyes he could almost feel the rope around his neck, almost hear the cheer of the crowd as he was turned off the cart and the rope tightened. Once he woke in the night screaming from a dream of crows flapping around his head trying to get at his eyes, then he felt the burn of the poultices and gave up trying to sleep.

It is not surprising therefore, that he looked a good deal worse when the following morning the doctor and Ann returned accompanied by an anxious gaoler. This latter would accompany them no further than the door of the cell, where he loitered uncertainly for a little while before he was called upon to assist. Jack winced when the poultices were removed. The doctor whistled between his teeth as Ann slipped them into her bag. "Most effective!" he said under his breath as he regarded the severe swellings they had left under Jack's arm and on the insides of his legs. "Most effective. Now, I am told they will last for a couple of days so it is time you took a turn for the worse. In a few minutes I am going to go and fetch the gaoler. You just lie perfectly still. He probably won't come much nearer than he did the last time, so we should have no trouble convincing him. The prison doctor might be a little more difficult, though I doubt it." Then they left again, the doctor's footsteps dogged this time by an almost hysterical gaoler. It was an anxious gathering that followed in the gaoler's room.

Tom stood in earnest conversation with the doctor; Ann stared out of the window with the look of a young woman facing death, and the gaoler wrung his hands as he awaited the arrival of Doctor Sanders who normally attended to the needs of the prisoners. This doctor took a while. When he did arrive it was clear he had been dragged from his bed. His eyes were red-rimmed, although this appeared to be a permanent condition, and his cheeks were unshaven. He winced slightly as Tom began to speak.

"Doctor Sanders, I have asked for you to be present so as to be able to explain to you why I insist that our family physician examine my brother first." The doctor's expression made it clear that he didn't give a damn who examined the prisoners as long as he could return to his bed. Tom continued, "The reason was that Doctor Stamford here was with my brother and I on our recent visit to Holland, and was able to observe what was happening there as closely as we were." At the word 'Holland' the gaoler's jaw dropped, and even Doctor Sanders began to take an interest.

"You were in Holland recently?" he asked, looking from Tom to his companion; both nodded solemnly.

"Then you think it might be . . ." spluttered the gaoler.

"Plague!" said Tom. The word fell from his lips like lead shot as both the doctor and the gaoler began to back instinctively away from the outsiders. "There is no reason to suppose," continued Tom, "that we are infected, but Doctor Stamford will need to know exactly who has been in contact with my brother since he arrived here." His words fell on deaf ears; the gaoler was already making for the door.

"I must inform the mayor, the constable, the . . ."

"I should think twice about doing that – " the gaoler turned at the sound of Tom's raised voice " – if I were you." The gaoler was by now well out of his depth, and prey to a thousand fears. "Why?" he asked despairingly, eager as soon as possible to hand over the problem to someone, anyone, in authority.

Tom walked deliberately towards him and lowered his voice. "As I said earlier, my brother and I were in Holland and saw the effects of the plague which is now rampaging there – Amsterdam, Rotterdam, everywhere. Do you know what they do to houses infected with it?" The gaoler shook his head. "Board them up and post armed guards around them. All inside, infected or not, are abandoned to their fate. I can tell you, Sir, the cries of those left inside will stay with me till the day I die. The cries of the sick are harrowing enough, but that healthy people should be given up to almost certain infection and death seems an offence against God. And yet, they say, it is the only way. No one leaves the house until all are dead. Is that what you want for yourself, your family and all of us, not to mention those poor wretches confined below?"

"But what else can we do?" wailed the gaoler.

Tom looked thoughtful for a moment. "There may be a way out," he said and paced off slowly deep in thought with the gaoler shuffling pitifully after him. The silence that followed was painful in the extreme for all present for different reasons. Doctor Winton had rejoined Ann at the far end of the room. Neither of them had ever been involved in anything like this before in their lives and the penalties if their imposture was discovered would be severe. It was not difficult, then, for either of them to appear nervous at the prospect of being immured alive with a diseased man. Though she knew Tom, Ann for her part knew him only as a free-spending libertine, addicted to drinking, gambling and buffoonery, and was unaware of his considerable talent for deceit. For Tom it was a difficult moment; everything depended on the gaoler falling in with his scheme. He seemed both witless and terrified enough to do so, but then there was the prison doctor to convince. This latter was leaning back against the wall now, his eyes closed and his brow furrowed, though whether from the effects of the previous night's debauch or the contemplation of the infinite, it was hard to tell. The critical moment had arrived. Tom turned.

"I have no desire for my family name to be remembered only for the reintroduction of plague into the country, and even less desire to end my days confined in your prison for whatever reason. Those are the choices that face us, unless . . ."

"Unless what?" It was the prison doctor who spoke this time, and Tom sighed inwardly with relief.

"Unless," he continued, "we keep my brother's illness a secret, and bury him as far away from here as possible at the dead of night. There is, as I have said, no evidence that any of us are infected. The two of you can certify that he died of some other sickness, and assuming that none of us develops symptoms in the meantime, no one need ever know."

"You're sure he will die?" said the gaoler. Tom looked to Doctor Winton who nodded, adding, "There is, I am afraid, no doubt of it." The gaoler was not at all happy. He clutched at a straw. "You are certain it is the plague?" Tom nodded gravely. "The doctor is quite sure. We both saw it at its worst in Amsterdam. My brother – I hesitate to say it, but – well, he was addicted to pleasures which I cannot mention in the presence of the fair sex, and which took him into quarters of the town I would not have entered for a hundred pounds. But to allay any doubts, perhaps Doctor . . ." and he turned to Doctor Winton, "you would like to take Doctor Sanders to see my brother?"

The prison doctor gulped, and his face indicated that the last thing he wished to see in all the world was the dying man upstairs, but he felt obliged to go along with this request; he would be able to see all he needed from the doorway. As they left, Tom continued to talk to, or rather at, the gaoler who had seated himself at a table with his head in his hands, and seemed beyond caring. "I have no doubt that my brother is guilty as charged, of course; he was wayward from his earliest days. But I doubt if he will live to stand trial. It will be a miracle if he lasts the night. And within days he will stand before a judge more stern than any this world has to offer. Oh, thank God our dear parents never lived to see these days!" Tom was warming to his theme now when his efforts were rewarded by the gaoler's next remark.

"Where will you take him?" he said, looking up from the table.

Tom tried his best to look mournful while his heart sang a 'Te Deum'. "Home, I suppose," he answered. "The family vault is the right and proper place for him in death whatever he may have been in life. We were never very close – natural I suppose between elder brother and younger." The gaoler nodded, then his face registered alarm as another objection occurred to him.

"What if one of us develops symptoms in the next few days? The truth will be bound to come out and everyone will know what we've done."

Tom smiled a little sadly. "If that happens, my friend," he said, "the wrath of the authorities will be the least of our worries!" and he clapped the gaoler on the shoulder, and the gaoler, anxious to avoid contact, leapt back. Further conversation was forestalled by the return of the two doctors. Sanders, as

Tom had gambled, had been content to carry out his examination from a distance of thirty feet and arrived back in the room as pale as a ghost. He said nothing but nodded at the gaoler who slumped back in his seat.

"Now then," Tom began once more, "I suggest we keep contact with him to a minimum. It is simply a matter of time now before he dies and there is nothing we can do to make his passing easier. As soon as he is dead, the two doctors can confirm his death and a certificate can be drawn up recording that he died of . . . Doctor Sanders, what do you usually say?"

"Goal fever!" answered the doctor, ignoring or not noticing the barb in the question.

"The gaol fever it shall be," declared Tom. "In the meanwhile I suggest we lie low and await events. I shall go into the town and hire a cart and some men; apart from that it's probably best if we keep away from people as much as possible. Doctor Stamford and I are staying at the Red Lion; you can contact us there. If nothing happens in the night, we shall see you first thing in the morning. Good day, gentlemen." With these words, 'Mr Wells', along with his physician and nurse, swept out of the room, leaving the gaoler and the doctor contemplating the magnitude of the deception into which they had been unwillingly drawn, and both firmly resolved not to pay the visitor upstairs any more visits until he was safely off the premises.

The following morning the doctor and nurse returned to visit the patient, escorted to the cell by the gaoler's assistant. If this young man suspected that something was wrong, and that the prisoner's illness was in some way connected with the package he had smuggled in to him earlier in the week, he kept his suspicions to himself. If this whole thing was an elaborate hoax, all well and good as far as he was concerned; he had no desire to see a man hanged for robbing a constable which was, in many ways, a laudable act. In short, it was a matter of supreme indifference to him, whether the prisoner escaped or not. What was certain though, was that if he were to tell the gaoler of his suspicions he would be forced to tell of his part in the business, and thus risk losing a secure and lucrative position. He decided therefore to keep quiet and let events take their course, and in the meantime, just in case the sickness was real, he wasn't going any nearer the prisoner than he could help. For this reason the doctor and Ann were able to work unobserved; she feeding him bread and milk to keep up his strength for the ordeal ahead, and he giving Jack precise instructions.

"At about five this evening, I want you to cease your thrashings and die. Turn your face to the wall, make sure you are in a comfortable position and lie perfectly still. You will have to stay like that for five, possibly six hours, and it isn't as easy as it sounds."

"Couldn't you give me a sleeping draught?" whispered Jack.

"Corpses don't breathe heavily, nor do they snore. Whatever you do, don't fall asleep. Just concentrate on being dead. As soon as possible I'll come in and declare you so, and then we can set about removing your body. There's no need to worry about the gaoler or the prison doctor; they won't touch you or come within a mile of you if they can help it. The box we're going to put you in is made loosely enough for you to breathe all right. Tom spent an hour in it last night to be sure, and you should not be in it above half. Above all remember, whatever happens, lie perfectly still, and with any luck we'll be on the road to London by morning." At these words they left, Ann pressing his hand as they did so, and then he was alone.

There had been occasions in Jack's life when it had been necessary to remain still for long periods: as a boy out hunting with a bow and arrow; the night after Worcester with Ironsides prowling every lane in the county, and subsequently in his new career; but never had he been faced with such a challenge as this. At half past five that evening the prisoner known as Mr Wells turned his face to the wall and died. His family physician was summoned, he was declared dead, and arrangements began for the surreptitious removal of the corpse as far as possible from Leicester Gaol. For the gaoler the ordeal of the past few days was almost over. For Jack it was approaching its climax. Within an hour he had developed an itch on his left cheek which in the course of a further hour became the focal point of his whole existence. His every thought was concerned with that itch; he longed to scratch it with an intensity that made him want to cry out in anguish; he dreamed of the moment when he would be free to do so, until this became the sole purpose for achieving that freedom. It became such an obsession that he was at one stage ready to throw caution to the winds and do it, gambling that there would be no one to see him. But what if there were? The whole plan would be revealed. His friends would return that night and walk straight into a trap. Then he thought of the hangman's noose and lay still.

To while away the time and take his mind off his torment he occupied himself with planning his revenge on the men who had sent him here, and then with plans for the future of the gang which had proved its worth a hundred times since its formation but never more so than now. This done he thought of what he would do the moment he was finally free, and after he had scratched his cheek. He planned it down to the last detail: the food he would eat, the wines he would choose, and the gifts he would shower on his friends who for his sake had risked so much. Then at last, almost reluctantly, he began to think of Ann. He had avoided the subject so far because it was beyond his comprehension why she, who almost from the moment of their first meeting had shown scant regard for him, should suddenly appear in company with his friends to effect his escape. Despite his early attempts to befriend her, she had seemed rather to wish to avoid too close an acquaintance with him; and yet here she was co-operating cheerfully with a band of men, who for all their admirable qualities, were nonetheless criminals.

Women had always been something of a mystery to him, but if he had expected any woman to put herself out on his behalf, it would have been Lucy. Not that he expected much from her; he had always been aware of her little ways and harboured few illusions as to what she got up to in his absence. He had no doubt that as soon as the news of his capture had reached her she had gone out to the park or somewhere to find a new benefactor. Nor did he blame her for that: she had to live. If Jack was cynical he had also the tolerance that goes with cynicism. What upset his whole view of the world was the appearance of Ann, and indeed so engrossed did he become in the contemplation of this matter that he failed to notice the time passing by, or mercifully, the racking cramp in his legs which was at its most acute by the time the cell door opened and two voices could be discerned whispering in the doorway.

"Now, I suggest we both go forward and examine the body,"

said one whom Jack recognised as his own doctor. Jack's heart beat so loudly that for a moment it seemed certain the men at the door would hear it.

"N . . . n . . . no need for that. I can see well enough from here that he's dead," replied the other voice, slurring his speech slightly.

"In that case," came the first voice, "let's waste no time, but get the men up here straight away," and the voices departed.

Jack heard a muffled cry from down in the depths of the building, and a few minutes later four men came into the cell cursing and bumping with a long box of coarse wood. Even in the darkness of the cell, Jack could recognise the faces of Hugh Jeffrey, Robert Warren and the unmistakable bulk of Will Reynolds. The fourth man was Noll, and once again Jack had to fight the urge to cry out in delight and embrace the man. They picked him up by the feet and shoulders and dumped him heavily and unceremoniously in the box.

"Show a little respect, damn you!" It was Tom's voice that broke the silence. "That's my brother!"

"That was your brother," replied Noll, before the gaoler's voice interrupted and bade them all be silent. The next few minutes were hot, sweaty and uncomfortable for Jack as he felt himself lifted on high and manoeuvred downstairs on the shoulders of his companions. His thoughts raced. God, but it was hot in here. What if they should drop him and he should cry out? What if . . . his thoughts were interrupted by the sound of horses hooves from nearby; they were close to the entrance of the prison. Never in his whole life, before or after, did Jack hear a sound which seemed to him so beautiful. The sound of those horses meant to him everything he prized, and everything he had seemed about to lose. They represented freedom, the road, fresh cool air and the sun in his face. He blessed those horses; he would buy them, and they would never work again but would live out their days in some sunny pasture decked with ribbons and worshipped like temple animals in some pagan land of long ago, if they would only take him away from this hellish place.

On the outside the four men heaved the box onto the back of a cart which had been backed right up to the main entrance of the gaol. The gaoler was everywhere at once, nervous as a cat, and glancing continually up and down the street. Beside him stood Tom looking as solemn as a man can be who is about to carry off his greatest-ever deception. In a few moments it was done, and Doctor Winton emerged from the gaol with the prison doctor, having signed a certificate to the effect that 'the prisoner Wells' had died of gaol fever that night. The box loaded, Tom turned to the gaoler who had joined his companion in the doorway.

"Well, that seems to be everything. Let us hope that this is the end of the matter. You may rest assured that my brother's body will be disposed of in such a way that there will be no risk of infection from it." The looks on the faces of the two in the doorway made it clear that they did not give a jot what happened to the body, as long as it happened well away from Leicester. Tom offered them his hand. Neither of them made any attempt to take it, so he merely smiled and bade them farewell. As the cart moved off, the gaoler shouted to Doctor Winton, "Doctor, how long?" The doctor turned, his brow furrowed. "How long before we know we're safe?" added the gaoler.

The doctor thought for a moment and then smiled, "If nothing has happened after a week or so, I think we can safely say that all will be well!" As the cart drew away down the street the gaoler and the prison doctor looked at each other and went back inside to begin their anxious vigil.

The cart with its attendant riders rattled off down the lane, turned the bend into the main street where it stopped for a few minutes to take on a solitary woman and some baggage, and then moved off once more past the forewarned and forepaid Watch and out of town on the main road towards Northampton. A mile out of town, they pulled over to a passing place in the road, opened the box, and with a good deal of hand-shaking and back-slapping resurrected its occupant. Amidst the cheering that greeted his return to the land of the living, Jack could do no more than smile weakly and raise his hand feebly in acknowledgement. Straight away the doctor took a hand, forcing a brandy flask between Jack's lips while Ann wrapped him in coats and blankets. After the doctor had made it clear in no uncertain terms to the cheering horsemen around the cart that all their efforts would have been in vain if Jack were to freeze to death, and that he was still very weak from his ordeal, they moved off once more.

Under his mound of coats and blankets Jack drank deeply from the flask and sucked in the cold night air. The feeling of relief which swept over him was almost like a physical force. In his weakened state the liquor lost no time in taking effect and, cold as he was, he soon began to nod. Just before he drifted into unconsciousness he remembered his earlier promise to himself and reached to scratch his cheek. To his immense frustration the itch was gone.

He was still asleep when at about midnight they arrived at an inn set back from the road slightly, whose host had been warned the day before to expect them. With no questions asked they were shown to an upstairs room where mulled wine was already prepared, and the host informed them that food would be on its way within minutes. Here the merriment began in earnest, merriment in which Jack, though he was the happiest man alive at that moment, took but little part. The effect of the wine on top of the brandy was to put him into a deep sleep very much akin to the death he had spent most of that day faking, and it was soon necessary for Tom and Hugh to put him to bed in a nearby room.

For the others, however, sleep was totally out of the question; the excitement of the last few days and the relief that their efforts had proved successful was such that no one had any thought but to drink, eat and relive their experience well into the night. For some there was simply the knowledge of another desperate venture carried off and no doubt another addition to the growing body of legend about Captain Coranto and his men. For others perhaps, there was the satisfaction of a debt well paid. Tom for example, had never quite forgotten that day on Shooters Hill and despite the assurances of the other two, secretly felt that he had somehow let them down. In this rescue, he had not only saved the life of a friend he prized highly, but redeemed himself in his own eyes. Small wonder then, that on this night he was at his most exuberant. Noll, for his part, had been on the verge of despair when the news of Jack's capture had reached him. A man who had lost many friends through violent death, he felt more for this one than he cared to admit. For him this had been more important than any of the coups he had achieved in his long career. As well as saving Jack, whom he had come to regard like a son, and paying him back for his own rescue on the Heath that day, he had shown them all that he was still a force to be reckoned with. Despite Tom's leading role the plan and organisation had been all his own. Ann and the doctor – neither of whom had ever performed a criminal act or even told a deliberate lie before – contemplated the enormity of what they had done, and marvelled that the heavens had not come crashing down upon their heads. Then as the drink took its effect, and the revelry of this band of robbers grew louder, they threw their consciences to the wind for one night and revelled too in their own resource and daring.

9

The day was well advanced before any of that little party felt disposed to move on, but Noll was keen to put as much distance as possible between themselves and Leicester, so by mid-morning they were on the road again. They were going to London via Reading; Noll was keen that Jack should get some clean air into his lungs before throwing himself once more into the life he customarily led in company with Tom. Jack was still too weak to stand a long journey, so they took it in slow, easy stages. That journey to Reading was one which Jack long afterwards remembered as one of the most pleasant he had ever made.

The first day was largely taken up with Tom and Noll recounting the tale of how the rescue had been conceived and put into operation. Tom, needless to say, took the major part of the tale-telling for himself. "It was fortunate your note reached us when it did, for it so happened that Noll was up in London at the time. We called the gang together and agreed that the first thing to do was to go and see Frost. Well, when he heard what we had to say he seemed most perturbed, but made it quite clear that there was nothing he could do to help. This came as something of a surprise to us, I don't mind admitting, as we had always thought that there was nothing and no place that was beyond his reach. Anyway, he was quite adamant that he had no contacts anywhere in this part of the country and that the best thing we could do was elect a new leader.

"By this time the news was quite widespread in the vicinity of the Dog and you would have been flattered by the distress it caused. Noll realised of course that this meant we had to act fast before word got out through some informer that the man held in Leicester gaol was none other than Captain Coranto. He had the germ of a plan in his head but wouldn't tell any of us what it was, which I think was a wise precaution considering how things are in London.

"Anyway, just as we were about to leave, up comes Ann – " and here Tom lowered his voice so that Ann, who was riding ahead of them talking with the doctor, would not hear, " – and announces that she is coming with us. Nor would she be put off, either. Said that like it or not, she was coming and simply marched off to the kitchens and told Frost the same thing. You should have seen his face! Didn't dare say a word though, not with all of us standing there, but you could tell he wasn't best pleased. My, but aren't you a dark horse?" and here he nudged Jack in the ribs. "You kept that one a secret. None of us even guessed. How did you ever keep it from Lucy? You must tell me how you do it sometime." Jack was just about to open his mouth to assert that there had been nothing between them when Tom was interrupted by Noll, "Get on with it will you? He wants to hear about my plan, not your sordid imaginings!"

"Well," Tom started once more, "it seems that Noll knew the doctor there, from – " he got no further.

"From having on pure impulse saved him from the bailiffs one day, when they were about to throw him into Reading Gaol for a paltry six pounds," said Noll. "It seemed a shame; Joyce told me that he was a good man, and I didn't much care for the bailiff; in fact, I robbed him a few days later out of sheer devilment. In any case, I thought that a tame doctor is always a useful commodity in our profession, though I didn't know how useful he would eventually be, nor how soon."

Tom took up the tale again. "I knew from the gossip in the cockpits and at the card tables that the plague was raging in Amsterdam, and I happened to mention it to Noll on the road, and that gave him the idea. With the doctor along to provide the expert knowledge, and a couple of poultices from those beggars that turn up at Joyce's from time to time, we were able to carry it off. Of course Noll decided that I should play the part of your brother; we look sufficiently alike and after all, Noll couldn't look like a gentleman if he tried!" They all laughed as Noll cuffed the younger man across the ear, almost unseating him from his horse.

As soon as the laughter had died down he carried on undeterred, "What makes me laugh is the thought of the gaoler and the prison doctor inspecting each other's armpits every day for the next week!''

Pleasant as this tomfoolery was after the dismal thoughts that had assailed him in prison, that part of the journey which he was ever after to remember fondly was the one he had spent with Ann. The others, showing more tact than he would have thought any of them capable of, left them alone as far as possible. Whatever the others may have thought, they were in fact virtual strangers to each other, and the next few days were for both of them a voyage of discovery. Jack found that in her company he was at once eager to talk more than usual whilst at the same time constrained as to what he could say. Neither of them had made any mention of Ann's sudden decision to come along to Leicester with the gang; her motives for doing so were understood between them at once and never again alluded to. Jack quickly learned also that any mention of the way in which he and his comrades earned their living met with a none too subtle attempt to change the subject. Although she had been prepared to become involved with them to save him from hanging, that was as far as it went. This came as something of a shock to Jack, who had been used to the adulation a 'knight of the road' could expect from women of all stations in life. Being forced to avoid the subject altogether left him at a loss; although he was not as addicted to boasting of his exploits as Tom, his career on the road had been the stuff of his life for what seemed like an eternity, and he had become accustomed to talking of little else.

He persevered, however, and soon found that in her company he was able to talk freely of subjects he had schooled himself to avoid. Ann had spent all her life in the city, and so knew little of the countryside; the sights and sounds all around them were new to her, and Jack – a countryman by birth, and by inclination – was able to enlighten her. He took great pleasure in this; although she was by no means an innocent she seemed to possess – Jack noticed almost with envy – a childlike sense of wonder at the world. At times too, her eyes would stare off over the horizon; she would seem lost in some dream, and he would wonder what she was thinking. Accustomed all his adult life to the company of the kind of women who hung around the camp or frequented the taverns of

Whitefriars and Billingsgate, the feelings she aroused in him were totally unfamiliar. Never before, even with Lucy – of whom, for all her faithless ways he was fond – had he given a moment's thought to what they were thinking; it had never seemed important. Now as he rode alongside Ann it was his main concern, and he fell ever deeper under her spell whilst Tom and Noll – who for all he was their leader, were in many ways far wiser than he – exchanged significant glances.

Inevitably as they talked he wandered onto the subject of his youth, of his home in the north, and the happy times before the wars that she could scarce remember. Ann proved a willing audience, and Jack found to his amazement that he was able to talk about those days without the feelings of bitterness that had always risen up in him before. This discovery was worth more to him than he could find words to express; it was as if a dam had burst. All at once, Jack, who had for the past three years lived in and for the present, found himself able to consider the past and even contemplate a future beyond the immediate concerns of the next expedition or the next debauch. Soon he was amazing himself with his own garrulousness. In between talking of his own hopes for the future, he listened to Ann's own story.

She told him of her childhood, and rehearsed for him the tragic history of her mother's final illness and her father's heroic efforts to save her which had left him bankrupt, broken and exhausted; and of their last days together in Whitefriars. On her father's death she had been forced to take whatever form of employment she could find. Caring for her father after her mother's death had taught her more than enough to find work as a cook, and she had taken a post at the Dog on the same day that Jack had first met her. It was when she talked of this that Jack began to discern that she was a better judge of character than others might have given her credit for. Jack had asked her how things were at the Dog.

"Oh as bad as ever," she declared, and seeing Jack's surprised expression she continued, "I suppose you think all's well there, do you? Well things may be from where you are."

"Well," said Jack, "I don't suppose Frost is the best man in the world to work for, but I've always found him friendly enough. Not that I'd trust him too far though."

"You'd be a fool to trust him at all," came the reply. "You probably don't notice the way he treats his family. Margaret lives in terror of him, Jack; she's a slave in that kitchen, and I sometimes think she goes in fear of her life. Hardly surprising when you hear what they say about his first wife, Jane's mother."

"What do they say?" asked Jack, remembering that this was one of the many subjects that Frost had avoided whenever they had talked.

"You know the Dog was hers? It had belonged to her father." Jack nodded. "Well," she continued, "it seems that he came along, swept her off her feet, and within a few months they were married. Now, she had a son from a previous marriage, and he and Frost didn't get on. This didn't worry him much though, because the boy was only young. Anyway, after about a year, she had a daughter – that was Jane – and after that she grew ill. She never really recovered, so they say, from her second child, and within a year she had sickened and died. Shortly after that the boy ran away, or 'so they say' again. Anyway, he was never heard of again, and since then Frost has been the sole owner of the Dog."

"So what conclusion do you draw from all that?" asked Jack, more amused than anything.

Ann looked at him in amazement, "Doesn't it strike you as odd? A man comes out of nowhere and marries a woman who owns a tavern which for all its faults brings in a tidy income. Then within two years she sickens and dies and her son and heir runs off to sea or somewhere and is never seen or heard of again? And that doesn't strike you as being very convenient for one man in particular?"

Jack was sceptical, "I hardly think it likely that . . ." he got no further.

"Why not?" said Ann. "It's common enough. He's a man with friends all over the city – as he's so fond of reminding everybody. And there is no shortage of so-called doctors, like that Doctor Stark who calls on him once a month as regular as a clock, and he never having had a day's illness as long as I've known him."

For some minutes Jack was too taken aback by Ann's accusations and the certainty with which they were made to say anything further. That this woman, whom he had considered so innocent, should turn out to be capable of believing such things came as something of a shock. She obviously sensed this, for after a few minutes she said, "I suppose you're shocked and think ill of me for entertaining such thoughts?" Jack was about to deny this but before he could say a word she went on, "All that proves is that for all your shining spurs, fine clothes and grand manner you're nothing but a simple country squire at heart. If you had lived in the city as long as I have you wouldn't be at all surprised at such things. Ask your friends back there," and she gestured over her shoulder at Tom, Noll and the others. "See if they're shocked. You ought to talk to some of the people around the Dog, not the swaggering fellows you go about with, but the poor folk, and hear what they have to say." Jack, by now a good deal discomfited and a little annoyed, stared ahead of him and said nothing. Ann laid a hand on his arm. "Don't be angry, Captain, just because I suggested you're not as worldly wise as you think."

"I'm not angry," he said, and she looked at him and smiled so that he conceded, "Well, maybe a little. But whether or not you think what you have said is true, I wouldn't go spreading it around. He's a powerful man, and not a man to make an enemy of."

"I don't intend to," she replied. "And anyway, most people think like you."

"Don't misunderstand me," said Jack. "I have few illusions about the man. But I must admit I find your conjectures – and that's all they are, conjectures – hard to credit. After all, he's been very useful to us in the past."

"Only because it suited him to be," replied Ann, warming to her subject once more. "Up to now he's had you where he wanted you – like everyone else – in the palm of his hand. But since you took over command of the gang, you've become less dependent on him. Why do you think he wouldn't lift a finger to help you when you were in gaol?"

"Because he didn't know anyone up there. There was nothing he could do!" answered Jack.

"Have you ever heard him admit that before?" was Ann's reply, and Jack was forced to admit that he hadn't.

"Even so," he said after a while, "I still can't believe he's as black as you paint him."

"That's because you haven't fallen foul of him. Just be sure you don't," said Ann. "Consider what happened to young John Simmons."

"Simmons?" cried Jack. "I suppose you think Frost got rid of him too?"

"Yes, as a matter of fact, I do. People who get in his way have a habit of disappearing. Surely even you have noticed that he and Jane were in love; everyone else seems to have known about it. Frost never liked the boy by all accounts, and always treated him like a dog. And when he noticed how things were between him and his daughter he became worse. Then all of a sudden the boy runs off without a word. I only know the boy from what Jane has told me, but did he seem to you the type to run away to sea or go for a soldier?" Again Jack was forced to agree.

"I know Noll has never trusted Frost," said Jack, "and I've tried as far as possible to get ourselves out of his way, but . . ."

"But it's easier not to," she butted in. "That's his way. He manages to make himself so useful to everyone that they don't notice that gradually they are slipping into his grasp. He won't rest until the whole world is sitting in the palm of his hand, and that includes you. He knows enough about you to hang you all five times over, and before long he'll be giving the orders, and then you try and defy him; he'll suddenly remember his duty as a citizen and it'll be Tyburn for the lot of you."

"If you hate him so much, why are you going back?" asked Jack after a long silence.

"Where else would I go?" she asked. "I have to live, and I have no money of my own." Jack opened his mouth to speak but before he could utter a word she spoke again. "If you're about to say what I think you are, Captain, don't bother. I don't want any part of your stolen goods, thank you very much." These last words hurt, and realising this she spoke again, more softly to him, "Don't take it to heart; you're just as helpless as all of us. What else could you do? You've loved this lawless life of yours because you think it makes you free, but can't you see that in the end you'll wind up a prisoner either in another stinking gaol, or in the pocket of the Frosts of this world? Oh, I'm sure it's a grand life while you're winning, but you can't win for ever. Eventually you'll have to pay the price, and the price is a dire one."

It was a thoughtful Captain Shipton that rode into Reading that evening, and his melancholy was only partly purged by the rapturous welcome they received from Joyce and her sons. His silence was put down by the others to tiredness, but two people knew the real reason. Late at night, and well drunk, he confessed to Noll who had seen all and guessed the truth, "I've been at close quarters with death a few times, Noll, but this time it was different. This time it touched me."

Over the next few days the party gradually dispersed. Doctor Winton returned to his anxious family with – though he had not asked for it – a torn up bond for six pounds in his pocket. Tom and the others were already growing impatient for the pleasures of London, and Ann announced that she was returning to the Dog.

The day they left Jack tried to dissuade her, but she would go. "It's more than just the need for a living," she said. "There's Jane to consider. God only knows what her father has in store for her, and I'm her only friend. She doesn't even fully understand what he's like; she still thinks that somehow he's going to find John for her. Every time he sends for her or someone knocks at the door late at night she half expects to see him again. I can't just leave her."

"How do you know he'll take you back?" said Jack, who had given up trying to defend Frost.

"Oh, he will. There's no doubt about that," she said. "He's got plans for me as well now he's thrown out that Alice," then she smiled, mounted her horse and rode down the road to where the others were waiting, leaving Jack more perplexed than ever. He watched them go, then went back into the house and told Noll that he would be returning to London sooner than he had planned.

It was late on a Saturday afternoon some three months afterwards that Robert Canvey was riding home in his coach after visiting a sick relative. He was immensely proud of his coach. It was not new of course, but its leatherwork was in reasonable condition, and few other gentlemen in the hundred could run to one. And although it was a rough ride as it rocked

on the leather straps that formed its only suspension he felt a
good deal less vulnerable in it than he was on horseback. In
truth he had never felt safe since that day he had been robbed.
It had severely damaged his standing in the hundred, nay, in
the county. A poor thing indeed, when a high constable is
robbed, and one who was known to be the best in the county.
The fact that the man had been apprehended the next day –
and in his own hundred – was it is true, some compensation but
not much. The scoundrel had died of gaol fever at Leicester
before he could be tried and hanged.

He had received his money back in full, but the robbery
looked like being the only thing that would be remembered
about his period of office. Already he was the butt of much of his
colleagues' humour. He bridled at the memory and cursed the
ill-luck that had deprived him of the pleasure of seeing the man
hang. Then he realised that he must be entering the village
where the miscreant had been caught. He was about to call to
his coachman to stop so that he could call in on the constable,
Mr Goss, and exchange a few words, when he became aware
that the coach was pulling up anyway. He leaned out of the
window to look up the road, and saw ahead of him in the
twilight a small group of men in the middle of the road flagging
the coach down with their lanterns. As the coach slowed, he
recognised the brown coats worn by all the watchmen in his
hundred. Canvey smiled and settled back in his seat; no doubt
there was some local alarm and Goss had called out the Watch.
A good man, Goss, a good man; a little over-zealous at times
perhaps, but it had paid off in the past, and he kept the Watch
on its toes. Like a little army it was, and the men always sober,
tidy and respectful. He would give them a few words of
encouragement, address the troops, as it were. The coach drew
to a stop and he leaned out. He did not recognise the watchman
who confronted him, and frowned for an instant to try and
recollect if he had seen him before. The frown was still on
his face when the man raised a pistol and thrust it under his
nose.

"If you'd be so kind as to step down, Sir," said the man,
"we'll have to search your coach."

"You'll do no such thing my man!" shouted Canvey
throwing open the door and alighting. "Do you realise who I

am? I am Robert Canvey, high constable of the hundred. Now put that thing away and take me to Mr Goss at once."

The man turned to the two who had joined him. "You heard what the gentleman said – take him to see Mr Goss."

Somehow someone had crept up behind Canvey and crouched behind him, for when the man shoved him in the chest he fell sprawling in the mud. Before he could even cry out, the two were on him, had ransacked his pockets, removed his boots, bound and blindfolded him, and were marching him off. They dragged him through a hedge and across a very muddy field to what smelled like a cow shed or sheep pen; he knew not which, he only knew that whatever it was that was on the floor oozed through his stockings. As they threw him full length in the stuff his blindfold slipped enough for him to make out a number of other figures similarly bound lying beside him. There, Mr Robert Canvey, high constable of the hundred, Mr Goss the constable and his entire Watch, as well as four other unfortunate travellers passed a most uncomfortable night. Canvey spent most of it wondering whether they would find the twenty pounds under the seat of his coach. He needn't have worried. They did.

10

On Jack's return to London it seemed at first as if everything would go on as before. Lucy had – as Jack had suspected she might – absconded as soon as the news broke of his capture, and was, by all accounts, living on the other side of the city with an officer of a foot regiment. Jack's rooms were empty now, but he didn't mind her having departed with such haste; after all she had taken nothing with her which was not her own – for which he gave her credit – and he doubted whether he could have continued to live with her now. The fact was that, as some of the more perceptive of his acquaintances had already begun to notice, things were not the same with Jack.

Outwardly, it is true, life carried on much as before; Frost welcomed him back to the Dog coolly, but showed no sign that he wanted to change those arrangements which had worked for so long to their mutual advantage. Ann was, as she had predicted, taken back at the Dog straightway, much to the delight of Jane who had grown to love her. Jack saw her therefore, nearly every day, but she showed no disposition to talk at these times or indeed at any time when there was a danger that Frost might see. Realising this, Jack respected her wish, and would wait until late at night when they could meet in the dark alley at the back of the tavern or she could come to his rooms. He found that he longed for these moments, and that the rest of his time seemed wasted. Most of the day he would wander the town scarcely aware of where he was going, simply whiling away the hours until they could be together again. In more ways than one she was responsible for his sickness at heart, although she remained largely unaware of it, and had perhaps only helped to speed a crisis that would have come anyway in its own good time. Her refusal to have any part in the life he led, or even to accept gifts that were the fruits of his robbing ways had caused him to think long and hard about matters that he had deliberately not dwelt on before. She had managed to get him talking about his past, which he had been at pains to suppress, for in his heart of hearts, despite all his swaggering, he was painfully aware of the degraded condition into which he had fallen. He began to wonder if his friends did not feel the same way. Noll with his other life in the country, Tom with his endless and feverish pursuit of pleasure; were they perhaps seeking to suppress the awful, inevitable fact that one day they would run out of luck, and end their days choking on the end of a rope in front of a cheering crowd.

It was with these melancholy thoughts that Jack was engrossed one morning several months later, as he sat in the window of his rooms staring into the street below, watching the rain sweep the refuse down the channel in the middle of the lane and the people dodging from doorway to doorway to avoid the downpour. His thoughts were interrupted by the arrival of Tom who shouted a greeting and crossed the room to stand steaming in front of the fire.

Tom had noticed the change in his friend; how he no longer threw himself into their old ways with such gusto; how the playhouse, card tables, and cock fights did not seem to hold the appeal for him that they once had. He put this down to the effects of the close shave he had had at Leicester, coupled with Lucy's defection, and was constantly trying to bring him out of this depression of spirits by steering new women at him, and suggesting new capers. Of course he knew there was something between his friend and Ann, but Jack had never been a man to take such matters seriously. Tom's remedy was simple. Jack was temporarily out of sorts, but nothing that a fresh round of debauches wouldn't put right.

"You should have some more light in here," he said as he dried the folds of his cloak in front of the fire, "it's no wonder you're melancholy."

Jack looked across at him and smiled. He had noticed how much more boisterous Tom had become in his attempts to cheer him up – he would rather have been left alone this morning, but he realised what his friend was trying to do in his clumsy way.

"No, I'm all right," he said in a tone that belied his words.

"Good," said Tom before he could go any further, "then you can come and dine with me. I need cheering up if you don't. I lost ten pounds at cards last night. There's a new ordinary opened off Fleet Street. I thought we could dine there and then go to the Bear Garden for the prize fight, and tonight I'll take you to an alehouse I've found in Billingsgate. I've taken to going there a lot lately while you've been moping around at home."

Jack groaned inwardly, but appreciating his friend's concern he rose and reached for his sword and cloak. Without a word Tom strode over and clapped him on the shoulder and they descended together into the rainy street.

In spite of himself, Jack was in a much better mood a few hours later. The new ordinary was a great success and they had dined well, and the prize fight had turned into a near riot between the opposing supporters, much to his amusement. Now he and Tom stood gazing at London Bridge; Jack laughed as Tom reminded him how they, along with Lucy and Eliza, had raced between its piers in a boat only two years earlier – to Jack it seemed like a lifetime ago.

As darkness fell they entered the murky world of Billingsgate – not dissimilar from Whitefriars or Southwark. Jack wondered why Tom had chosen this of all places to drink that evening. He was still wondering when, after leading him through an unlit labyrinth, Tom brought him to a building, well lit on its upper floors but in an otherwise darkened alley. Once inside they ascended a steep wooden staircase with the help of a rope nailed to the wall. An old woman at the top of the stairs lighted their way with a candle. The room they entered was like any alehouse in the city, but the shrill laughter and sounds of carousal from the floor above indicated wherein lay the difference between this and some of their more regular haunts. The old woman who had lighted their way returned to the bar, and buried her nose once more in an astrologer's almanac. Two watermen were in one corner, guzzling broiled herrings and thus unable to spare a glance for the two girls in faded finery who were eyeing them coyly from an adjoining table. A group of sailors sat near the head of the stairs arguing cheerfully but noisily about which of them had been in the hottest or coldest climes, or who had been in the greatest danger in such and such a sea fight.

Tom led Jack in and ordered Nantz brandy from a pretty little girl who could not have been older than fourteen. By the time she had gone the two girls across the room had turned their attention to the newcomers, and with a cry of recognition the youngest of them rushed across the room, kissed Tom on the cheek and sat down beside him. She was small and pretty and looked scarcely older than the child who had taken their order.

Jack saw now why they had come here. In answer to Jack's smile Tom winked and indicated with his eyes to the girl's companion. Jack saw at once that he had got the worst of the bargain. She leaned across and breathed lewdly in his ear. Having been laid low in Holland once with a swingeing clap, Jack had always been inclined to caution in such matters. Now, with the entry of Ann into his life, he had lost all taste for such pleasures. He shook his head and raised his cup to indicate his preference. She leaned forward once more and whispered, louder this time, "I do have a brother . . ." and fell about giggling drunkenly. Then, giving a dismissive shrug she left him and went upstairs to join her sisters who seemed to be having a better time. Left to his own devices – Tom and his friend had eyes for no one but each other – Jack returned to his brandy. He was quite happy to leave Tom to his pleasures – no doubt he would have to lie to Eliza for him tomorrow.

His thoughts and most other activity in the room ceased seconds later, when from the upper floor clumped a figure who might have doubled for Goliath in a country play. The stone buckles on his shoes, his buff coat and the cropped hair on his cannonball of a head proclaimed him to be an apprentice boy, a slightly misleading term at the best of times, but especially so in this case. The floorboards shook as he heaved over towards the old woman and ordered more ale in a voice thick with drink. Even the sailors paused for a moment in their bantering as he swept the room with a surly and threatening gaze before making his way unsteadily back to the stairs. The implicit challenge did not go unheeded and Jack closed his eyes and groaned as one of the sailors announced loudly, "He's tacking against the wind!", to which another replied, "He must be a weaver's apprentice." The apprentice stopped halfway up the stairs, but did not turn his head. Then he continued on his way followed by redoubled mockery.

For a short while it seemed as if all would be well. Jack was returning to his drink and Tom to his fumblings when there was a renewed clattering on the stairs. 'Goliath' had returned with a clamouring crowd of his fellows. He stopped for an instant before hurling a green glass bottle at the heads of his tormentors. The drink had affected his aim and the bottle smashed on the wall; its contents steamed. In a moment one of the sailors had sprung to his feet and, nimble as a monkey, slipped down the stairs into the street. The remainder stood their ground and prepared to repel boarders. Grabbing the girl by his side Tom flattened himself against the wall as the apprentices, by far the larger party, rushed past them to the assault. As they did so Jack was able to see Tom pointing in the direction of the stairs to indicate that they should make their separate ways out of there as soon as they could. Parted from his friend by the brawling mob, Jack joined the watermen and their herrings in the corner.

The fight ebbed and flowed across the room as each side in turn fell back and rallied. It was brutal close-quarter work with cudgels, chair-legs, bottles, fists and feet; a sort of fighting with which Jack was unfamiliar and intended to remain so. Several heads had been broken and eyes gouged before the nimble sailor, who far from abandoning his friends had gone to a nearby tavern for reinforcements, returned with a dozen sailors at his back. It was the apprentices who now fell back, making their way towards the staircase from which they had descended and from where the whores, out of loyalty to their customers, were pitching bottles into the ranks of the sailors below. On the fringes of the fight, the old woman and the child were sheltering under the bar, Tom and his girl were hiding under the stairs, and Jack was sitting under a table with the two watermen who, in the spirit such intimacy engenders, were sharing their herrings with him.

With neither side appearing likely to win outright, and casualties being roughly equal, the fight might have petered out there and then, had not one of the apprentices, after felling a sailor with a stool, rushed to the window and, leaning out, shouted, "Clubs! Clubs!"

"Clubs!" the cry was taken up further down the street and again a few streets away, "Clubs!" – the rallying cry of the

London apprentice. Minutes passed and the garrison of the upper storey was on the brink of defeat when relief arrived from below. A clamour arose from the street as first the bottom floor, then the stairs, then the room itself filled with fresh draughts of apprentices, and the engagement threatened to turn into a massacre of the maritime party.

It was at this moment that Jack decided to execute that military manoeuvre appropriate to a man in danger of being caught up in someone else's battle – the *sauve qui peut*, and he made his way to the stairhead, closely followed by the watermen who reluctantly abandoned their last herring. Drawing his sword he managed to struggle down to within three steps of the bottom by kicking and cracking heads with his hilt. Just then, however, he tripped and fell to the foot of the stairs in a tangled heap of apprentices and watermen. Emerging from this heap of humanity he saw that the constable and the Watch had arrived, and anxious to nip this trouble in the bud before the whole city took fire, were laying about them indiscriminately with their staves. To the right, struggling through a window, he saw Tom and his companion who had somehow managed to descend the stairs as well. Meanwhile in the street outside it seemed to be raining whores, sailors and apprentices as all upstairs abandoned ship to escape the Watch. Jack fought his way towards a window and had laid his free hand on the sill when something struck his head from behind. His last sight was of Tom being swept up the street by the crowd, looking anxiously over his shoulder towards him, then the tumult faded and he pitched forward into the darkness.

Jack awoke to the realisation that he was cold; the hardness of his bed and the throbbing of his head dawned on him later. For a while he lay in that half-sleep, normally pleasant, but this morning accompanied by the vague feeling that all was not well. Pressing in on his befuddled senses were all the sounds and smells of the camp, and for a few moments he assumed he was a soldier again before realising that all that was behind him now. Even so, there was no mistaking that old familiar smell, a mixture of cheesy stockings, armpits and stale breath which even in this cold air was beginning to grow oppressive. He stirred, his head screamed and he lay still again, taking stock. This was not the first time he had awoken in strange surroundings with an aching head, and he groaned when he saw where he was.

The sight that greeted him was not a soothing one. He was in a large, bare, flagged room with a pitiful fire in its centre which warmed only the two or three who lay around it wrapped up like bundles of dirty washing, covered in ashes. The remaining thirty or so occupants were variously attempting to keep warm. Some were still asleep, screwed into tight, uncomfortable knots on the raised platform on which Jack found himself or under benches and tables in the main body of the room. Others stamped up and down the flags, rubbing stiff joints and watching their frozen breath rise to the ceiling. One large group was already mustering by the fire, and others clustered near the large, studded oak door, or added their names to the thousands that covered the timber on the walls.

Jack rubbed some life into his limbs; his hip ached from the hard floor. He felt something wriggle inside his shirt, removed a louse, cracked it with familiar ease and began to survey the room. His fellow inmates (for he soon realised himself to be enjoying the hospitality of the constable) seemed, as might be expected, to be the sweepings of the city. The clothing of the largest part of them was frayed, filthy, and barely adequate for the time of year; others were dressed in rags. Before he had time to observe much more he noticed that the large party by the fire was moving round the room from group to group, and that coins were changing hands. It became clear that those still on the platform were mostly newcomers and that this marauding band were acting in the role of tax-gatherers. As they approached each new inmate they set up a cry of "Garnish, garnish!" whereupon their victim was expected to pay two shillings. As each man paid up the leader of the band stepped forward. He was a powerfully built man with a pock-marked face and a badly broken nose. When he smiled, Jack noticed that only the left side of his mouth had any teeth.

"You are cordially welcome to this, the King's ward of Poultry Compter," he would say, "and admitted to its protection and privileges." Then he would move on to the next man, collecting tribute from each. Occasionally some poor soul would turn out empty pockets or attempt to stammer an apology, only to receive a cuff across the ear and immediate relegation to the meanest class of subject in this dungeon kingdom.

As they made their way towards him Jack reached into his purse for the money; two shillings seemed reasonable enough, and as a natural supporter of kings he had no desire to subvert the established order. Before he could withdraw his hand from the purse, however, the leader of the mob smiled ingratiatingly at him, gave a slight bow, as much as his standing with his fellows would allow, and muttering, "Good day to you Captain," passed him by. Surprised and gratified by this effect of his reputation, Jack took the compliment as though it were no more than his due, and turned his attentions to the state of his clothing. As he brushed off the straw and worse that clung to him, Jack eyed the door through which the turnkey would shortly appear. He was no stranger to the Compter; nights with Tom had ended up here before, but this time Jack was keener than ever to pay the turnkey and the constable the customary bribes and be off. The fetid air and studded door had dreadful associations for him now.

Over to his right the mob had come up with the main group of new arrivals, who were huddled together at one end of the platform. As Jack watched without much interest one poor wretch was receiving a buffet across the head, to the cheers of the rabble, as the remainder fished into their purses or prepared for the worst. A second man had found the money and was being admitted to the protection of the crowd when one face among the many caught Jack's eye. It was a long sallow face, thin-lipped and red-eyed beneath a mat of pale red hair. It was a face that Jack had not seen in many years, and those years had made their mark on it, but he recognised it at once. It was the same face he had seen as a boy, smirking down at him and his mother as she had pleaded with the commissioners. As Jack darted forward into the crowd the face disappeared from view. Jack shouted, "Overton!" but his cry was lost in the general clamour. Shouldering his way unopposed through the press he saw that his quarry had fallen to his knees and was now coughing into a dirty handkerchief, unaware of his presence. Jack stopped and stared, still unable to believe what he saw.

Although the face was thinner, ravaged by sickness, and the once fine black suit was rusty and soiled, the man before him was unmistakable: Thomas Overton, bailiff to Martin Bracewell, and the agent of Jack's dispossession. All question as to how the man came to be in London and in this state were forgotten as Jack moved forward to obey his immediate impulse; to throw himself on the man and tear him to pieces. Before he could do so the crowd had come between them once more, and Overton found himself confronted by the leader of the mob, who strode forward to collect his dues. Unable either to pay or resist, or even care what befell him, Overton looked up with lack-lustre eyes, resigned to his fate. Nor did his expression change, apart from a slight sagging of the jaw, when a well-dressed stranger parted the crowd, and threw two shillings into the straw in front of him. The gang leader turned and regarded Jack who nodded to where the coins lay and grunted, "There's his due. He's mine."

Overton looked from one to the other as the leader indicated to one of his cronies who stooped to pick up the coins. In an instant the crowd had melted away, and Overton faced his rescuer. The man who towered over him regarded him with an expression far from friendly, and there was something familiar about him. Overton prided himself on his memory and he had detected some traces of the speech of the North country as the man had spoken. His eyes narrowed as he peered up under the brim of the man's hat; then recognition dawned and hope died within him.

Nevertheless he smiled a bitter defeated smile.

"It does you great credit, after all this time," he said, "that you can still take pity on an old neighbour."

"Pity!" Jack spat the word back at him. "I'm surprised you can say the word without choking. My first thought was to kill you."

Overton looked up suddenly, "And your second thought?"

Jack looked into his eyes; there was fear there, certainly, but there was something else too. The man's mind was working fast, seeking for advantage.

"My second thought," said Jack, "was that you may be of use to me."

"In return for what?"

"In return for passage out of this place . . ." He was interrupted by Overton's renewed coughing, "and the services of a doctor."

Behind him Jack could hear the sound of bolts being withdrawn and a large key turning in a lock. As the crowd surged towards the door, Jack reached down and hauled Overton to his feet. "Stay close by me," he grunted.

Overton managed a weak, sly smile, "Have no fear, I shall be your shadow."

Without a word Jack turned on his heel and marched up to the door with the crowd parting before him, and passing through it with Overton close behind, descended the stairs to the cellar, which was the object of the general stampede.

There in a room dimly lit but a good deal warmer they were able to purchase two mugs of ale and some toasted bread by way of breakfast. Overton accepted eagerly whatever Jack gave him, and ate and drank feverishly, never for a moment taking his eyes off Jack who never once looked at him. The room was filling up now with the occupants of the other wards including the women. All who had either money or credit were quaffing and chattering; sailors and apprentices rubbed shoulders, the previous night's quarrel forgotten; whores and drunkards, pimps and pickpockets mingled with the ragged, regular inmates and the usual debtors. These last presented a most affecting sight, and with the arrival of the women and children pitiful little reunions took place as far as possible from the remainder of the prisoners. Looking at them, Jack thought of his mother's last years, falling ever deeper into debt, believing her son to be dead, and suffering the persecution of Bracewell and this man who now hung on his elbow. When the turnkey appeared once more at the head of the stairs, Jack beckoned to him, and after a few whispered words and the exchange of some coins, the man left them.

Seeing that his benefactor was in no mood for conversation, Overton remained silent – the food and drink had revived him somewhat, and there was no doubting that his fortunes had revived also. Shipton wanted something from him – he had a good idea what – and he was sure he could use that fact to his advantage.

The two continued to drink in silence until the arrival of the constable; the needles tucked into his sleeves showed him to be a tailor by trade. After exchanging a few words with the turnkey he began the business of sorting out those who would go before the justices. Jack waited for what seemed like an age, finally darting a glance at the turnkey, who at once whispered in the constable's ear. The constable listened for a few moments, then nodded and turned towards Jack and his companion.

"What, Sirs, you still here?" he said and inclined his head towards the stairs. Jack needed no further prompting, but raced up to them, closely followed by Overton and the turnkey who returned Jack's sword and led them both out through the main gate and into the morning sunshine.

It was an hour later in the upper room of a nearby tavern that Overton, fortified by a bowl of gravy soup and a jug of mulled sack, was ready to tell his story. "I was still bailiff to Bracewell until six months ago," he said, "when he threw me out. Certain ... er ... irregularities in the book-keeping finally came to his notice. He sent me out on the road with no more than I stood ... *stand* up in. I had to walk to London. I could tell you tales of how I suffered upon the road that would ..."

"Spare me them," said Jack curtly.

"Well, the rest is quickly told. I arrived in London all but penniless. I had not been here a week when I lost what little remained in a crooked card game – " at this Jack smiled for the first time that morning, " – and was reduced to stealing my bread. I was taken up by the Watch two days ago, and was in the compter till this morning. My health is ruined, I ..."

"That's enough!" Jack interrupted him, "I'm not concerned with you. Tell me about Bracewell."

Overton smiled. "Well, he's much as you remember him; a little stouter, perhaps, and a lot richer. He has all your father's land, you know, and the Denbys' and a few others' besides. He's done well out of them, thanks to me, for which much gratitude I got. No more than I had in my purse, all because of a few pounds here and there ... set me walking upon the road, after all those years ..."

"So now you know what it's like," snapped Jack, "I don't want to hear that either. How did he come to own my father's land?"

"Well, your going paved the way."

"My going? I was little more than a boy. What difference could I make?"

"You were man enough to go and join the King, and thus add your Malignancy to that of your father's. Things couldn't have fallen out better for Bracewell. He was a commissioner, don't forget. His committee set the fines to be paid by Royalists. Yours was a notoriously Malignant family. Your lands were sequestered and the fine set at . . . one third if I remember rightly. Your mother had to pay half straight off just to get the land back."

"How did she manage that?" Jack's voice choked as he spoke.

"Bracewell lent her the money."

"Bracewell?"

"Yes, it was the usual way with him. He came at night offering to lend the money. Told her he was keen to mitigate the effects of these sad times on local gentry. From then on she was in his debt."

"But how did he get the land?"

"It was easy enough for a man in his position to keep turning the screw: timber-felling on your land, provisions for the army. It all helped to make sure she never recovered. Then, when the time came for the remainder of the debt to be paid . . . the well ran dry."

"He refused to lend her any more?"

"He claimed he couldn't. It came to the same thing. The land was sequestered and granted as payment of debts to her main creditor."

"Bracewell."

"Exactly. Your mother probably died thinking he was her friend."

Jack was on his feet now. "Then the land wasn't sold voluntarily?"

"It wasn't sold at all. His right to the land died with the republic. But with you dead, who was there to challenge him for it?"

"So I have a case at law?"

Overton smiled. "Ah well, if it's legal advice you want, that will cost a little more . . ." The rest of his words died in his throat as Jack pounced on him and dragged him to the window.

His head was out of it as Jack yelled at him, "Take care how you speak to me, or I'll pitch you out into the street."

Overton offered no resistance; he lay limp in Jack's arms and smiled up at him. "I think not," he said. "I think we have both acquired a little wisdom upon the road. A man who means to enjoy his own again is not about to commit a murder. Besides, all I have told you is worthless until I swear to it before witnesses. Oh you have a case at law, but it will take time and money, and a lot more without me."

Jack released his grip on the man, and walked back to the centre of the room. "I haven't forgotten your part in all this," he said.

Overton was confident now. "I merely did my master's bidding, as befits a good servant. And was I not always polite?"

"Polite enough, yes. In case our side should prevail again."

"Well, now you have." Overton crossed the room, sat down at the table, and reached for his cup. "But to have what is yours, you need to use the law." He massaged his arm where Jack had gripped him. "Force will not suffice. More sack, I think." He held out his cup, and Jack poured for him, filled with grudging admiration. Whatever else he was, Overton was no coward.

Overton went on, "Bracewell has become very fond of your house. He has others of course, but that's the one he chooses to live in most of the year." He was buoyant now, cheered by the prospect of freedom, profit and revenge on his former master. "I may even come north with you to see him thrown out. But of course, what I do will depend on you." His every word drew Jack deeper into his power, and they both knew it.

On Jack's orders a boy was sent across the city to the home of an attorney known to specialise in cases of this nature, and some hours later, in the fading light of the afternoon, Overton repeated his story in greater detail. The attorney, a slight, unsmiling man with a badly pocked face paced the room, interrupting occasionally with questions as his clerk wrote the account down. The whole matter having been committed to paper, sworn to, and signed in front of witnesses, Overton was conducted to an adjoining room, and, still weak and exhausted from his experiences in captivity, put to bed.

As he slept, Jack and the attorney discussed the matter in

hushed tones. "It's a good case," said the attorney, at the same time throwing the document almost dismissively onto the table. "We could swear out a writ of trespass and ejectment, and have him out of there right enough if . . ."

"If what?" said Jack.

The attorney looked him up and down before answering, "If you have the money to fight such a case."

Jack nodded in understanding as the attorney went on, "Why do you think these cases are not pursued more often?"

"Because men in my position have been well rewarded for the most part."

"For the most part, yes," agreed the attorney, "but those who remain often lack the funds to get back what is theirs. Yours is an uncommon case, and this Bracewell an uncommon rascal, but it will still be a costly business to remove him."

"How much?" asked Jack.

"That is difficult to say. Bracewell is clearly a powerful man locally. He will fight, try to impose delay, in the hope you will give up or run out of money."

"But all that aside, if I have the money, you can get him out," said Jack.

"Undoubtedly," said the attorney, and smiled for the first time.

Jack considered his position. For the past two years he had lived like a lord, and like a lord he had spent heavily. He had fine clothes, richly furnished lodgings, the best horses – everything in short which denoted a gentleman, and like a gentleman he had almost nothing set by. It seemed that his career in thieving was not yet about to end. Now, when he was keener than ever to leave this life behind him, he would have to take to the road once more in order to do so.

As he turned to face the attorney, Overton's words echoed in his mind, "Bracewell has become very fond of your house."

"I'll find the money," he said.

For the next few days, having procured lodgings for Overton, and ensured via the attorney that he would be provided for until he was required, Jack spent his time locked away in his rooms. Tom, having seen that his remedy to Jack's ills had failed, stayed away, and even Ann could not gain admittance to his rooms. He spent his days and nights in mental turmoil. Ever since Ann had entered into his life, a profound dissatisfaction had set in. He considered the world; everywhere he looked the strong seemed to be preying on the weak.

He had justified himself on these grounds. In his own way, he had argued, he was following the way of the world. Everyone was doing it – courtiers, lawyers, merchants, farmers, doctors, gaolers, watchmen – all of them taking bribes, betraying friends, preying on the weak and helpless; none of them honest, none of them trustworthy. Where did he differ from any of them? It was an old formula; he had used it many times, even lectured his victims on it, if they complained at his depredations; only now it did not suffice. There was another side to the story, another world – the world of his family, the world he had been born into, the world he had once set out to defend on a stormy night a lifetime ago, and had lost forever. From time to time things had happened which had reminded him of this fact; the time he had spent with Joyce and her sons; that Puritan the day he was captured. Then there were Doctor Winton and Ann, both representatives of a world which was now, for the first time in years, exerting its pull on him. Yes, it was true that men preyed on one another, that men were unscrupulous and cruel. Most of them had been born into a world where they had no choice; he had not been, but his world had been snatched from him. He had been cast out of his Eden, and feared that the road back was for ever closed to him.

What troubled him the most was the paradox that in order to escape this life once and for all, he would first have to embrace it once more. To raise the money he would need could take weeks, months, longer perhaps, and he would be drawn once more into a life for which he had lost all appetite. In the meantime there was Ann to consider; she had begged him to leave off this life. How could he make her understand his motives in taking it up once more? If – as seemed likely – she did not understand, was there not a danger that he might lose her forever? Yet life without her was for him unthinkable. Without her the vision of the future which now presented itself faded once more; what comfort could he draw from his own personal restoration, if in the process he lost her?

He continued in this vein day and night for almost a week,

drawing up plans, and discarding them almost at once. Then one night as the candle burned low, and he slumped unwashed, unshaven and despairing in a chair, a new thought occurred to him. He stood up and began pacing the room. He paced for almost an hour as gradually, the outlines of a plan began to form. Finally, as the sky outside began to grey, and the birds began to sing, he stood in the window, threw back his head, and laughed at the beauty, simplicity, and above all the irony of it all.

For years he had nursed a sense of grievance, a grievance he still felt, and he had taken his revenge on the world, yet never had he taken his revenge on the instrument of his family's downfall. He had punished hundreds for his family's ruination without once punishing the truly guilty. The man who had dispossessed his family had grown fat on the proceeds, while he, Jack, had taken it out on everyone else. Yet if this plan could be made to work, and he picked his moment, he could at one stroke have enough out of Bracewell to fight his entire case for him. One last robbery, taking money that in any sense but the strictly legal was rightfully his, and he would be able to leave this life forever and take Ann with him.

That evening he took the opportunity to mention his decision to Noll, who being about to return to Reading, had insisted that they spend the night drinking together. He resolved not to tell him the full extent of his plan, in particular the fact that he intended this to be his last robbery; there would be time enough for that later. It was not a good time to raise the subject though, for they were both well drunk when Jack said, "Noll, I'm going back to Yorkshire. I've been thinking about it for some weeks; there's something I must do there."

"What's that?" grunted Noll, looking down into his tankard.

"You remember I've told you about my father's estate? Well, I want to see it again, and . . ." he leaned closer to Noll, "I mean to rob the man that's on it."

"Is he so wealthy as to be worth a journey all the way up there?" asked Noll. "I should have thought there were rich enough pickings down south without taking the trouble to go all that way. Remember they're a good deal less meticulous how they do things up there. If you get caught they'll hang you before you have time to put pen to paper!"

The reference to his last capture rankled slightly, so Jack said a little irritably, "You don't understand. That man's living on what is my birthright, and I mean to have it, or at least a portion of it. When I've got it I thought I might – well, maybe leave the business altogether." Jack had already said more than he meant to. Noll snorted. Jack's words confirmed his suspicions. Jack went on, "What's wrong with that? You're keen enough yourself to vanish into the country at every opportunity. I'm surprised you haven't done it yourself."

"The reason I haven't done it, my friend," said Noll, "is that however pleasant it may be to take one's ease in the country, I am at heart a robber. I've always been one and I always will be. I'll never leave, not till they hang me." There was an edge to his voice that Jack did not much care for.

"Well, I'm going to do it anyway, whether you like it or not," he said. Noll shrugged and then smiled, "If you're set on it, I'll come with you. Just to make sure you don't land yourself in any more trouble." It was an unfortunate choice of words, but Jack swallowed his anger and simply said, "No! I'm going alone."

"Don't be stupid," said Noll. "It'll be easier with two. Anyway, I've a mind to see the North country again myself. I might . . ."

"No!" said Jack, more forcefully this time, "I'm doing this alone. It's my business, my birthright, and I'll finish it myself. It's a ghost I must exorcise."

"You mean you don't want me along because you've grown ashamed of me, ashamed of your old friends." Noll suddenly didn't seem drunk. "What's the matter, afraid you'll meet someone you know? Or is it that there's some vision of your past and maybe your future up there that you don't want sullied by the likes of me?"

Somehow Noll had hit closer to the mark than he realised. Jack looked down at the table. "That's not true," he said quietly, failing to convince even himself.

"Yes it is!" Noll was shouting now. "We're all right for robbing and roistering with for a while, good enough to get you out of a scrape when you walk into one, but when it comes to it we're not good enough for anything else. As soon as you find a girl that isn't a whore or a thief you suddenly remember your scruples that are packed down somewhere in the bottom of your portmanteau, and you want to become a gentleman again!"

Jack growled, "That's enough!"

But Noll was in full flight now. "It's all so simple for you, isn't it? You think you can just step into this world, dabble in it for a while, and step out when it suits you, your lily-white hands unsullied. The gentleman high-pad! You've indulged yourself in our grubby little lives as another gentleman might collect paintings or breed racehorses. Well, don't be deceived, Captain; you're no better than any of us, and it may not be as easy to get out as you think."

"That's enough, old man!" Jack shouted.

"Old man!" laughed Noll – it was a humourless laugh. "Not too old to come and get you out of prison where you landed yourself through your own sloppiness."

"You owed me that, and you know it!" Jack rose to his feet.

"Well, now the debt is paid," said Noll coldly, "and neither of us owes the other a thing. Go on up north; it'll be better for the others than having you moping around here like a sick girl. And don't be in a hurry to come back. You'll not be missed. In future we'll stick with our own kind; the bogus captains of St Paul's. At least we'll be spared all the cant and hypocrisy! Captain!" he spat the word out. "When I think of some of the captains I've known."

"Spare me the reminiscences, old man, I've heard them all before. I've heard all I ever want to hear about Captain Hind, and about the Whitecoats. You're the only one I've ever met; the rest saw fit to leave their bones with their comrades on Hessay Moor – like my father!"

It was a stupid and cheap remark; Jack was not even sure what he meant by it, but it was one he was to regret for the rest of his life. In a second he and Noll were facing each other across the table, their hands on their sword hilts. Across the room a couple of drinkers turned from their ale to watch the two; the host considered intervening and then thought better of it: better to pick up the pieces afterwards. They stood for a while both swaying slightly, both a little surprised that somehow, suddenly, they had come to this. Nothing happened; there was still too much between them for that. Without a word Jack stalked out of the tavern and away; Noll slumped back into his seat and stayed there staring into space; it was a long time before the host dared to disturb him with the bill.

Early the following morning Jack arose and completed his preparations for the journey. His head screamed from the drink, and he remembered with shame the things that had been said. Of course they would patch it up – they were too close to bear grudges – but once a thing was said it could never be unsaid. He knew he had hurt his friend; knew too that Noll had been partly right in what he had said. In his shame he almost went over to the Dog, to where he knew Noll would be up and making ready for his own journey. Then he thought again; he might still be angry – better to leave it a while. He would only be up north for a couple of weeks – he would call in at Reading on the way back. By that time it would all have been forgotten and they would like as not laugh about the whole thing. Packed and ready he rode out of Southwark across the Bridge and made for Bishopsgate and the Great North Road. He had not told Ann any more than that he would be gone for a couple of weeks. When he came back he would have a lot more to tell her.

Although he did not know it, Jack did not depart Southwark unobserved. Always an early riser, Frost had seen him leave; he had stood at an upstairs window in the Dog and had remained there for a long while after Jack had disappeared from view. Shipton had been much on his mind lately; for some time now the man had seemed to frustrate him at every turn. He had received the news of his capture in Leicestershire with mixed feelings. It is true, he had been deprived at a stroke of the handsome reward he had been looking forward to collecting some day, but at least he had been freed from a man who had become a thorn in his flesh. Ever since he had taken over the gang, Shipton had led them further away from his clutches. They had eaten and drunk less frequently at the Dog, come to him less often for information. As soon as he had been captured, however, what had they done? They had come straight to him for help. That was how it should be, how it had always been until Shipton had come along. That was why he had refused them help. It suited him to be rid of Shipton. Of course, he had been unfortunate; there had been no way of knowing that they would simply walk into Leicester and carry him off as easily as blinking. And they had done it without his help. Frost did not like people to manage without him; it gave them ideas.

Now he was confronted once again with the problem of Shipton. In the long term it was no problem at all; Shipton would hang and he would collect the reward. The problem was one of timing. The beauty of his position was that there was profit to be had whatever he did; the disadvantage was that the best time to turn a highwayman in was when he was at his most profitable. Whatever his faults, Shipton had brought prosperity to the gang and to J Frost, Esq. They had built up quite a reputation for themselves and quite a price on their heads, but the trick was to turn them in at precisely the right moment. Too soon or too late and you were the poorer for it. A delicate problem indeed. Perhaps it was time to be rid of them all, for there was no shortage of new blood to replace them. No doubt some of Tim Willis' pickpockets would be keen enough to graduate to higher things with a little help from him. No, that would be a waste; the old gang could go on quite nicely without Shipton at their head.

He came to a decision; as soon as possible he would peach Shipton to the authorities but hang onto the rest. Of course they would have to go too eventually, but not for a couple of years at least. With Shipton out of the way he could take a more personal hand in the running of the gang. They wouldn't suspect his part in their leader's betrayal, and even if they did, what of it? It would serve as a useful reminder to them where the power lay. So Shipton was to go! He crossed the room and poured himself a glass of sack. It was a pity in some ways; he had invested quite a lot in Shipton – Lucy hadn't come cheap in the first place and the information he provided cost a lot also. Still, with the reward money, he could be sure of a profit. That was why highwaymen were such good business; as long as they thrived so did you. You could provide them with everything they needed and make sure they paid through the nose for it; you could unload the valuables they brought in, watches, snuff-boxes, jewellery; and you could sell them the information they needed. Then as soon as they became a burden, a word in the right quarter took them off your hands and put a tidy sum in your purse at the same time. He toasted Shipton in his mind as he raised his glass to his lips.

There were other reasons for getting rid of Shipton too. Things were not all well downstairs. Ann's going off like that had completely thrown him; he had never suspected that there was anything between them. He knew now though: Wicks had confirmed that. He had seen her going into Shipton's rooms late at night. It just showed how things could go wrong. He had laid on Lucy for precisely that purpose, and very useful she had been for a while; then she had slipped away without so much as a by your leave. He would settle accounts with her later.

But he had had plans of his own for Ann, once he had offloaded Alice onto Mr Richardson. Jane seemed to have grown fond of her; that could have proved useful – it still could. But just lately Jane had been acting strangely, asking a lot of awkward questions about that boy Simmons. It was just possible that she suspected something. If so, someone must have put the idea into her head: that could only have been Ann, her single friend. No doubt Ann was too witless to think up such a thing by herself; she must have got it from Shipton. It all came down to Shipton every time. Once he was out of the way there would be nothing to stop him; Ann would either accept his protection or pay the price for her meddling, and he could get Jane married off to Richardson's boy. She would understand one day. She may hate him for it now, but he would learn to live with that. She was only a child; she hadn't yet learned that you either have the world by the throat or it has you. If his plans for her came to fruition she would never have to learn. Married to Richardson's boy she would be safe; she wouldn't have to fight tooth and nail every inch of the way as he had done. Whatever happened he would leave her secure, and wealthy too.

In the meantime however there were a number of things that needed settling, and most of them could be settled by removing Shipton. As long as the man remained alive he had the feeling that he was losing control of events; it was not a feeling he was accustomed to and it was not a feeling he liked. The sooner he was free of it the better.

11

It was market-day and as if in celebration of the fact, a watery sun had crept out from amongst the clouds and lent its approval to the proceedings below, smiling on the rooftops of the small town and the surrounding moorland. The centre of the town seemed to be a turmoil of men, women, sheep, some cows, pigs, geese and hens all crammed together without plan or purpose. In fact, to the experienced eye, all was as it should be, and everywhere men prodded animals, exchanged comments and passed judgements. Sellers praised and buyers disparaged until bargains were struck, hands were shaken and both parties repaired to the inn or alehouse to seal the contract. Rich and poor, landlord, tenant and serving-man all rubbed shoulders freely. On the fringes of the throng young lads and girls crowded round the pedlars eyeing the lengths of ribbon, combs and gloves displayed on their trays and listening to their seemingly endless funds of jokes, stories, and snippets of news and gossip.

Seemingly oblivious to all this, and intending to rub shoulders with no man, Martin Bracewell strode into the crowd, gratified to feel it part as usual before him. At his side, though a little behind, walked his friend Edward Greene. The two wasted no time on the livestock, but made straight for a small group of men who were standing rather forlornly to the right of the old Market Cross.

Bracewell glanced up at the cross; he always felt there was a special bond between him and that cross. During the War an over-zealous officer of the parliament army had wanted to pull it down as a popish idol; Bracewell, as a member of the local committee, and therefore not without influence in local parliamentarian circles, had brought his influence to bear to prevent this, pointing out that the removal of the cross would do little to prosper the Parliament's cause in an area still prone to Malignancy. In later years, at the return of the King, this sole act had gone a long way to obscuring his less savoury activities during the Protectorate. He was remembered not as Bracewell the sequestrator, but as Bracewell who saved the Market Cross from the Ironside captain. The fact that he ended the Wars the richer by the purchase of the estates of a number of Royalist families, whose ruin he had speeded along while he was a parliamentarian county commissioner, was by no means forgotten. However, the fact was that nowadays his was the power locally, and it had to be lived with. In the way that people will, they tended therefore to concentrate on his more laudable actions in those troubled times, of which the saving of the Market Cross was the most memorable. Bracewell was fond of that cross. Although he was not normally a whimsical man he liked to think that, in a way, each of them had saved the other.

Reaching the little group who stood in the shadow of the cross, Bracewell stopped, stepped back one pace and considered them. They stood mute and eyed him hopefully. They were a group of about ten men, varying in age from sixteen to fifty, all similarly dressed in coats of coarse cloth and carrying staffs or crooks. After surveying them for a moment or two he stepped in amongst them, grasping an arm here, prodding a chest there. Although all of the men were of sturdy build none made any move to check his progress or resist his manhandling. For a few minutes he continued his researches before singling out two men from their fellows and taking them to one side. The others groaned with disappointment but continued to watch to see who would be chosen. Bracewell eyed the two candidates.

"Have you all your teeth?" he asked the first, who nodded and grinned hideously in confirmation of the fact. The other followed suit. "Well," Bracewell looked them both in the eye. "Let's see your legs!" The two men gaped at him, then at each other; a small crowd gathered and began to grow as Bracewell said over his shoulder to Greene, "It's the only way." He turned back to the two men who stood uncertain what to do, and plainly discomfited by the growing crowd. "Come on!" he shouted impatiently. "I haven't all day; hoik up those coats and let's see your legs." The two men did as they were bidden. The crowd stood silent. At the back a couple of youths attempted a humorous remark but were angrily silenced by the others.

"Right!" said Bracewell after a minute or two had passed. "You see that boulder over on the moor side?" he pointed to a large grey stone alone amongst the heather some five hundred yards distant. "First one of you there and back gets the job." Without a second's hesitation both men sprinted off in the direction of the rock; the crowd parted before them, and some began to shout encouragement. All eyes in the square were now on the two men as they raced off up the hillside. It was neck and neck as they reached the rock, but on descending the hill, the taller of the two men began to gain the advantage; he fell several times as he careered down the steep slope, but each time he tucked his chin on his chest, rolled forward, and came up running. By the time they had regained the edge of the square he was fifty yards ahead of his rival, whose face clearly showed the strain he was under. Yet with the desperation born of hardship he managed to put on a burst of speed and had closed the gap by half as his opponent dashed triumphantly past Bracewell to be caught in the arms of the by now cheering crowd. Bracewell smiled at the multitude like a Roman emperor at the games, and turning to the winner, said, "You'll do. Meet me outside the Red Lion at four."

As he said this, the loser, who had kept running, slithered to a halt beside him and crashed in a heap on the cobbles at his feet, gasping for air. Without so much as glancing at him, Bracewell strode off followed by Greene. "It's the only way, Edward," he maintained as they left the square. "Always check their legs."

"I didn't know you needed another shepherd. Is old Matthew Sharpe dead then?" asked his friend.

"Good as," grunted Bracewell. "Old! Worse than useless, he is now. I warned him if he couldn't keep up I'd have to be rid of him, but it was no use. It's his own fault. Should have had a couple of sons, instead of which he has two daughters, and one of them an idiot."

"What'll become of him?" asked his friend. Bracewell looked at him as though he were an idiot too.

"I don't know. He'll have to find somewhere else. I've been as generous as I can – I've given him a month to find somewhere, but I can't keep this fellow waiting too long. He's no doubt a family of his own he wants to move in. I'm already employing Sharpe's other daughter up at the house – she'd better buck up as well or she'll go the way of her father. I'm not running an almshouse up there, you know." Bracewell was unaware as he walked towards the Red Lion inn of the stares of the crowd. He would have paid them no regard if he had been. He was unaware also of the stranger in the high-crowned hat and black travelling cloak, who had been leaning against the Market Cross all the while, and who had watched the proceedings in the market square with interest and who, as the two friends entered the Red Lion, walked across towards it himself.

Seated at a table near the fire inside the inn, neither Bracewell nor his companion looked up as the stranger entered the crowded room; nor did they notice him talking to the host. They were far too wrapped up in their own affairs. "Now then, Edward," said Bracewell as soon as the bottle of wine they had ordered appeared, "about this grey mare of yours – I think my lad is just about big enough to ride her now, so what are you asking for her?"

Greene considered the matter for a minute as if the idea of selling her had only just occurred to him; in fact it had been on his mind all day, and was one of the main reasons he had come over all the way from York to see Bracewell. "Fifteen pounds!" he announced after a while, and reeled as his friend exploded.

"Fifteen pounds! You must be out of your mind! Either that or you think I am. Fifteen pounds for that . . ." he got no further than that before his friend interrupted sharply to point out that he had already been offered twenty for her by a near neighbour and had only turned him down as a favour to Bracewell and from the affection he had for his son. Bracewell replied to the effect that if that was Greene's idea of a favour, he'd be grateful if in future he refrained from doing him any, and the conversation continued in this vein for some time while the two tried to agree on a price. It was not very difficult, therefore, for the stranger, who was over at the other side of the room, to listen in on this not very edifying conversation, whilst at the same time carrying on a conversation of his own with the host. After a while the two disputants across the room had reached an agreement, and Bracewell called loudly for pen and paper, causing the host to break off his talk and rush over with them. When Martin Bracewell called for something it was as well to be quick about it, he explained to the stranger, who nodded, smiled, and crossed the room to warm his hands by the fire.

"Here's my bond for ten pounds, and you can think yourself lucky I have a sense of humour!" said Bracewell as he scribbled on the paper and shoved it across to his friend. "It's payable as usual by Isaac Fisher of Stonegate." Greene tucked the paper inside his doublet and raised his glass to Bracewell in a toast.

"Here's to the mare. You couldn't have got yourself a better for the money, Martin, if you'd searched the whole county. When are you going to come over and fetch her?" Bracewell thought for a moment.

"I've got some business with Fisher so I'll be over in York next Thursday. I'll call in at Whixley on the way back. And have some of that Navarre wine ready for me. It'll be some compensation for having been robbed by you!" Both men laughed and neither noticed the stranger smiling too.

In all the performance of paying the bill and calling for their horses neither Bracewell nor his guest saw the stranger leave ahead of them. Nor were they aware, as they climbed the moorland road to Bracewell's home, that their every move was being closely observed. They passed below a small copse unaware of the solitary horseman who watched them from its shadows. There in the half dark the horse – true to its training – was still as the figure in the saddle leaned forward to catch a moment of his quarries' conversation. Suddenly, as if on impulse, the shadowy figure drew two pistols from the long leather holsters on each side of his saddle-bow. The horse, knowing what came next, edged forward. Then, as if recollecting himself, the man checked the forward movement, whispered to his mount, and slid the pistols noiselessly back into their holsters. By now the two men below had reached a bend in the dirt road, and it was not until they had disappeared round it and the sound of their voices no longer carried back on the wind, that the horseman left his vantage point.

The house was an irregular stone building which, with the exception of the rugged, embattled west tower, dated from the reign of Elizabeth. Of no great beauty, it was nonetheless comfortable and well situated, south facing, and sheltered from the prevailing winds. Tonight as the two men entered the courtyard to be greeted by the household servants, grooms and an assortment of dogs, its aspect could not have been more pleasing. The light from its windows seemed to warm the night air as they dismounted and strode towards the main door, Bracewell already bellowing for his supper and a pint of his best wine.

An hour later and supper over, Bracewell was still shouting. He and Greene were seated in the large fireplace of the hall. His wife had retired, and the servants had been dismissed for the night, all except one who was now the object of her master's wrath. Presently a stout, plain girl entered silently and placed a tray, on which were a bottle and two glasses, on a small table in front of the two men. As she did so Greene couldn't help noticing her red-rimmed eyes. "That's old Matthew Sharpe's girl, I suppose," he said as she left.

"That's her," said Bracewell. "Been crying all day no doubt over the fate of her father, which she'd do well to remember!" He shouted these last words in her direction as the door closed behind her.

"How long has old Sharpe been on this estate?" asked Greene.

"Oh, a good few years," answered the other. "Since before I owned it, when the Shiptons were here."

"The Shiptons?" Greene had not heard of them.

"Yes." Bracewell poured wine into the two glasses and offered one to his friend. "They used to own it before the Wars. John Shipton's, it was. Rode off with two of his tenants to join the King at York, fine as you like. You'd have thought they were off to fight in the Holy Land; never came back though. Nor did that damn fool son of his who did the same thing when the present King came down from Scotland. You'd have thought they'd have learned their lesson by then, but no!" He drained his glass and poured himself another. "Too busy being noble to hold on to what they had. That's why I have it now!"

Outside, on a hill that overlooked the house, the lone horseman huddled deeper into his cloak as the wind lashed the rain into his face. He remained staring at the house in silence for over an hour before turning his horse's head and galloping off into the night.

A mile away in a crudely built one-roomed cottage with a leaky slate roof and a battered wooden door, Matthew Sharpe heard the sound of horse's hooves coming in the direction of his house. It would be truer to say that his dog heard the sound and alerted its master. The dog was marginally less deaf than Matthew; in his long life as a shepherd, Matthew had outlived many dogs, but he had grown old with this one. Matthew looked at his wife and both turned wonderingly towards the door. It was unusual for anyone to be out riding at this hour. Rather reluctantly master and dog rose and walked as fast as their old bones would take them. Before they could reach the door something hard hit it, and the sound of hooves receded and grew fainter. By the time Matthew had opened the door and peered out into the night, the horseman had gone, and the old man almost fell over the bag of silver coins that lay on the threshold.

Later that same evening in London, Jonathan Frost was returning to the Dog from an evening at the cock pit. He was in a good mood, though his wife did not know it. He had lost his temper with her earlier that day, and had thrown a pan of scalding water at her, which fortunately had missed. Now she was lying awake in her room dreading his return. As it was, however, he had forgotten his anger and even whistled to himself as he entered the tavern. Rogers' young cock had improved no end since he had trimmed its jollops, and had killed Williams the Welshman's bird stone dead, providing an evening both entertaining and profitable for Frost. He crossed the front room, empty now save for Wicks snoring under a table near the dwindling fire, and headed for the kitchen. Ann was working alone there, clearing away. She paid him little attention when he came in, walked rather deliberately over to the fire, and threw himself into a chair. After watching her for a while he spoke. "Fetch me a bottle of canary wine," he said, adding as Ann descended the stairs to the cellar, "and two glasses!"

In a few minutes she returned with the bottle, opened it and placed it on the table in front of him, all without a word. He poured himself a glass, smiling strangely at her, and then said, "You'll join me?" It was difficult to say for certain whether this was an invitation or an order, and no doubt the ambiguity was intentional.

Ann merely answered, "Thank you, Mr Frost, but I have still much to do," and went back to her work. Frost's smile did not alter as he watched her moving about the kitchen, tidying away the pots, pans, dishes and knives. There was no denying that she was a beauty; he could see what Shipton saw in her. Proud, too; plenty of spirit – no harm in that. She would lose some of that when she had seen her gallant captain hang, and she was alone again. As for the rest, he would beat that out of her once he had her where he wanted her. He had no doubt she would come round eventually. He had never failed to get what he wanted one way or another. All that was required was a little patience. He was a patient man. Even so, he wished now he hadn't been so quick to get rid of Alice. He could have done with her tonight. Refilling his glass he spoke. "You seem to be working alone tonight. Where's Jane?"

Ann scarcely offered him a glance as she answered, "She was tired, so I told her to go to bed. I can manage here by myself."

"You are good friends, aren't you?" he said, filling a second glass with wine.

"I'm very fond of her, yes," said Ann, not noticing that he had risen from his seat and was advancing towards her with a glass in each hand.

"I'm glad about that," he was saying, "I want you to be friends." Ann turned. He was very close now. He smiled once more and held his smile as she brushed past him, murmuring that she was very busy, and wanted to get away to bed. "And I want us to be friends," he continued as she brushed past him once more and began clearing things from the table. "You'll find I make a good friend." He grabbed her arm and spun her round, pulling her close to him. She was as close to him as she had ever been and in his excitement Frost did not at first notice the knife. It was a long, broad-bladed carving knife, its handle in her right hand and its point under his chin. She hissed at him, and the venomous tone in her voice startled him.

"Step back a pace, Mr Frost. You may own everyone else here but you don't own me." Now fully in control of himself once more, Frost could see that there was nothing to be gained from this situation except possibly a knife in the ribs. Without a word he turned and left the room. He was not a man to issue threats. Outside he raised his hand to his chin and then looked down at it. On the back of his hand was a small drop of blood. He cursed himself as he climbed the stairs to his own rooms. There were certain things in life which had never happened to him. One of them was that he had never acted impulsively. He had broken that rule for the first time tonight, and had paid for it. As he examined his chin in the mirror he reminded himself that there were other things in life which had never happened to him. For example, no one had ever threatened him with a knife, let alone drawn blood, and got away with it. He would see that it stayed that way.

The next morning Ann, who had decided overnight that she would surely be dismissed, already had her bags packed. To her surprise, however, when Frost came into the kitchen he completely ignored her, issued a few instructions to his wife and then retired to his private rooms. With Jack away, Noll in Reading, and Tom – as was quite common with him – nowhere to be found she really had nowhere to go, and so, since Frost seemed content to let the matter drop, she resolved to stay at least for the time being. Nevertheless, she was anxious to avoid Frost as far as possible, and managed to communicate this to Jane without being too specific about why. Frost was slightly surprised but not displeased that it was his daughter who brought him his breakfast and morning draught, and tended his fire while he ate. He had been meaning to speak with her for some time, but various matters had intervened.

"Jane," he said after a while. "I've been thinking. That dress of yours is looking a little ragged. You really should have some better clothes. Why don't we go into the city sometime soon and look for something? And you can choose some lengths of ribbon and lace to trim your old dresses with."

"If you like, father," her voice sounded dull and unenthusiastic, and she did not look up from the fire as she added fuel to it. "Anything you say."

Frost tried again. "Or perhaps there's something else you'd like?" She did not answer and he rose from his table and walked over to where she was crouched by the fire. He reached out to touch her, but failed, as she rose and turned towards the table.

"Jane," he said, and his voice softened almost to a whisper. "I don't say much, but I . . ."

"Have you finished with this food, father?" she cut him off in mid-sentence. He nodded, and she picked up the tray and turned to go. As she reached the door she turned and said, "Is there any news of John yet, father?" He could only shake his head, not trusting his voice; she stood and looked at him for a full minute, a minute that seemed like an hour as he stood avoiding her gaze. She left and closed the door quietly behind her.

Frost crossed the room and sank into a chair. His mind raced. The fire began to burn brightly as he stared into its flames. Someone who knew him well – had there existed such a person – would have known from the look in his eyes and the working of his jaw that he was growing angrier by the second. The girl; she was responsible for everything. Not content with setting him at defiance, she was poisoning his daughter's mind against him, trying to take from him the thing he valued most in the world. All of a sudden he leapt from his chair, grabbed his beaver hat and silver-topped cane, threw a cloak over his shoulders, and crashed down the stairs. Passing the door to the kitchen he kicked it open, shouting to his wife, "I'm off to see Mr Richardson. Tell Wicks I want to see him when I get back, and he'd better be sober!" With that he swept out into the street ignoring the greetings of sundry drinkers in the tavern as he did so.

As he marched down the cobbled street his spirits soared. Used as he was to waiting, there was something deeply satisfying in the feeling one got when the crisis was reached and a decision had been made. He loved the knowledge that his actions could, in a moment, change his world for the better; it gave him a feeling of power to which there was no equal. What he had in mind struck him as especially fitting, given the girl's obvious interest in the whereabouts of Simmons. He was going to visit Mr Richardson to enquire about his interests in the West Indies.

Things had gone very well indeed for Jack. The alehouse was unprepossessing to say the least, but it was ideally situated a couple of miles east of the Great North Road, and not ten miles from Mr Edward Greene's house at Whixley. Jack had been given an Irishman's name by Hugh Jeffrey who, unlike Jack, had operated in the north before. It was one of a dozen names he had memorised in case he should need help. The Irishman, Hugh had said, was a reliable man, game for anything and trustworthy, a good man to have at your back. He had also warned Jack not to be put off by the man's appearance.

As he waited in the fading afternoon sunshine for the man to emerge from the house and come into the orchard where he was waiting, Jack wondered what to expect. He had been reluctant to go inside, not wanting to be seen by any more people than he had to, and so had given a boy a penny to go in and summon him. Presently the boy reappeared in the company of a man well over six feet tall, lean, and broad-shouldered, with a mop of greasy, straw-coloured hair. When Jack mentioned Hugh's name he grinned, revealing a mouthful of rotten yellow teeth, and invited him to come inside. Jack hesitated, but on being assured that the place was empty, followed him and the boy, who seemed to be his son, into the house.

It was a low-ceilinged, one-roomed building, which had been partitioned with a length of dirty curtain into two parts. The front portion of the room was obviously for the use of the customers. Posting the boy at the door, the man led Jack straight through, past the curtain, into the living-quarters. There beside the fire a woman as thin as a wraith in a grimy grey shift looked at him. An infant girl clung to her neck and a baby lay in a cradle close by. Two more young boys played over in a corner. The Irishman briefly introduced Jack to his family, who showed scant interest and then invited him to sit at the table and share a cup of something warming. This proved to be a glass of some raw spirit, presumably brewed in the backyard. Jack drained it and held out his cup for another. Gratified, the man grinned and poured him another. Jack sipped this one a little more gingerly. He had won the man over; he only wished he wouldn't grin so much. Unfortunately the man proved to be most good-humoured and grinned frequently as Jack told him what he had in mind.

At the end of their conversation, he took Jack outside, and led him through the orchard and up a narrow, rocky lane between two rows of stunted trees. They climbed for several minutes until the track levelled out onto the rough pasture above the road. There, tucked into a fold on the hill, was a small, crude, stone construction with a turf roof and one small entrance. The interior of the hut was strewn with copper boiling vessels, ladles and other implements of the distiller's trade, but it was roomy enough for their purposes. Again the man listened as Jack talked, and confined himself to nodding occasionally. At length they descended once more to the roadside and Jack, having paid him the first instalment (which brought forth another hideous grin) shook his hand. He declined his offer to stay there and announced that he would be back with the horses in two days' time. It was Tuesday afternoon.

Ann was working late at the Dog again, tidying the kitchen and preparing it for the morning's early start. She had sent Jane up to bed; these days the girl seemed always to be tired. She threw herself into her work now in a way she never had before, as if to take her mind off her troubles, and when she was alone Ann often heard her weeping. It must seem a cruel world to her, she thought. Margaret was kind but ineffectual, and too afraid on her own account to pay much heed to Jane's worries. Her father was the cause of them, and apart from Ann, the poor girl had no one to turn to. That was partly the reason for Ann's decision to stay at the Dog. To leave would have seemed like desertion. But for that consideration she would have thrown caution to the winds and left. No doubt she would have managed somehow until Jack returned. The tavern was empty now, save for Wicks and his two cronies in the front room. The sounds of their muffled conversation and occasional laughter intruded into her thoughts; it was not pleasant laughter and she wondered about them often. They never seemed to do a hand's turn about the place, and yet it was obvious they were retained by Frost for some purpose. She wondered what it was, then decided it was probably better not to know.

She thought about Jack. It was strange that he had just decided to go away like that on the spur of the moment so soon after his return. Why had he been so secretive about it? She had tried repeatedly to get him to tell her, but in the end had given up when he became irritable and moody. Noll had seemed most reluctant to talk about it on the morning he had left for

Reading, saying merely that no doubt she would find out soon enough. Jack's secrecy had annoyed and slightly wounded her. She knew he had suspected Lucy of passing information to Frost; surely he did not suspect her also? Or did he think her incapable of holding her tongue? Either way it was not very flattering. She wished he would leave this place and go wherever he wanted. As for Jane – well, they would have to sort that problem out as best they could. The front room was silent now as she finished off in the kitchen and prepared to go up. As she turned to go, Wicks was standing in the doorway.

"Mr Frost wants to see you out in the yard," he said. "He looks mighty angry; I'd hurry if I were you!" With that he turned and went back into the front room. Ann considered what he had said. What would Frost be doing out in the yard at this time of night? She had hardly seen him since that incident a few nights ago, but he had seemed disposed to forget it, and earlier he had talked quite pleasantly to her and even managed a smile. On the other hand it would not be the first time he had come back drunk, and rampaged about the house making complaints to all and sundry about the standard of their work, turfing people out of bed and making them mop floors or clean pots and pans in the middle of the night. She walked into the corridor and looked out at the yard; in the dim light of the moon she could just make out a figure that looked like him standing with his back to the house. She hesitated, then deciding it wise to keep the peace, stepped lightly out into the yard. Alone in the front room, Wicks stood up and followed her out quietly.

Once in the yard she approached the figure at the entrance to the yard. "You wanted something, Mr Frost?" she began to say, and the figure turned. She recognised the face, and it was not the face of Frost. From behind, her arms were pinioned and a rag was stuffed into her mouth. She began to choke as a blanket was thrown over her head. It was pointless screaming; there was no one to hear her even if she had succeeded in making a sound. As she was slowly dragged, kicking, away from the house and towards the lane, she fumbled for the knife she had made a habit of carrying since her brush with Frost. For a moment panic seized her and she grew weak, but as her hand found the handle of the small kitchen knife, her mind took over once more. She could only move her right arm from the elbow, her upper arms being held fast by the man behind her. Turning the knife handle in her hand so that the point was behind, she stabbed backwards and upwards with what little strength she could muster. The knife struck and she felt its point grate against something hard with such force that the weapon was wrenched out of her hand. At the same moment a high-pitched shriek deafened her left ear and the enclasping arms released her.

Weakened as she was, and taken by surprise, she fell forward onto her knees just as a blow caught the side of her jaw, knocking the sense out of her. Ann had never been struck before in her life. She had never known before how such a blow saps the strength and numbs the mind leaving the victim helpless. Out of pure instinct she ripped the rag from her mouth and tried to scream, but her mouth was too dry. Her head swam and she had all but given herself up as lost, when she became aware that someone was shouting. Stunned as she was she knew that whoever was shouting like that must be on her side. Her attackers had been silent until one of them had received her blade in his ribs. The shouting subsided now to a sound of scuffling punctuated by grunts which lasted for only a few seconds before at least two people ran off down the lane.

Someone grabbed her by the arm and dragged her to her feet. She could not make out who it was, friend or foe, and was too weak and dazed to resist as whoever it was pulled her out of the yard and away down the lane. As she left the yard she glanced over her shoulder and could just make out the figure of a man crawling across the cobbles, sobbing and gasping for breath. His head was drooping as though he were searching for something he had lost. Bruised and breathless, she followed in the wake of the shadowy figure whose grasp on her arm never weakened for a moment. A hundred yards down the lane was a pool of light from a nearby window and it was there that the figure was leading her. As they reached it, they both stopped, and she turned to face the man. Recognising him at once, she almost fell into his arms with relief. After a three day debauch in Billingsgate, Tom Ratcliffe had come home.

12

Martin Bracewell did not leave Mr Greene's house at Whixley until the day was well advanced. They had sat up till late, drinking Greene's excellent Navarre wine, and Bracewell's head was paying the price for it now. Even the hooves of the mare, which walked patiently behind his own horse, sounded loud as they bit into the hard surface of the road. Mr Bracewell had only been riding for twenty minutes and already he was perspiring from the midday sun. Despite his headache, however, he was in a cheerful mood as he rode along; it had been a good few days all in all. Admittedly he had had to pay out ten pounds for the mare for his ungrateful wretch of a son, but he had been willing to pay twenty had Greene but known it. Yesterday in York he had concluded a successful deal with a merchant friend of his, and given the scrivener, Fisher, a good roasting about a couple of mistakes in a document he had had drawn up. It never hurt to let these sorts of people feel the weight of your anger from time to time. That way you were guaranteed their very best service next time. And the eviction of old Sharpe had gone smoothly enough. It had promised to be difficult but the old man took it all quite casually in the end; said he had got a bit put by from when the Shiptons had owned the place. Damn his impudence! Still, it was better than an ugly scene. Such a thing on your own doorstep could make one very unpopular locally.

"Mr Bracewell!" his thoughts were interrupted by the sound of his own name being called softly from the trees to his left. "This way, Mr Bracewell!" said the voice as he turned to look for its owner. He could just make out a cloaked figure sitting his horse in the shade, and had turned his own horse's head towards it, when he saw the figure was levelling a pistol at him. He was too stupefied to resist as the figure, whose face was

158

concealed by a scarf, said, "Keep coming, Mr Bracewell, or I'll blow your brains out." Still stunned by the fact that this person knew his name, and half suspecting that this was some sort of joke, he walked his mount slowly into the shade of the trees. Once in the gloom of the small wood it became clear that this man, whoever he was, was not alone. There was another, a monster of a man from the look of him, on his right, similarly masked and cloaked.

"Who are you? What do you want?" said Bracewell, though had he stopped to think for a moment, he would have realised that they had no intention of answering his first question and no need to answer the second. By way of an answer the man with the pistol said, "You have nothing to fear from us, Mr Bracewell, as long as you do what we say. You will raise your hands, please." As he did so the other moved in, and removed his purse from his belt. Bracewell thanked the Lord that he hadn't decided to carry more than ten pounds for his journey. Nevertheless he began to complain to his robbers.

"I beg of you, don't take from me all that I own in the world." Further entreaty was prevented by a piece of wadding which was straightway thrust into his mouth, and secured by a cloth gag. Expecting at any moment to be pitched from his horse, Bracewell was surprised when instead his hands were tied around the horse's neck and, the monster having dismounted to complete the task, his feet were tied under his horse's belly. They were obviously going to carry him off somewhere, but where? And why? His last sight as the sacking hood was pulled over his eyes was the cold gaze of the man with the gun. It turned his blood to ice in a moment and stayed with him for the rest of that day. The hood having been secured none too gently round his neck by a thong, they began to move.

Bracewell clung to the horse's neck and tried to remember as much as possible of the journey so that he might be able to work out where he was being taken. Already he was storing in his mind every detail of the men's appearances so that he might give a full report to the constable as soon as he was released. He would move heaven and earth to have his revenge once he was free. Martin Bracewell was not a man who was free with his money, nor was he prone to invest money without a good return, but to see these two hang he would spend every penny he had. It offended his sense of propriety as much as anything else, that anyone should dare to defy him, let alone manhandle him and drag him round the countryside like a piece of baggage. It upset the natural order of a world in which he had always been the master, and others had always fawned on him or paid the price for it. Well, they would learn the cost, as others had, of offending Martin Bracewell.

He was already thinking on the wording of the reward poster he would have drafted, and how much the reward should be, when the thought struck him that he might never make that report to the constable or publish that poster. His mind went blank. For the first time in his life, Bracewell was in danger; for the first time in his life he was terrified. If he had at any time dared to hope that this was all a terrible dream, the reality of the situation was brought home to him by the injuries he sustained in the course of his first brief journey. Tree branches scraped along his back, and thorns and brambles scratched his legs before he realised that he was climbing and then felt the sun on his back.

After about half an hour they stopped and he heard his fellow travellers dismount. The bonds that held his feet underneath the horse were cut as were the ones at his wrists, and he was unceremoniously thrown to the ground face down. There he lay for what seemed an eternity. He heard the sound of a stream running nearby, felt bracken underneath him, and was aware of the buzzing of thousands of bees – or was it flies? – which seemed to fill the air. After a while, lulled by the sound and in spite of his fear and the thirst which now tortured him, he fell asleep. When he awoke he was cold, the sound of insects had ceased, and he guessed it was night. Eventually he was dragged to his feet, set on his horse, and tied as before. This time it was a longer journey, over an hour before they again stopped and he was once more cut loose and sent sprawling, this time on soft earth. Before he could rise to his feet the hood was removed and he felt the cool night air on his face. Cold as he was, it was a relief.

As his eyes adjusted to what little light there was from the moon he saw that he was facing a stone hovel with a turf roof and a low entrance such as he used at home to keep sheep in. With no ceremony he was thrust into this entrance, and fell onto the bare earth floor inside. The other two followed him in. The inside of the hut was lit by a solitary candle, and as his huge captor untied his gag, Bracewell could see a platter with some bread on it, and a jug beside it. Without waiting to be invited he reached at once for the jug and all but drained it, before falling on the bread like a starving pauper. His captors watched him impassively, then the smaller of the two, who was no small man himself, came forward. Bracewell remembered the man's look just before his hood had been lowered and his heart quailed, but to his surprise the man leaned down and offered him a flask which, when Bracewell drank from it, proved to contain brandy. It was brandy of good quality, though had it been rot-gut, Bracewell would have drunk it with relish. It coursed through his body and immediately he felt better, partly from the effect of the drink, and partly from the reflection that one does not give brandy to a man one is about to kill. Before he could take another pull at the flask, however, it was snatched from his grasp.

"There'll be more of that later, Mr Bracewell, after you've done some writing," said the man who had done all the talking.

"What sort of writing?" croaked Bracewell.

"Oh, simple enough for a man of your learning," replied the other, "and familiar enough too, to a man of business like yourself."

"What do you mean?" said Bracewell weakly, although he had already guessed.

"A bond, Mr Bracewell, made out to Mr William Simpson for the sum of two hundred pounds, payable by Mr Isaac Fisher, the scrivener of Stonegate, York."

"But I haven't got anything like that amount," began the prisoner. He got no further.

"You're not at market now, Mr Bracewell," said the man. "We'll have no haggling here. If you haggle I'll kill you. If you refuse I'll kill you. It's that simple." He turned and drew the candle closer to Bracewell, and from behind him, the other produced a board, a pen and some paper. "Now Mr Bracewell – if you'll be so good as to set down what I say, we can conclude this deal with all dispatch."

The man dictated and Bracewell, now thoroughly dejected, wrote. It only took three minutes; three minutes to sign away

what it had taken years to amass. The man took the document
and perused it for a moment or two before saying, "Splendid,
Mr Bracewell, splendid. I think you'll agree I've been generous. I don't suppose you'll starve on what's left." Then his eyes,
which were all Bracewell could see, narrowed, and his voice
took on an unpleasant tone as he went on, "That is if you live to
enjoy it."

Bracewell began to stammer, "For pity's sake!"

"Pity!" said the other. "Not a subject of which you can claim
much knowledge, I think. You will wait here with my friend
until I return from York tomorrow. If all goes well with me, it
will with you. Otherwise . . ." he left the rest to Bracewell's
imagination, which was by now filled with the most dreadful
visions. The large man threw him a blanket which was none too
clean; as he caught it the first man spoke once more. "Don't
even think of trying to escape or my friend here will surely make
an end of you . . . Sleep well, Bracewell." With that the first man
left; the other settled himself at the door, and Martin Bracewell
wrapped himself in the blanket and tried unsuccessfully to get
some sleep.

He was still trying, hampered by the coldness and hardness
of the earth below him, as dawn came up. Outside he could
hear the larks singing as they ascended the morning air. He
wished they wouldn't. To Jack Shipton who had passed a much
more comfortable night than either Bracewell or the Irishman
who guarded him, the sound was a good deal more pleasing.
What he was about to do was not without risk of course. The
scrivener might suspect something, or he and Bracewell might
have some agreed sign by which a genuine bond could be
recognised from a false one. He felt sure, however, that they had
put the fear of God into Bracewell sufficiently to ensure that he
had not tried such trickery as that. Of course, Bracewell would
try to bribe the Irishman while he was away: that was a risk he
simply had to take. He had Hugh Jeffrey's assurance that the
man was reliable, and that assurance, he knew, was not given
lightly. In any case, no doubt the Irishman had gathered
enough about Bracewell's character, from what he had seen
and what Jack had told him, not to put too much trust in him.

Jack had not seen York since, as a little boy, he had ridden
through Micklegate Bar on the back of his father's horse. It was

a poignant moment for him, therefore, to ride through that same gate on this fine summer morning. Memories of that visit which had been such a treat for a boy of nine came flooding back and with them, as was the way with his memories, a host of others less pleasant. He fought them down, reminding himself of the task that confronted him, and taking care – one of the first things he had learned in London – not to stare about him in wonder like a stranger. Certain sights as he rode along brought back memories, but he told himself as he fought to restrain them that he was on his father's business, and that once he had finished it and reclaimed at least part of his inheritance, there would be time enough for such self-indulgence. Stonegate, in the shadow of the minster, was not difficult to find; nor was the dwelling of Isaac Fisher, scrivener. Jack rode past it, dismounted at the bottom end of the street and walked back down to the shop with a nonchalant air. Hardened though he was by the dangers to which he had been exposed over the years, there was something cold-blooded about this that made great demands on his nerves. He opened the door and swept in, a man in a hurry. At an oak desk at the end of a dim room sat a young clerk toiling painstakingly at some document. He looked up as Jack entered. "I wish to see Mr Fisher," said Jack before the clerk could open his mouth to speak.

"Mr Fisher is busy upstairs at the moment," said the young man, wiping the ink from his fingers as he rose. "Perhaps I can . . ."

"Upstairs, you say," said Jack. "Then that's where I shall go. He'll want to see me, I'm sure!" He barged past the youth and stepped smartly upstairs, ignoring the bleatings from below. The stairs led into a comfortably furnished room whose walls were lined with books. The centre of the room was taken up by a large round table of dark wood at which stood two men perusing a roll of parchment. They had not seen Jack enter the room, and had been too engrossed in their conversation to hear him coming up the stairs.

"Mr Fisher!" shouted Jack and both men started and turned. As if in shock, the parchment on the table rolled itself shut. The older of the two, a grey, nervous-looking man, nodded. The other, a plump, pink merchant, seemed annoyed at the interruption and was about to protest when he saw the look in Jack's eye. "I have a bond here from Mr Martin Bracewell," said Jack, noting with pleasure that the man almost winced at the mention of the name, "and I want it paying with all speed." He presented Fisher with the document, and watched first Fisher's then the merchant's jaws sag.

Fisher peered at it through his spectacles for a moment or two more before saying, "Well, Mr – er – Simpson, it's not that simple. I mean, two hundred pounds – we don't usually deal in . . ."

"Come now, Mr Fisher," said Jack. "I am sure you would not want to fall foul of Mr Bracewell. He assured me that you would pay me promptly. However, if you refuse to honour his bond, I suppose I shall have to go and tell him that in future, as far as you and I are concerned, his bond is worthless." He paused to let the words sink in, and sink in they did. Through Mr Fisher's mind flashed awful images of Bracewell's last visit; of how he had stamped around shouting at him over a small mistake in that document, berating him for a fool in front of his clerks and his family. He was not eager to risk again falling victim of Mr Bracewell's ire. Jack had snatched the bond from Fisher's hand and was preparing to leave when the scrivener spoke.

"I didn't mean to say that we wouldn't pay, Mr Simpson." Jack turned, thankfully; his bluff had paid off and he laughed inwardly at the irony that Bracewell's fearsome reputation should be his undoing. "I merely meant to say that it would take a while." Jack took out a gold watch and studied it for a moment.

"I will return at four o'clock," he said. "I trust it will be ready by then?" Fisher nodded once more and shook his head as Jack turned away and descended the stairs. It was amazing the things that man Bracewell demanded. He hadn't even mentioned this on Wednesday. Then, shaken from his thoughts by the urgency of the task that awaited him, he rushed into a back room where sat three more clerks, and began frantically issuing instructions. The merchant, realising that he would receive no more attention that day, left unnoticed by anyone.

By four o'clock, Jack had engaged a stout, honest-seeming fellow to carry the two portmanteaux he had brought along for the task, and reappeared at Fisher's house, where such was the terror of Bracewell's name that the money was ready for collection. Jack stood affecting nonchalance as two clerks placed the bags of coins in the portmanteaux, and the remainder crowded round and goggled at the sight. Relieved that he had been able to cope with this latest demand, Mr Fisher became expansive and attempted several times to engage this Mr Simpson in conversation. "You must have had many dealings with Mr Bracewell," he offered.

"No, this is my first," said the other, "but I shall be seeing him again soon, and I shall be sure and tell him how promptly you were able to produce the money. I am sure he will be well pleased." Greatly relieved, Mr Fisher became solicitous for the welfare of this associate of one of his best customers.

"Are you not afraid, Sir, to be carrying so much money about you?" Mr Simpson smiled condescendingly.

"I shall not be travelling far, and of course I never travel alone. The roads are so dangerous these days." The other agreed that indeed they were, and added, as the job was completed and Mr Simpson and his man were leaving, "Please give my regards to Mr Bracewell – " his words were interrupted by the closing of the door, " – if you see him before I do."

It was growing dark when Jack reached the little hut where Bracewell was confined, and found to his relief that all was as he had left it. The Irishman emerged as he approached, and grinned on hearing that all had gone according to plan. Before they re-entered the hut Jack asked him, "How much did he offer you?"

He grinned once more. "Ten!" he said.

"Cheapskate!" grunted Jack and ducked into the entrance to tell the disconsolate prisoner the news. Bracewell's heart sank as the masked man informed him that he was now the poorer by two hundred pounds, but he comforted himself with the reflection that at least it meant his freedom was close at hand. He was tired, dirty, and had not slept a wink. After he had failed in his attempt to bribe the brute who guarded him, he had whiled away the time by dreaming of the revenge he would exact on the two of them as soon as he was free.

Now he was roughly hauled to his feet once more and gagged and hooded as before. Once outside in the field he was hauled into the saddle of a horse and bound again. There was a brief delay and he could hear the two talking in muffled tones and the chink of money – his money no doubt. Then he felt his horse being led and they were off. They travelled for hours and the night grew colder. He felt that they were climbing, though he had long since abandoned any attempts to work out where they were going. There was a bitter wind blowing and he thought he heard the rumble of distant thunder when they at last stopped. Bracewell turned his head this way and that, trying to listen out for the movements of his captors, but there was no sound until he felt the bonds that held his hands and feet being cut, and before he could recover his balance, he was sent sprawling to the ground. As he stood, he pulled the hood from over his eyes and saw a little distance away a solitary horseman who was now leading Bracewell's own horse away. For as far as the eye could see in any direction, Bracewell saw, by the light of the thin moon which peeped out between the gathering clouds, miles and miles of moorland. The horseman had now reached a small rise fifty feet distant, and turned once more to face Bracewell. Panic seized the man's heart.

"Have you brought me here to kill me?" he wailed. "You said . . ."

The man on horseback shook his head. "You have fulfilled your part of the bargain, Mr Bracewell," and he patted the portmanteau across his saddle. The clinking sound was torture to his victim. "And I shall fulfil mine. You are free to go." Bracewell looked around him in despair. His voice was more subdued when he spoke again.

"There was more to this than just the money, wasn't there?" he said, and the other nodded. "What did I do to you?" he asked. The man thought for a moment and then answered, "I doubt you would remember, Mr Bracewell – just another of the people you walked over to make yourself rich."

"And what was I supposed to do, starve to death? What right have you, a highway robber, to lecture me?" There was no answer as the man turned once more to go. "You're not going to leave me here?" Bracewell's voice reflected his panic. "I could die!"

"You could indeed, if you stand around here talking much longer. I think the weather is going to turn," came the reply, and as if in confirmation the sound of thunder grew louder.

Bracewell looked around him, but every direction offered the same grim prospect and he could still hardly believe that this was happening to him. He surveyed the expanse of heather, vast as the sky above, which stretched away into the distance. He started to run, stopped, changed direction and stumbled forward again, hardly even looking where he was going.

"Mr Bracewell!" The man's voice stopped him in his tracks, and he turned to where the horseman was standing – perhaps he had relented. "How are your legs?" said the man, and as he rode away, Bracewell could hear his laughter floating back on the wind.

13

The gang had made an early start, leaving the Dog at six, and taking the Windsor road. From his upstairs window, Frost had watched them go. Only Noll had had any enthusiasm for this venture; the others had responded reluctantly to his call, preferring to await Jack's return. Noll had been evasive when pressed as to Jack's whereabouts, or when he would return, and this had served to dampen spirits further. It was a bad day from the start; there was hardly any traffic on the road, and nothing that any of them considered worth the effort. The early morning drizzle had settled down to a steady rainfall, and the murmurings of discontent grew louder as the morning progressed. Noll was worried; it was important to him that this went well. Before too long the gang might have to get used to operating under his leadership once more. If Jack was serious about leaving, then the gang was in danger of falling apart unless they could find a new leader. He was Jack's lieutenant, and command fell naturally to him, but only Tom had ever worked under him before. He had to prove his worth to the others. There was more to it than that; he knew Jack's words to him on the night he had left had been no more than angry jibes uttered in the heat of the moment, but many true words were spoken in jest. Perhaps he was too old for this life, perhaps it was time he too retired. The difference was that he didn't want to.

Tom was not at ease this morning either. He had moved Ann to a safe apartment on the other side of town to await Jack's return, whenever that would be, but the implications of what he had stumbled on that night disturbed him. It was difficult to escape the conclusion that Frost was at the back of it all, though it was also possible that Wicks, whom they had left grovelling on the floor of the yard and who had since vanished, was acting

168

on his own account. Half his mind was on that for most of the morning as they waited around in the rain.

Just after one o'clock it seemed their luck had changed. They had moved into Belfont Lane just outside Staines, where from the direction of the village they saw a coach approaching their position. There were no accompanying outriders, and at the prospect of such easy meat their spirits rose. According to a well-practised drill they moved into position: Reynolds down the road towards the approaching coach, Warren back up the road towards Windsor. Hugh would block the road and cover the driver and his mate, while Tom and Noll dealt with the passengers. Oblivious to their presence, the coach rolled forward; Noll raised his pistol to fire the signal shot – Hugh was already urging his horse into a trot. Just as Noll fired he heard Reynolds' warning shout from the right. Both he and Tom turned in the direction of the cry. What they saw appalled them.

Down a grassy slope from the direction of the village, tightly bunched and without a sound, rode a dozen horsemen. Hugh was already shouting "Stand!" when the first shots came from the coach, and Noll shouted, "Get out! Follow me!" Within seconds the whole gang had assembled on the road and had made off in the direction of Windsor. The pursuit was on.

After two hundred yards or so Tom looked over his shoulder and saw to his dismay that they were still close behind. The pursuers had left the coach far behind and came on relentlessly. Noll shouted, "Off the road. We'll make for Harrow on the Hill," and turned his horse right off the road and down across a field, the others following close at his heels. He had half hoped that whoever was after them would pull up once they had left the road and abandon the pursuit. If they were just a band of travellers they would probably do that, and resume their journey, congratulating themselves on a job well done. When he reached the bottom of the slope he looked back; as he feared they had left the road and were still close behind. This was no group of travellers. Still, there was no reason to suppose they could not outdistance them. The gang were mounted on the best horses money could buy. It would be unfortunate indeed if whichever justice or constable this was had such mounts at his disposal.

They splashed across a little stream and ascended a steep rise on the other side. As they breasted the rise their pursuers were already through the stream and beginning to climb; there was no doubt that they were well mounted. Noll's mind was racing. If they could not outrun them, they would have to gain a little ground and then slip off to one side and lie low to let them pass. Provided the ground favoured them it was a simple enough trick and had foiled more than one hue and cry. Minutes later the chance came; they vanished down a steep slope losing sight of their pursuers for a few precious minutes, and saw over to their right a thick wood ideal for the purpose. Waving his arm, Noll veered to the right and plunged into the trees. Within seconds all were clustered round a large oak, dismounted, calming their horses, drawing in great gulps of air through their mouths.

Tense moments passed as the horsemen halted on the skyline; one or two left the main group and rode right and left, scanning the horizon. Down in the wood the gang fought for breath as they watched. All prayed silently for the men on the hill to descend into the level ground and go racing by, on to Harrow on the Hill. Then there would be time for a leisurely ride south and a quiet entry into London, to a warm fire, dry clothes and hot mulled wine.

After a while the detached parties returned, and the fugitives saw to their horror one of the group point in the direction of the wood. The horsemen began their descent, and the gang saw that their ruse had achieved nothing except to allow their pursuers to gain on them. Noll led them down to the end of the wood. If they could reach the village they might be able to shake them off there or lose them on the open ground beyond. They raced across an open field and began the ascent to the village whose rooftops they could just make out through the rain. The climb was a steep one and the horses were tiring as they reached the summit of the hill and approached the village. They were riding down a narrow lane and could hear, close behind them, the hooves of their enemies. As they turned a sharp corner they saw before them a sight that caused them all to rein in hard.

Gathered in the road some fifty yards distant was a group of about thirty or forty men, variously armed with clubs, pitchforks, scythes, some pikes and the odd musket. Behind them was a lone man on horseback who was trying vainly to muster them into some sort of formation. The gang stood dumbfounded, unable for a moment to take in the import of what they saw. Suddenly the crowd in the road was wreathed in smoke, and almost simultaneously two bullets sang past Noll's head. Without a word they turned and galloped back the way they had come, hoping to find a way out of the lane before the party behind caught up.

Only a hundred yards down the lane at the crest of the slope they pulled up again; their pursuers were halfway up it and they were not alone. Close at their heels rode a troop of dragoons and on the open ground to the right, working their way up the hill on foot, they could see a number of red-coated figures trailing pikes and muskets. Hugh Jeffrey turned to Noll. "They've got us bottled up here," he gasped. "We'll be slaughtered like rats in a pit!"

Noll nodded. "We'll have to try and break through the villagers. They didn't look too steady. Let's go!" He turned his horse once more and as the others followed they drew and cocked their pistols. By the time the gang were within fifty yards of the villagers once more, their constable had chivvied them into some sort of order. "Right!" shouted Noll over the din. "At them at the gallop; keep close together, and if anyone breaks through, just keep going." Then without allowing any of them time to think, Noll led the gang at a hard gallop straight at the already wavering crowd before them. Knee to knee they rode, firing into the crowd as they went. From the front of the body came a scattered volley of answering shots and Will Reynolds clutched at his side and swayed in the saddle, but the remainder of the shots whistled harmlessly overhead and seconds later the tightly packed mass of men and horses crashed into what was left of the crowd, sending dozens sprawling and even more diving into doorways and hedgerows for cover. A few stalwarts struck at the passing horsemen who for their part lashed out with clubbed pistols as they dashed down the street. In seconds it was over and, scarcely able to believe their luck, and with hardly a scratch, the gang found themselves on the other side of the village with nothing between them and London. It was then that they noticed Will Reynolds was not with them; they turned and saw his riderless horse coming down the street.

Beyond was a scene of confusion. Dead and wounded lay scattered in the wake of their charge and in the centre of the street the constable was trying to force his way into the midst of a large group of villagers who were clustering round something which lay in the road. Before any of the gang could think of riding back into that turmoil they saw clubs rise and fall as though the men were threshing corn, and they knew that it would be futile. None of them had time to utter even a curse before Noll pointed beyond the villagers to where the horsemen and dragoons were entering the village. It was time to be moving and they raced to the open ground beyond as the pursuers crashed through the villagers with almost as little regard for their welfare as had the gang, and continued the pursuit.

The dragoons' horses were fresher than either the gang's or the justice's men's, and several times during the cross-country race to Kilburn they drew near enough to fire their pistols. It was with relief, therefore, that the gang reached the relative safety of the village, and with even greater relief that they found their way through it unopposed. From there it was on to Hendon. Always the dragoons were at their heels, and not far behind them, the horsemen who had begun the pursuit. At Hendon the Watch were drawn up across the road reinforced with a few of the locals armed with the usual assortment of weapons. These made no attempt to retard the gang's progress through the village but retired into the houses on either side and fired a few shots in their direction after they had gone. As they left the village behind them, Noll glanced backward; he was surprised to see that the pursuit seemed to have slackened. No one had emerged from the village. He reined and moved off to a rise on the right side of the road from where he could see down the village street. Surely it was not possible that they had given up the chase at last?

It took him only a second to grasp the meaning of what he saw. The view down the street was not as good as he expected, but he was just able to make out the figure of a man climbing into the saddle. They were changing horses; someone had planned this operation thoroughly and had prepositioned fresh horses along their likely escape routes. He rode back to the gang. "They're getting fresh mounts," he shouted, and raced off down the road towards Hampstead with the others in his wake. The village seemed quiet as they entered it from the south end. Noll led them up the main street and for the second time that day was forced to rein sharply.

At the top end of the street were some two hundred men, better armed and better formed than their counterparts in Harrow. There was a greater number of pikemen in this band, and above their heads hung the smoke from musketeers' slow matches. The gang turned as one man, and clattered back down the way they had come. It was too late.

The dragoons were already drawing up a hundred yards away, unhurriedly dressing their ranks; they had their quarry trapped and they knew it. The gang turned again and gathered in a group around Noll, looking in to him. "Well," he said. "We have two choices. We can mix it with the dragoons and those others that have been on our heels all day, or we can test the mettle of the bumpkins up the road there. I suggest we put them through their paces." He tried to sound confident, but nothing could hide from any of them the hopelessness of their situation. They walked their lathered horses slowly up the street towards the mass of men at the north end, loading their pistols as they did so. The waiting body of men stood silent as they approached. Tom brought his horse alongside Noll's.

"They knew we were coming, Noll. Someone betrayed us. They must have alerted the militia and constables in every town for fifty miles around here."

Noll looked tired and suddenly very old as he replied, "It was bound to happen sometime, Tom."

"But Noll," Tom's voice was like a little boy's as he spoke, "what I meant was – well, you know what I'm like when I've been drinking . . . I think – well, I told Eliza where we were going. Do you think she . . .?"

Noll smiled sadly. "Don't worry about it, boy," he said, and clapped Tom on the shoulder. It was a kind of farewell.

The four of them urged their horses into a trot and then into a gallop; men who saw it said they were cheering as they came. From upstairs windows in the street, the fire of a dozen muskets blanketed the scene in smoke as the front rank of the militia broke away to reveal the chains stretched across the street, anchored to the buildings on either side. There was no time to

stop, no room to change direction, and the four horses, one of
them already with an empty saddle, crashed to the ground in a
kicking, shrieking mêlée. For a few moments all was confusion
as men tried to pull themselves clear of the rolling press of
horseflesh and the lashing hooves. Then from all sides men
closed in, pikes and pitchforks jabbing. Only Tom even got to
his feet, dazed and with his left arm broken. His sword was in
his right, and at first men backed off as he swung wildly in all
directions, but seeing that he was too weak to resist for long,
they soon closed in again. He was still swiping the air with his
blade when a pike caught him in the back; as he turned another
pierced his breast, and a blow from a watchman's halberd cut
him down. By now the dragoons had come clattering up the
street and, true cavalrymen as they were, leapt from their
saddles, pistols in hand, to put the horses out of their pain.
Halfway up the street lay Robert Warren riddled with bullets;
under one of the horses was Hugh Jeffrey with a broken neck;
Tom's body had already been dragged clear for identification
when, with a cry, two militiamen dragged Noll, still breathing,
from the carnage.

14

A week passed before Jack returned to London. He had taken his time on the journey down, feeling as if a great weight had been lifted from his shoulders. The prospects for the future seemed excellent. With the money now in his possession – money he felt he had as good a right to as any man – he could break free from the life he had led since returning to England. With Overton safely installed in rooms in London, and the attorney ready to go to work as soon as the money was forthcoming, he had much to tell Ann. So keen was he to see her that he cancelled his plans of calling in at Reading to see Noll, and pressed on into London. He felt no sense of foreboding as he entered Crooked Lane where both the Dog and his lodgings lay. Nor was he unduly alarmed, therefore, when a man stepped out into the road in front of him before he had gone a few yards and taking his horse by the bridle, said, "I think you should read this before you go any further, Captain." He handed Jack a note; as he opened the note, Jack looked down at the man. It was a man he recognised, one of the regular drinkers at the Dog. The note was written in Ann's uncertain hand. It said, "Do not go to the Dog there is great danger. Come quickly to the white house, close by St Botolph's, Bishopsgate. The man needs paying five pounds. Ann."

Mystified, and by now thoroughly alarmed, Jack paid the man and left, scarcely heading his cry of "Good luck, Captain!" It took him half an hour to find the house which was in a poor but respectable quarter, a little off the main street. The door of the house was open, and as he entered he was met by a stout, grey-haired woman, her eyes red from weeping, who led him up the stairs to a room overlooking the street, and left him. Seconds later the door opened once more and as Jack turned he saw Ann standing in the doorway. She rushed into his open

175

arms, shouting, "Oh, thank God!" and then the fortitude that had sustained her through the most difficult week of her life crumbled, and she wept, gasping between agonised sobs, "Oh, Jack, they're dead, all of them – Noll's in Newgate – Tom, the others, all dead . . . it was Frost." Jack gaped at her in disbelief, and it was some minutes before he could get anything out of her that made any sense to him. When he did, the effect was as if she had stabbed him to the heart. He staggered, clutched at the table edge for support, and then fell weakly into a chair. A painful silence followed, punctuated by Ann's sobbing. Jack sat and stared into the middle distance as the enormity of what he had heard sank in.

Suddenly he was on his feet, incoherent himself now, making for the door and shouting as he went, "I must get to Newgate – Noll, he needs me!" Ann leapt across the room and reached the door before him. Pressing her back against it she grappled with him as he tried to fight past her.

"You can't go out again. It's a miracle you got here without being seen. I've had men on the lookout for you all week. Every constable and watchman in London is after you. They know you'll come back. If you go down to Newgate you'll hang alongside Noll!" Gradually the sense of her words prevailed; he gave up the struggle and turned away.

"But I swore an oath; we all did," he said, as much to himself as to her.

"You didn't swear to throw your life away pointlessly, I'm sure," Ann replied, following him back into the room. She was about to continue when she saw that he now was weeping, and rushed to his side. He sat and wept unashamedly for the men who had been his only friends for what had seemed like a lifetime, men with whom he had ridden, fought, laughed and drunk. Men who had trusted him, and men whom he felt he had failed when they needed him most. "I should have been there," was all he could say when finally he had regained control of himself. Ann had her arm about him.

"If you had been there you would have been dead too, or waiting to be hanged, like Noll," she whispered. "And I, for one, thank God that you weren't." Nothing more was said for some time.

Later, Ann told him the whole story, starting with the night she had threatened Frost with the knife, and then telling of her rescue at the hands of Tom. "It was pure chance that he happened to come home that night. He had been away on one of his long drinking bouts. If he hadn't, Jack, God knows where I'd be now. Anyway, he cut one of them, and I'd wounded Wicks. Tom brought me here to his aunt's house; that was his aunt that brought you upstairs. I told Tom that I thought Frost was behind it all, that he had ordered Wicks to do what he did as a way of getting revenge for what had happened earlier, but I'm not sure he believed me. He thought Wicks was acting on his own account, though it seemed obvious to me that Wicks never did anything without being told by Frost. What became of Wicks after, I don't know, though I know he didn't die. He must have told Frost what had happened, and Frost informed on the gang to get his revenge on both of us. They were betrayed, Jack. The authorities knew exactly where they would be. They had alerted the whole county. The militia were turned out, dragoons had been drafted in and every Watch for miles around was stood to. They had no chance. I was sure it was Frost; I was even more sure after I went to see Lucy."

"You went to see Lucy?" gasped Jack, who had already heard enough that day to rob him of his reason.

"Yes," Ann answered, a little impatiently. "She wasn't difficult to find. Her sort generally know each other's business, so I made a few enquiries. She is living with an officer near the Guildhall. She received me kindly enough. She heard the news and was as desolated as I was; for some reason that surprised me." Ann looked across at Jack, who was still gaping at her in wonder, before carrying on, "Anyway, the most important thing is that Lucy was not alone. Eliza was with her; that was Tom's girl." Jack nodded as Ann went on, "Eliza was almost out of her wits, and looked about to make away with herself. It was some time before I could get her to tell me anything, but when she did it confirmed what I had suspected all along. She was passing information to Frost in the same way that Lucy had. She had been doing it for years, and saw little harm in it. Frost paid her a little extra. He liked to know what people were up to. She had no idea it would end up like this. It seems that Noll came back from Reading with the idea of an expedition to Windsor in his head. The others were not so keen, but in your absence he was the leader, so they went along. I think he wanted to prove that he could lead them as well as you. Well, two days before they left, Tom told Eliza, and she, as usual, told Frost." Here she began to sob once more. "He must have gone straight to the justices, Jack, and told them all he knew. No doubt he's collected the reward . . ." and once more she broke down. Jack comforted her as best he could, though his own thoughts were far from comfortable. They both sat in silence for a while and contemplated a world that almost overnight, it seemed, had become more bleak and hostile than they could ever have believed possible. It was Jack who spoke first.

"If I had only listened to you, I would have got all of us out of Frost's reach." Then his voice grew angry, "And if I'd only stayed here in London, instead of dashing off on some scheme of my own . . ."

"You'd be dead now with the rest of them," Ann interrupted harshly. "This is no time for self-recrimination," she went on. "Save that for when you get out of here alive, if you ever do. The dead are dead, and all the tears in the world won't bring them back. You've got to think of the living, yourself and Noll."

"Noll!" shouted Jack. "You're right! I've got to help him. We've got to get him out of there."

Ann's voice was almost scornful as she spoke, "This is no time for idle dreaming either. How could you get him out? All the gold in the world won't buy him out of Newgate, and you have no time for anything else. He went to the Old Bailey on Friday; he's been sentenced to death and he's to be hanged the day after tomorrow."

"Then we must attempt a rescue." Jack was almost frantically clutching at straws now, as the realisation of his helplessness dawned on him. "We!" said Ann. "You and I? What can we do? There's a price on your head, and if you so much as go within a mile of Newgate someone is going to want to claim it. You daren't even set foot out of doors. That leaves me, unless you have any other men to call upon, that I don't know about." Jack hung his head and sat down once more. Ann crossed over to him and took his head in her hands. "I don't mean to hurt you, Jack, but you have to face facts. In any case, Noll has expressly forbidden any such attempts on your part."

Jack looked up at her. "You've seen him?" he said, past being surprised by her any more.

"I've been twice," she said. "I shall be going again tomorrow night, for the last time.'

It was late at night, and the light from the street lamps glistened on the heads of the nails, large as a man's thumb, which studded the great gate of Newgate Prison. Ann's heart sank as she approached it, although she was innocent of any crime; the gates loomed above her like the entrance to some dark, forbidden city. Although it was early autumn, and the cold weather had not really set in, she wore a velvet mask and fur stole to disguise her appearance. She had nothing to fear for herself, it was true, but she did not wish to be recognised, and so help others who might be looking for Jack. It was not her first visit, and the gaoler opened the wicket gate to admit her when she asked to see the condemned man. The hinges on the gate screamed as though in agony as the door opened, and she stepped into the darkness with the same sense of foreboding as on her previous visits. Before Jack had been imprisoned at Leicester, such things as this had been totally outside her experience. Even Leicester gaol could not compare in horror with this awful place.

As she followed the turnkey down the dark passage towards the condemned cell, she had an almost overwhelming desire to turn and run back to the gate and hammer on it until they let her out. Only the thought of Noll kept her going. The air in the corridor was damp and Ann could feel the effect on her lungs already. What must it be like to live here, she wondered? From what seemed like far away, though it was in fact only a few walls distant, came the sound of laughter, singing and revelry. It echoed on the stones and at this remove sounded anything but cheerful. The gaoler looked over his shoulder at her and smiled. "They're having a fine old time in the King's ward tonight," he said, but seeing that Ann was not to be drawn into conversation, he turned once more and led on. From elsewhere came the sound of drunken laughter, like the cackling of so many geese. Someone else was raving, until another cut him short with a foul oath. All these sounds coming as they did from unknown regions, distorted by the echoes, and each in its own way a cry of despair, produced in Ann the feeling that here was hell on earth.

The gaoler, hungry for any anecdotes or snippets of information that could be traded later in the taverns and ordinaries, sold for a drink or two to the hacks and pamphlet-writers, tried once more to talk. "You his daughter or his doxy?" he asked. Ann shook her head. "Just a friend of the family," she answered, and the gaoler looked disappointed for a moment, then seemed to realise something and nodded at her, adding with a wink, "Say no more!"

The sounds from elsewhere in the prison began to recede, though the smell did not improve, and Ann sniffed at an orange she had brought with her for the purpose. The gaoler was talking again as much to himself as to her. "Quiet one he is, this one," he was saying. "Usually a lot more demanding than this, they are. Music, dancing, girls, fine foods and wines brought in by their friends. Regular banquets they usually have. Not this time though. Still, it takes all sorts. We had Captain Webster in here, you know. You won't remember him. Long before your time, he was. What a boy he was! Feasting and drinking right up to the last moment. And on the cart when the hangman knelt to ask his forgiveness, he kicked him in the stomach! God, but he was game," he finished as they arrived at the door of the condemned cell. On entering the cell, Ann saw that Noll was not alone.

At the table beside him sat the chaplain, a fat, elderly man who, despite his florid face and toper's nose, had about him an air of permanent sadness. They had been sharing a bottle of wine, but as soon as Ann entered he stood up and left without a word, save for promising to return later. As he left he dragged the reluctant gaoler with him, and Ann and Noll had the cell to themselves. It was a bare room with a cot, a table, and two stools. On the table was the bottle of wine and two cups, a half-eaten meal, some writing materials and a bible. A solitary small window looked out onto the yard, across which Ann could just make out St Sepulchre's church. Noll looked at Ann and smiled. He seemed to have aged twenty years in the past few days.

"I think I have convinced the chaplain he is wasting his time," he said. "I am not about to repent now, and forswear a life I enjoyed to the full when it was going well for me."

Ann simply said, "Jack's back," and Noll's face changed from resignation to alarm. "It's all right; he's safely hidden up at Bishopsgate," she said, and Noll sighed with relief and sat at the table once again. Ann sat down opposite him. "His head is full of schemes, as usual," she said, and Noll shook his head.

"No scheme in the world can save me now, and with half London after him he'd be a fool to even try. I hope you told him that." Ann nodded. Noll leaned over and grasped her arm so tightly it hurt. His voice was low when he spoke and she had never heard him speak with such urgency before.

"Keep him away tomorrow. They'll be looking out for him at Tyburn. Frost'll want to collect on him too, and he's not the only one. Get him away from here as soon as you can. Out of London and never come back. Promise me!" Ann nodded and her eyes filled with tears as the old man revealed his love for Jack. After a while he asked her, "Did he have any message for me?"

Ann tried to smile. "He said to say that he loved you, and I was to say that he never meant those words that passed between you the last time. He said you'd know what that meant."

Noll nodded, and reached across the table to where the pen and paper lay. "I've written two letters," he said, and smiled. "Didn't know I was much of a one for writing, did you? Well, I'm not, but I had plenty of time here, though it took me most of it. There's more here than I ever wrote in my whole life before." Once more Ann tried to smile, but it was futile. Noll went on, "One is to Joyce – I know you'll deliver it for me. The other is for Jack."

Ann took them and tucked them inside the folds of her cloak. She was about to speak when the ringing of a hand-bell directly outside the window cut her words off. They both turned to look out through the tiny space as the ringing continued. Just outside they could see a solitary watchman who looked in at them as he worked the bell. Presently he stopped, and producing from his pocket a piece of paper, proceeded to read from it with a voice as imposing as he could muster, as follows:

> All you that in the condemned hold do lie
> Prepare you, for tomorrow you shall die.
> Watch all, and pray, the hour is drawing near,
> When you before the Almighty must appear.

Examine well yourselves, in time repent;
That you may not to eternal flames be sent.
Forswear your sins, trust in Christ's merits,
That heavenly grace you may inherit.
And when St Sepulchre's bell tomorrow tolls,
The Lord may have mercy on your souls.

The watchman folded the piece of paper, thrust it in his pocket, and taking up his halberd once more, cried out, "Past twelve o'clock!" and went on his way. As soon as he had gone, Ann looked to Noll in amazement. He smiled grimly. "I'd forgotten, you wouldn't know about these things," he said. "They've been doing it for over fifty years now. Some merchant left a grant in his will for it, that condemned men might hear his poem, and thus be led to repentance. He could have saved himself the expense for me!"

The horror of it all threatened to overwhelm Ann, but for Noll's sake she fought to restrain her feelings. She could see that it had shaken him too. He did not look at her when he spoke again. "I'm an old man, I don't greatly fear death; it comes to us all eventually and I've outlived a good many of my friends. But the manner of it, that I fear. It's a hard death when there's no one to help it along." Then he remembered himself and clutched at her arm once more. "Don't misunderstand me! Keep Jack away at all costs!" Ann promised him once more. Then he asked the question he had been trying to ask for some time. "Will you be there?"

Ann faltered. She had never been to a hanging before and the thought of it horrified her. She would have given a king's ransom to stay away, but she asked him, "What do you want me to do?"

Noll spoke as though he were ashamed at what he was saying. "It will be hard tomorrow. Oh, the crowds will cheer me to the echo, and I'll put a brave face on it, never fear. But . . ." he lowered his voice so that she could hardly hear him, "it would help me to know that there was at least one person out there who was truly on my side." Ann leaned across and took his hand. "I'll be there," she whispered, "I promise." This seemed to comfort him, for when he spoke again it was in his old voice.

"When you've been in here a while you learn the meaning of freedom. Jack would know what I mean. It's strange that freedom was always one of the great joys of that life of ours; the freedom to go where we pleased, and do what we pleased. But it was an illusion. I mean, there we were, free as birds, free to roam the country, take any road we pleased. If we met up with a traveller on the road, and we asked him which way he was going, we were always going the same way, for a highwayman is never out of his way. And yet, for all that freedom, we were all going to the same place in the end. Jack used to say that he envied no man in the world, because he called no man master, but we were no more free than an apprentice or a serving-man. In the end the Frosts of this world own you, and if you fall foul of them, you pay the highest price there is to pay. Before he went away he talked of leaving off this life altogether; I poured scorn on him at the time, but he was right. You make sure that he does. And now," he stood up, "you must go; I have a speech to write. Mustn't disappoint the public – some of them will have paid high prices for the best seats. And I must get a good night's sleep. Can't go before my maker with bags under my eyes."

He did his best to sound jaunty as he walked Ann to the door of the cell, and he almost succeeded. When the gaoler came in answer to his knock, he took Ann in his arms and held her close to him. He clung to her as though she were life itself for what seemed like an age, then suddenly released her and turned away without a word. Ann did not hear a word of the gaoler's chatter as she followed him, her eyes blinded with tears, down the vile corridors and into the night.

15

As the early morning sun filtered in through the panes of the small window overlooking the street, Jack looked down at the gathering crowds and wondered how many of them were going to the hanging that day. He turned and looked over at the bed against the far wall, where Ann lay sleeping. Asleep, she seemed childlike and vulnerable, which had always been the way he had thought of her. Always, that was, until now. He had been accustomed to think of himself as a battle-hardened man of the world, and her as a poor innocent in need of protection from the cruel world which surrounded her. This illusion had, however, been destined to join so many others of his. It had been shattered by the events of the past few weeks. Although he had always admired Ann, he had been amazed by the resource and courage she had shown. For it had been she who first defied Frost to his face; she who had left Wicks bleeding in a gutter; she who had confronted Lucy and rooted out the truth about Frost; she who had hired men to look out for him day and night, and prevent him blundering into the Dog; and now, at last, she who had nightly braved the hell of Newgate to bring comfort to a dying friend. All this while he had been either absent on some hare-brained scheme of his own, or reduced to the role of helpless spectator. As he gazed at her sleeping form he marvelled at the mettle of this young woman who had twice saved his life and was now, at his time of direst need, his right arm. His world seemed to be changing faster than he could comprehend.

He had Noll's letter on his lap. He had read it several times already, although every sentence of it seemed to tear at his vitals. He read it once more.

Jack,
    Hard words passed between us when last we met. Forget them, for I meant none of them and no more did you. You

184

were right, my friend. If I had left when I should have done, I would not be in the hard case I am now in. We had a good life, you and I, but it is over. Mine must end upon the morrow, and yours must change before it is too late. I beg you for both your sakes do not go to Tyburn in the morning. They will be looking for you, Jack. As soon as it is over, take Ann, like who there is no other in the world, and leave this city forever. I know I do not need to ask you to look out for Joyce and her boys, though the Lord knows she has done well enough without me all these years. I thank God for the good times we had. You were the son I never had. Until we are together again, God bless you.

Noll.

Jack, don't go after Frost for God's sake!

Jack lay the letter down gently on the floor as the tears burned his cheek. Noll had begged and Ann had ordered that he stay away from Tyburn that day. This was what he was reduced to, sitting around weeping like a woman while his old friend died a hideous death alone amongst a howling mob without a friend to make his passing easier. Quietly he stood up and tiptoed over to the door. Ann was still sleeping as he crept down the stairs and out into the street, closing the door of the house softly behind him.

Noll was awoken at dawn from a dream of a meadow at the back of an alehouse. It had been a sunny afternoon years ago. Joyce's boys had been scarcely able to walk, but he had hoisted them both into the saddle in front of him and ridden round and round the meadow, whilst she had laughed and waved from the back of the house and the boys had cried out in delight. It was a bitter cold morning as Noll hauled himself from the hard cot, the sort of morning men curse not realising how precious each of them is. He put on his best suit of blue silk that Ann had brought in two days earlier; he had hardly ever worn it. Outside it was a bright day, despite the cold, and the sun shone down on him as together with the gaolers, he crossed the yard to St Sepulchre's for holy communion.

It was still shining as they returned, leading Noll to comment that there would be a good crowd today. The gaolers nodded

185

and smiled to each other behind his back in silent approval of his spirit. Back in his cell, a splendid late breakfast was laid out for him with several bottles of wine, which he shared with his captors. He was perfectly calm, or rather numb, as he ate. Late the previous night he had done with reminiscence, and now considered neither the past nor the future, but savoured the few moments left him. He lingered over each mouthful of food, and each of the many glasses of wine he drank in the time allowed him. At the gate, as the shackles he had worn for a week were removed, he even managed to joke with the gaolers, and walked with a jaunty step towards the street where the city marshall was nervously bustling about on horseback trying to get the procession into some kind of order. The sight of the cart with its escort of soldiers stayed him for a moment, and his resolve almost faltered, but from the shadows of the lodge gate emerged his friend the chaplain, who had drunk with him most of the previous evening, and who now presented him with a nosegay of hedgerow flowers. They climbed into the cart together, joining the waiting hangman. A substantial crowd had already gathered and they cheered as Noll shook the hangman's hand and then reached into his pocket and produced an old clay pipe which he stuck in the corner of his mouth. The city marshall, looking harrassed, rode by, and the cheering grew tumultuous as Noll shouted to him, "Hurry it up, will you sir, I haven't got all day!"

Jack had made straight for the nearest tavern and now sat, sipping at a cup of ale and regarding the other drinkers. The tavern was mostly full of workmen, apprentices and journeymen. He knew he was taking a risk being out at all, especially in this place where he was, in his fine clothes, most conspicuous, but his mind was wholly taken up with the task in hand. Presently he saw what he wanted, a man close to his own height and build seated at a table on the other side of the room. He was wearing a workman's leather jerkin, breeches of coarse cloth, linen stockings and a pair of buckled shoes. Beside him on the bench lay a crumpled woollen cap. Jack picked up his cup and crossed the room to join the fellow at his table. The man eyed him suspiciously as he sat down.

"Do you want to earn some easy money?" Jack said.

"That depends how much and how easy," replied the other.

"Couldn't be easier," Jack smiled at him. "Just sell me your clothes!"

The man stared at him open-mouthed for a moment, then frowned. "Are you mad?" he said.

"Does it matter?" said Jack, throwing a pound onto the table. "That's yours if you give me them now." The man thought for a second; the man was clearly mad, but with the money he was offering he could buy a dozen sets of clothes far finer than these, and much more besides.

"Round the back," he said, and Jack followed him outside. Within minutes the exchange was complete, and as Jack adjusted the woollen cap on his cropped head, he looked for all the world like an apprentice. The other sat on the step, wondering at his sudden good fortune and shook his head in disbelief as he watched. "Just tell me one thing," he said as Jack was about to leave, "What's it for?" Jack stared absently down the street.

"To play a joke on a friend," he said and was gone. The man shook his head and smiled.

The procession was led by the marshall, followed by a party of mounted constables, then the cart surrounded by troopers, and finally more constables. As it proceeded up Snow Hill, over the Fleet Bridge and up Holborn Hill, crowds lined the street on both sides, cheering and waving at the prisoner, who smiled and waved back. At the City of Oxford tavern on Oxford Road, the procession stopped in accordance with custom, and a beaming landlord brought a pint of ale to the prisoner in the cart. A hush fell on the crowd as Noll drained it at great speed and held it upside down to show that it was empty. The crowd cheered once more, and then fell silent as the landlord approached to collect the mug. "That'll be a penny, if you please, Sir," he smiled up at Noll.

Noll smiled down at him. "I'll pay you on the way back!" he announced to the expectant crowd, who howled with laughter at the old joke. Then the procession went on its way, pursued up the street by cries of "Good luck!" and "God bless!" from the crowd now filing back into the tavern.

The large open space which was Tyburn Fields was crowded

by the time the procession reached it. Even the anglers who fished in the stream that gave it its name had abandoned their rods and joined the heaving throng which pushed and shoved this way and that to get a better view. An earsplitting cheer went up as the procession arrived and the crowd parted before it as it made its way towards the great, three-legged gallows. Hundreds had come from miles around to view the spectacle. Most were on foot, some in coaches or crowded onto carts, others had paid for their seats and were packed together on raised banks of benches. Around the foot of the gallows, watchmen with halberds kept the crowd back as best they could as the cart halted underneath. Noll was by now quite drunk. He had imbibed well at breakfast, had drained the pint of ale at the tavern at an astonishing speed, and had been fortified liberally with brandy from the chaplain's flask. It was not difficult for him, then, to raise a smile at the vast crowd that had come to see him off.

Of course he did not know that out there somewhere was Jack, fighting his way to the front; nor that sitting on a bench with a select group of friends was Frost; but he knew that Ann was out there somewhere and the thought comforted him greatly.

The crowd, quite close now and pressing closer, was clearly on his side. The men cheered and shouted encouragement to him; women and girls threw kerchiefs ribbons and flowers in his direction. Below the cart a man released a pigeon from a basket; it climbed the air above the gallows and circled above. The sight seemed to attract the gaze of everyone as it circled once more in the bright blue sky and flew off in the direction of Newgate, carrying the message that the prisoner had arrived safely. A hush fell.

As the rope was lowered from above and the noose descended by Noll's head, he stepped forward; it was time for his speech. A murmur ran amongst the crowd as each told his neighbour to be silent. Noll spoke. His voice was clear and confident.

"My friends! I would be guilty of the crime of ingratitude, which among persons of quality is a greater crime than the one of which I stand here convicted, if I did not thank all those of you who willingly or unwillingly have helped me in my rise to fame and fortune." The crowd roared with laughter, and

Noll acknowledged their appreciation with a smile. "And most especially the ladies," there was more cheering, "who at one wave of my weapon have yielded favours too numerous and too particular to mention here. Gentlemen, I commend them to you." The crowd roared its approval, and after a few moments Noll gestured for silence. "I also commend to you, my friends, our Sovereign Lord the King, to whom I have been a more loyal servant than many who do now presume to be my judges!" There were cries of "Shame!" and "God Save the King!" Noll continued, "Lastly, my friends, I bid you, whether you love me or hate me, to raise a glass to me tonight. Farewell!"

Tumultuous applause rang through the air as Noll stepped back and gave a last wave. Over the benches, Frost turned to his friend Mr Richardson and nodded in grudging admiration; elsewhere in the crowd, Ann buried her face in her hands and was comforted by an old woman who stood beside her; and right under the gallows, at the front of the crowd, stood Jack who, like many others, was pushing against the halberds of the Watch. The noose was lowered over Noll's neck, and a black kerchief tied round his head. Beside Jack a powerfully built man with the arms of a blacksmith was arguing with the young watchman, who with his halberd was keeping both of them back. "Let one of us through for pity's sake," he was saying. "He'll kick for hours if you don't. Do you want that on your conscience, boy?" Nearby, constables who were mingling with the crowd hoping to catch sight of any accomplices of the condemned man, were taking a special interest in the gathering at the foot of the gallows. Up on the cart Noll seemed already to have left this world far behind him as he nodded to the hangman, who lowered the kerchief over his eyes. Jack looked the young watchman in the face; he was a beardless youth, probably at his first hanging. "Please!" whispered Jack desperately, "he's my friend!" The young lad said nothing, but indicated with his eyes towards the butt of his halberd; it was raised, and in a second Jack had slipped under it and reached the foot of the gallows itself. The cart had begun to move and Noll, blindfolded, suddenly had a vision of a line of pikemen in undyed white coats rushing forwards at the charge on some forgotten moor many years ago. As his feet felt the empty air beneath him, and before the noose tightened, he cried out "Vive le Roi!"

Jack heard nothing as he grabbed the kicking legs of his friend and heaved downwards on them with all his strength, but the crowd were roaring at the tops of their voices now. Suddenly he heard a choked cry from Noll; it was almost inaudible, but clear enough for Jack to make it out. "God bless you, my boy!"

Suddenly he was not alone; the blacksmith was by his side and pulling at Noll's legs. Looking over his shoulder Jack could see that the crowd had broken through the cordon in a number of places and he could hear an authoritative voice shouting "Stop that man!" Noll was still now; the combined weight of his closest friend and a total stranger had ended his death agony. The blacksmith whispered in his ear, "You'd better be off; it's you they're after!" and Jack, with one backwards glance at the body of his friend, vanished into the crowd one step ahead of two constables who were converging on him. The crowd, who had guessed what was afoot, closed ranks, and the constables raged ineffectually as Jack was swallowed up in their number.

In different parts of that same crowd, Ann and Jack were swept along by it as it began to move slowly back towards the city. Gradually, as it got further from Tyburn, it spread out and began to disperse. Jack took shelter in the company of a large group of apprentices who laughed and joked as they descended the hill; in their number, he thought, was complete anonymity. Confident in his disguise he completely failed to notice the tall, thin man, dressed entirely in black, with a low-crowned hat, who a few yards distant pointed him out to two others with him, before all three set off to follow him at a discreet distance. Jack was still numb from the events of that morning, and scarcely able to think of the future. For him the future consisted of getting back to Bishopsgate as soon as possible; Ann would know where he had gone and would already be half out of her mind with worry. Had it not been for her, he reflected as he re-entered the city, he would no longer have cared whether he lived or died.

He left the safety of his apprentice band, and took the most direct route to Bishopsgate; the three men who had never been far behind him closed up as he turned off the main street. Jack was thinking of Ann and the plans they would soon have to make, but there were two things that had to be done before he could make any plans, two things that were at the moment more important to him than life itself.

He was in a part of town unfamiliar to him and he stopped to consider the way. As he stood looking around him, the man in black crossed the street so as to get a better look at him. Then he nodded to his two companions who, quick as a flash, ran to Jack's side and without a word grasped his arms and steered him up a small side street. Jack kicked and thrashed in their grip, but to no avail – they held him fast. With the third man following they ran him halfway up an alley, and then turned into a small yard similar to that at the back of the Dog, using Jack as a battering-ram as they crashed through its wooden gate. Weakened by his ordeal on the hill, and unwilling to draw attention to himself by crying out for help, Jack was helpless as they threw him against the wall and held him for the third man to see. The man approached and, reaching over, pulled off Jack's woollen cap.

"Oh yes!" he announced with evident relish, "it's him, it's definitely him!" Jack lowered his head to look under the brim of the man's hat and into his face. At once he knew he was doomed. It was Bancroft, the actor. "You remember me, I'm sure," he said. "The Scythian king. Only last time we met, as I recall, you were unable to stay for the end of the performance. Such a pity! Allow me to introduce two other members of the company, stalwart Scythians both." The two men who held Jack grinned unpleasantly at him. Bancroft hissed, "Search him!" and the two obeyed, removing Jack's weighty purse and throwing it to Bancroft who tucked it away inside his doublet. Jack's heart sank; his world had been turned upside-down just when it had seemed possible that all would be well. The events of the day, crowned by this, quite unmanned him and only pure pride kept him from breaking down there and then. He grieved not so much for himself as for Ann, who would now be all alone, and for the things he would now have to leave undone as he went to a death as grisly as that to which he had been a party this day. The irony that it should have been this, of all his crimes, that should have caught up with him brought a smile to his lips; this, which had become one of his favourite stories, was to send him to the gallows. He looked up at the actor.

"So, Mr Bancroft, you finally reached London!" he said.

"Yes," replied Bancroft. "Finally reached – that is, returned to – London. And we would have got here a good deal quicker if you had not made away with our money." He began to pace up and down the yard, working himself up into a frenzy as he spoke. "How could you! When I had befriended you, taken you into my private apartments, helped you to wine at my own expense and, what is more than all this, was treating you to a private performance of one of the most affecting – "

Jack interrupted him, "Spare me your sermonising, Mr Bancroft. Call the constable and let's have done with it!" The actor stopped in his tracks and stood for a while looking at the ground. When he looked up once more his face was quivering with emotion. His voice shook as he spoke. "Do you think after what I have seen today," he said, "that I could give a man over to be hanged?"

Seconds later Jack was thrust unceremoniously into the alley, and after staring back into the yard for a moment, stumbled off in the direction of Bishopsgate.

Ann was not yet back when he arrived at the house and he whiled away the time until her return in bathing and changing out of his workman's clothes. He was adjusting his periwig when he heard the door open behind him, and turned to present his excuses to Ann for breaking his promise of the previous night, and going to Tyburn. The day, it seemed, had not run out of surprises for him, for instead of Ann, he found Lucy before him. He had not seen or heard from her since he had been captured in Leicester, and he clutched at the mantelpiece for support as she walked towards him. She looked as though she half expected some rebuke from him, and stopped before she was within arms reach. Finally Jack found his tongue. "Why have you come here?" he asked.

"To bring you some information and some advice," was the reply.

"Information for me?" said Jack, with a sarcastic edge to his voice. "Now there's a novelty. What information?"

Lucy looked at the floor. "It's Eliza. They fished her out of the river this morning. I thought you might want to know – we had some good times together."

Jack's voice was softer when he spoke again. "Lucy, I'm sorry. It was good of you to come."

Lucy sighed. "She never recovered from Tom's death. I was afraid she'd do something like this but I couldn't watch her all the time. I know what you think of us and our sort even when you flatter us and buy us things, but we have our feelings too. You probably hate me for what I was doing, but what choice had I? Frost hired me to spy on you right from the start; he wanted to know everything; he always did. Oh, you were always kind and generous, Jack, better than any before or since, but I needed more. I have to think of when I'm old. I won't always be young or pretty and I don't want to end up like Mrs Stanway, or worse. I want something better."

Jack smiled sadly. "I don't hate you, Lucy. And as to the rest, I knew. I knew right from the start. You said you had some advice. What is it?"

Lucy looked at him uncertainly. "Don't go up against Frost, Jack. I know you, I know what you're thinking. Don't do it. He's too strong for you, too powerful. Nothing can stop him, and anyone who gets in his way is destroyed. Your friends – Noll, Tom and the rest – they were some of his victims; so was Eliza, in a way; and there have been many more. You're not a part of this world of ours; you don't belong, neither does she. So both of you thank God for that, and get away from here. Even if you did beat Frost, there would be another to take his place. There are always Frosts and there always will be. Don't throw your life away on him – he's not worth it."

Jack eyed her coolly for a moment. "Did Frost send you?" he said.

Lucy winced. "I suppose you had a right to say that," she said, "but it's not true. I know Frost paid me to like you, but I didn't have to pretend. You were kinder to me than anyone else has ever been; you deserve better than me, and now you've got it. I just want you to live to enjoy it." She turned to go, but before she could reach the door Jack had caught up with her and took her in his arms.

"You deserve better, dear Lucy," he said, "than to be insulted by the likes of me. You're just another of Frost's victims like the rest of us. Are you happy with your officer?'' She smiled and nodded and Jack went on, "I was always fond of you, Lucy. We did have some good times together, and I for one will never forget them. And I'm taking your advice – Ann and I are leaving London tonight and never coming back.'' And with that he leaned over and kissed her tenderly on the forehead. She left without a word but with tear-brimmed eyes. Halfway down the stairs she met Ann coming up; the two women stopped and a look passed between them of perfect understanding and sympathy. They clasped hands for a second, and then went their separate ways.

Noll's body was taken from Tyburn back to Newgate, where, having been dipped in a vat of boiling pitch, it was clamped into an iron frame and conveyed to a spot known as 'Wildwoods' on Hampstead Heath and there hung on the gibbet. It hung there for the rest of the day, exposed to the incurious glance of the seasoned traveller and the startled gaze of the casual passer-by, until the hour of midnight, when its peace was further disturbed by the arrival of a long cart of the type used to transport hay in country areas, driven by two country lads, accompanied by a gentleman in a dark cloak and plumed hat. This latter, mounting the cart, proceeded to hack at the cross-bar of the gibbet with a woodsman's axe until it gave way completely and the obscene frame and its contents fell to the ground with a clatter. The two lads then hoisted it onto the back of the cart, remembering perhaps a long time ago when the man whose remains they handled had hoisted them both laughing into his saddle, and with their grisly burden they drove by the light of the moon back to a small village just outside Reading.

The following night the frame received the attentions of the local blacksmith, and the body, free at last from its iron cage, was wrapped in a linen shroud and laid gently in an oak coffin. Within the hour it was driven to the local churchyard where the sexton, a friend of Joyce's with a partiality for her ale, led the bearers to a freshly dug grave in the corner of the churchyard where the turf had been rolled back. There, attended by a small party of mourners who huddled together in the darkness, the body was finally laid to rest with dignity. By morning the turf had been rolled back into its proper place and there was no sign that anyone had ever been to that forgotten corner of the churchyard.

Early next morning, Jack arose and left the house silently while Ann still slept. He had left beside the bed the portmanteaux containing the money, a note and a letter which she was to open if she heard that he was dead. Before the night sky had begun to show grey over the eastern horizon, he was leading his horse out of the farmyard and down onto the road. In spite of all the promises he had made to Noll, to Lucy, and above all to Ann, he was going back to London.

16

Jonathan Frost reached across the table and pulled towards him the letter that had been the object of his thoughts all morning. Beside the fire, ill at ease despite the mug of warm ale in his hand, sat a man in working clothes. Frost spared him not a glance as he read the letter yet again:

Frost,
I know you would hang me if you could. But think again; I have eyes in my head and a tongue too. I know sufficient about the disappearance of J Simmons, about your first wife and Doctor Stark, and about our own dealings with you, to bring you to Newgate with me. And if I am taken I shall have nothing to lose. If I dance the Tyburn jig, you shall be my partner. But that proverb is not true which says that two of a trade shall never agree. We have a mutual interest in forgetting the past. I would be free of you, and you of me. I would leave London and never return but that my purse is empty. A moderate sum, however, would help me on my way. I will be at the small wharf west of the bridge on the city side at the stroke of midnight tomorrow. Meet me there. Come alone and no trickery.

J. Shipton

Frost looked across at the man by the fire. "You are the lamplighter for Thames Street?" he asked him.

"Yes Sir," replied the other.

"Do you know the small wharf on the west of the bridge?" said Frost, and the man nodded. "Is there a light there?"

"Yes, Sir; at the top of the street that leads down to it. It's about fifty yards away, but it lights up the whole wharf."

"And is the wharf deserted?"

"It's used by the watermen until about ten, Sir, but it's as quiet as the grave after that." Frost smiled at the words.

"How long do those lamps of yours last?" he asked.

"All night, Sir," then the man grinned. "Usually, that is."

"You can control them?"

"Oh yes, Sir; if I don't fill them right, they sometimes go out in the middle of the night. It's awful dangerous to be abroad then, Sir!"

Frost smiled once again. "How closely can you time them?"

"What time do you want?" asked the man. Frost slid a small purse across the table at the man.

"The stroke of midnight," he said.

The man pocketed the purse and smiled confidentially at Frost. "I can guarantee it," he said. Frost's eyes were daggers as he smiled back at the man.

"I hope so. There'll be more in this for you if it works. If it doesn't . . ." the look on Frost's face took the smile off the other's. Frost pointed to the door and the man got up to leave. "On your way down, tell the two who fetched you here I want to see them," said Frost and turned once again to the letter. It had disturbed him deeply. How much did Shipton really know about Simmons' disappearance, and worse still, about Doctor Stark? Of course he might be bluffing, but that was not a risk he could afford to take, and in any case, even so much as a hint in the wrong quarters could set off a train of very awkward investigations. Nor could he be sure that Shipton was serious about the money; it may just be a ruse to lure him out to kill him. On the other hand he may really be desperate and in need of money. It was certain at any rate that Shipton wanted one or the other, money or revenge, and Frost intended to make sure that he got neither. Shipton was in many ways a loose end. That business with the girl still rankled of course, but there were other girls, and with any luck Shipton might lead him to her before he died. If they could take him alive, it would be simple enough to get him to talk before they killed him. But that was not as important as ensuring that this time Shipton died.

Further thoughts on the matter were prevented by a respectful knock at the door, and the entry of Wicks' two cronies, Gog and Magog. Frost looked them over as they stood before him. It was a pity that Wicks had not recovered yet; the wound was not a serious one but it had festered. Doctor Stark was an incompetent idiot when it came to curing people. "I have a simple task for you," he said. "I am going to meet Shipton tomorrow night at a small wharf by the bridge just off Thames Street. Do you know it?" They both nodded and he went on, "I shall meet him there at the stroke of midnight, and there, with your help, I shall kill him." The two showed no reaction as he went on, "I want you two to be there by ten o'clock, armed, ready and sober. Get yourself in the doorway of one of those buildings on the right-hand side as you approach the river, and watch out for us. Shipton will probably be early; just lie low until I arrive. I will talk to him for a moment or two, and then the street light will go out. That is your signal. I will attack him while he is still distracted and you come in from behind and grab him. If possible, drag him into the shadow of one of the buildings. Don't kill him unless you have to; that pleasure is to be mine! I shall finish him off with this!" and he reached behind him and produced his silver-topped cane.

In his room above a tavern in Fish Street Jack loaded his pistol. It was the small pocket pistol, which was the first thing he had ever robbed from his first victim that day on Hounslow Heath; the gambler who had talked him out of half of his winnings. He rammed two balls down the barrel. At close range there was no doubt that this would make an end of Frost and he could use his sword to deal with anyone else Frost brought with him. He had no doubt that Frost intended to kill him, or that he would bring others to do his dirty work for him, but first he would have to come to the wharf alone, and Jack would need only a few seconds to kill him. No doubt the advantage lay with Frost as far as numbers went, but Jack had one advantage – Frost wanted to kill him and get away with it. Jack was not so particular.

At five minutes before the appointed time Jack stood on the wharf in the light from the street lamp in Thames Street. He was unaware that only a few feet away in the darkness of a doorway lurked Frost's two accomplices. Nor did he notice that the light in which he stood was beginning to flicker. All his efforts were concentrated on listening for the sound of footsteps coming towards him from the direction of the street. It was a strain listening, as nearly all sounds were muted by the roaring of the white water between the piers of London Bridge only a hundred yards distant. With only a minute to spare, Jack discerned the unmistakable figure of Frost at the top of the lane. After regarding him for a moment as if to make sure he was alone, Frost began to walk the fifty yards or so down the lane towards his enemy. He was almost certain that Shipton was alone, but he was taking no chances. As well as his cane he had a small pistol in his pocket. His padded doublet had strips of metal sewn in the lining, and his low-crowned hat was of metal covered with felt. As he walked unhurriedly down the lane he noted with satisfaction that the light behind him was starting to flicker.

Jack stood with his back towards the river, and waited while Frost approached. Under his cloak his hand felt for the pistol and quietly cocked it. When they spoke their voices were almost drowned by the roar of the cataracts under the bridge and the bumping of the boats tied up at the wharf below them; it was high tide. "I had not looked to see you again," said Frost.

"Let us hope it will be the last time for both of us," answered Jack.

"That it may be," smiled Frost, waiting for the light to go, "but if you think I am going to give you money, you are wrong. You couldn't betray me without giving yourself away."

"You're forgetting something," said Jack slowly drawing the pistol from his pocket. "Ann. She knows as much as I do, and isn't involved in anything. She could inform on you without any harm to herself."

"Ah yes, dear Ann," Frost's smiled broadened. "Where is she now?"

"Somewhere safe from you!" replied Jack.

"Are you sure there is such a place?" said Frost, and then the light went out. Jack heard the sound of running feet behind him; so that was where they were! He drew his pistol clear, pressed it against Frost's side and fired. Frost fell backwards without a cry and Jack turned, just drawing his sword clear in time to spit the first of the two, who curled up at his feet like a dog. The other was slightly behind his companion and so was able to check his headlong rush and engage Jack at sword's point. He was no fencer, however, and Jack was starting to gain the upper hand when from behind he heard a pistol shot and something passed through the folds of his cloak and shattered his left hand. Out of the corner of his eye Jack saw to his amazement Frost sitting up with a smoking pistol in his hand. He had no more time to take in the scene, however, for his opponent, realising that he was outmatched and that his advantage lay with his weight, closed with Jack and began to grapple with him at close quarters. Jack wrestled with the stronger man, hampered by his damaged left hand, and trying to draw his right clear so that he could strike the man's head with his sword hilt. Suddenly something hissed past his left ear and smashed down between them, snapping Jack's blade three inches from the hilt. It was Frost's cane; he was on his feet and had crept up on them while they struggled. Jack's opponent leapt back, and looked past both Frost and him in the direction of Thames Street, from which came the sound of shouting and running feet.

Not waiting to see what the cause of the commotion was the man stepped back into the shadows and, grasping his comrade who had struggled to his feet and was staggering about, dragged him off into the night, leaving Jack and Frost alone in their arena. Down the little lane behind them two lanterns came bobbing, as a group of men ran towards them. Before either of them could move they were caught in the light; Frost replaced his hat and Jack just had time to shove his sword hilt into his scabbard, before they stood revealed. Someone was shouting, "Ho there! Stand for the Watch!" and onto the wharf came four watchmen, two with lanterns, and a constable. Jack controlled his breathing and turned to face them, and Frost came up to his side, smiling. Jack wondered that he could stand, let alone smile.

The constable eyed them suspiciously. "We heard shots," he said. It was Frost who spoke.

"Are you sure, constable? We heard nothing."

"Well, it certainly sounded like shots," replied the constable, still examining the two by the poor light of the lanterns.

"Perhaps it was the boats banging," offered Jack.

"Sounded like shots to me," said one of the watchmen.

"Who are you anyway?" asked the constable.

"My friend Mr Simpson and I live near here," said Frost, who had noticed that the light from one of the lanterns was shining on Jack's sword blade, lying on the ground at their feet. "And we have just been drinking in the Ship in Fish Street. We have been taking the air by the river here, and discussing a little business matter." He turned to Jack. "Did you hear anything, friend?"

"Not a thing," said Jack, "but I did see two rough-looking fellows running off in that direction a few minutes ago." A drop of blood dripped from his hand and landed on his boot with a splash. No one noticed.

"That's strange, I never noticed that," said Frost, leaning against Jack for support. "Mind you, Simpson, you always were a most observant fellow. Now my good man," he smiled at the constable, "I hope you don't intend to keep us here all night?"

"Well, no Sir," stammered the constable. "That direction you say, Sir?" Jack nodded. "Right, come along, lads. Good night, Sirs!" and the constable and his men ran off the way they had come and darkness engulfed the two men again. They stood side by side until the Watch was completely out of sight, then Frost stepped to one side and swung his cane at Jack's head. Automatically, Jack raised his left arm to ward off the blow; the cane connected and he felt his wrist snap. Sickened by the pain Jack staggered backwards towards the river as Frost, walking with some difficulty, closed with him. Jack groped for his sword hilt, and using it like a knuckle-duster darted forward and struck at Frost's head. The blow caught the brim of his hat which sang metallically. Frost raised his cane for another blow, and Jack backed away unwillingly towards the shadows, afraid that the other two might still be lurking. Frost advanced; he could feel the path that one of the pistol balls had traced through his body burning like fire. The other had smashed into one of the steel plates in his doublets, shattering it and forcing fragments into his left side. His cane grew heavier; he could feel his strength draining. All he needed was one clear shot and Shipton would be finished.

He swung at Jack's head; Jack stepped back and stumbled,

falling flat on his back on the slippery cobbles. In a second Frost was over him, raising his cane for the killing stroke. Just as he did so a window opened in a house not ten yards away, and a beam of light shone out into the night between them. Frost sprang back, stifling a cry of agony; Jack drew his feet in and both fell silent in the darkness on either side. A young woman came to the window and talked over her shoulder to someone inside the room. "Look at the river," she said. "It's beautiful at night." On one side of the beam of light Jack tried to struggle to his feet; on the other Frost flattened himself against the wall and tried to creep under the window. "You can see all the lights of Southwark," the woman was saying. "Do come and look John, it's beautiful." Jack was on his feet now, as a man's voice said, "Yes, it is beautiful dear, but do come inside and close that window. You know how bad the night air is for you." The window closed and as the woman drew the hangings over it and darkness fell once more, Frost, with the last of his strength, ran at Jack, cutting down murderously with the cane as he did so. Jack ducked and side-stepped and the cane cut through the air beside him before striking a bollard on the edge of the wharf. The impact jarred Frost's arm, and the force he had put behind the blow threw him momentarily off balance as he followed it through. As he tried to recover he already knew his opponent's next move, for as Jack ran towards him, he shouted, "No!"

Head lowered, bent double, Jack cannoned into Frost, at the same time with his good arm scooping the man's legs up into the air, sending him pitching forward over the edge of the wharf and down into the dark waters, ten feet below. The water hit Frost like a stone wall, and then folded around him like an icy fist. Weak through loss of blood though he was, he managed to reach out with his left arm and grasp at one of the supports of the wharf. It was wet and slippery, and he felt his grip weakening as he tried to free his right arm from the heavy folds of his cloak which clung to him under the water. He tried to kick his legs, but found he could hardly move them; he could feel the current dragging him out towards the centre as the river rushed eagerly towards the bridge. Slowly his fingers slid over the green slime that clung to the post, and he lost his hold.

All at once the river claimed him, carrying him into its midst. Encumbered by his cloak and the weight of his doublet, it was all he could do to keep afloat as he spun in the water and found himself staring at the cataracts. Their roaring filled the air; like lions, he thought, white lions that were rushing at him. They were on him! His last thought was of Jane.

Leaning on the railing, Jack saw him vanish and sank to the floor in a swoon. How long he lay there he did not know, but it was still dark when he awoke, shivering from head to foot, and the pain engulfed him. He pulled himself to his feet, and was about to go when he saw, lying at his feet, the black, silver-headed cane. Picking it up, he weighed it in his hand for a moment, considered keeping it, then changed his mind and threw it as far out into the river as he could. Ten minutes later, on Thames Street, the watchmen hardly gave a second glance to the drunken gentleman who barged past them without a word and vanished into the night.

Three days later outside the Dog, Jack sat on horseback talking to Jane. The conversation was friendly, but punctuated by strained silences; whatever had happened in the past, there was a gulf between them now that could never be bridged. They had pulled her father's body from the river the previous day. Jack was uneasy; although it was early morning the street was gradually stirring to life. "I came to say goodbye," he said. "I can't stay long."

"I shouldn't worry, Captain; my father had many enemies. I think half of London had a reason to wish him dead. I doubt if the authorities will trouble themselves overmuch about him."

"What will become of you?" he asked.

"Oh, we'll be all right," she said. "My father was nothing if not thorough. He made full provision for me. Margaret will run the tavern for me until I come of age. Then it is mine." A long silence followed, which was broken when Jane said, "When Ann stabbed Wicks, I had the job of tending him in between Doctor Stark's visits. The wound was not serious but it festered and he became feverish. He talked a lot as he tossed and turned. He knew a lot about my father's business, and he told me what happened to John Simmons. Mr Richardson, my father's friend, had some interest in the Barbadoes, and knew a number of merchants who shipped out there regularly. It seems that when he saw how things were between John and me, my father arranged to have him kidnapped and sent out there to be sold as a slave.''

''Is there anything you can do?'' asked Jack.

''I've already done it. Mr Richardson himself is working on it. I told him that if John was not found, or if anything had happened to him, he would find himself explaining his recruitment methods to the justices.'' Jack smiled and shook his head in wonder. Jane continued, ''I did not love my father, or even like him, but I am his daughter, as his friends will discover if they get in my way.'' There was another silence. Jane began, ''You know he killed my mother?'' but broke off when she saw Jack looking into the tavern where Gog and Magog were humping barrels. ''Don't worry about them,'' she said. ''They work for me now.'' Again Jack shook his head. ''What will you and Ann do now?'' asked Jane.

''I don't know,'' said Jack. ''It didn't seem worth planning for the future before now.'' He did not relish lying to the girl, but he was determined from now on to cover his tracks.

Jane smiled. ''I wish you luck; Ann was a good friend to me. The best I ever had. Give her my love.'' Jack turned his horse's head to go and Jane said, ''My father was an evil man, but I think he loved me in his own way.''

Jack nodded. ''I don't suppose we're any of us wholly bad or good,'' he said, then, ''I hope you find John.''

She looked up at him. Her voice was a woman's as she spoke. ''Oh don't worry, Captain,'' she said, ''I'll find him.''

As Jack rode off she ran into the middle of the street and shouted after him, ''Mind how you go! I hear there are some dangerous people on the roads these days!''

It had been several weeks since Martin Bracewell had arrived, footsore, feverish and on the point of collapse, tapping feebly on the door of his house in the early hours of the morning. This day, market day, was the first since then on which he had ventured out of doors. His health had not yet fully recovered from his ordeal on the moors, nor, despite his attempts to keep his household servants quiet, had his reputation. It was now common knowledge that he had been robbed of an undisclosed but large sum, and according to what Bracewell had heard the news had not been unwelcome to some. The fact that the scriveners had so readily paid the vast sum over, and the fact that this had been due in great measure to his own fearsome reputation galled him as much as it had amused his many enemies.

As he entered the outskirts of the town he could hear the sounds he associated with market day, though they seemed this morning to be rather louder than was usual, this early in the day at any rate. The streets through which he now rode, by contrast, were strangely quiet, save for one man who appeared from round a corner and tottered towards him. Bracewell recognised the man, and was not surprised to see *him* drunk so early. What did surprise him though, was the look the man gave him as he approached, and continued to give him as he passed by. Accustomed to deference from one and all, he was somewhat taken aback by the man's insolent, knowing smile. Despite his resolution not to do so, he looked over his shoulder as he continued down the street; the man had stopped and was still staring at him, still with that infuriating smile. Bracewell was shocked; his standing had evidently suffered in his absence; he would have to put that right and soon.

Entering the town square it was immediately clear that all was not as it should be. It was as if the whole market had shifted ground to the environs of the Red Lion, leaving the animals largely unregarded in the centre of the square. Keen to find out whatever it was that was going on at the inn without his knowledge, he pressed forward through the crowd, who as usual made way for him. Yet even here, things were not as they had been; he could read it in the faces of the crowd that looked up at him as he made his way through them. It was as if they found it somehow amusing that he should have arrived at this moment.

By the entrance to the inn there stood a coach and several horses attended by the hostler and the grooms. All eyes in the crowd, however, were on the couple who stood at the door of the inn receiving the plaudits of the crowd. The lady, prettier and dressed in finer style than any Bracewell had seen in these parts, seemed a little abashed and looked blushingly across at her companion from time to time. He on the other hand was revelling in the moment, smiling, waving, addressing friends in the crowd, and directing the operations of the innkeeper and his servants, who were working their way through the throng dispensing ale with a free hand. Bracewell leaned forward in his saddle, trying to get a clearer look at the face of this man who seemed so intent on rendering the entire town incapably drunk. The face seemed familiar, but for a few moments the name eluded him. Then he heard it from the crowd, whispered from somewhere behind him – 'Shipton'. He looked again, startled, disbelieving, then he saw the man's face clearly for the first time, and he rode forward slack jawed and slack reined.

Shipton was still talking to someone in the crowd, but as Bracewell approached he looked at him and spoke, "Martin Bracewell!" The man's voice sent a chill down Bracewell's spine for some reason which he did not understand, and never did, although he puzzled over it for years afterwards. He was standing now with his hand on his sword hilt, proud and confident like his arrogant damned father.

"I see you have done me the honour of coming in person to attend me. You might have saved yourself a journey – we were about to visit you in my father's house."

"Your father's house!" Bracewell started to splutter. He was up against the side of the coach now and before he could say another word, a thin, unsmiling man with a pock-marked face had leaned from its window and tapped him lightly on the arm with a roll of parchment. Bracewell snatched the parchment from the man and brandishing it like a weapon advanced on Jack. "If this is what I think it is . . ." he began.

"A writ of trespass and ejectment from the house and lands formerly held by my father, and granted illegally to you by Parliament," said Jack.

Bracewell looked from Jack to the man in the coach; both were smiling at him now, and the crowd had fallen silent.

"You'll have a fight on your hands," he bellowed, "you'll need proof!" The man in the coach leaned back to reveal that he was not alone. In the shadows as it was, the pale face that leered out at him seemed disembodied. It was as though the attorney had cut off Overton's head and brought it, alone, to testify.

"You!" Bracewell shouted, and tried to move nearer, but his horse, as though startled by this second ghost from the past, shied away, and careered, with Bracewell out of control, almost to the Market Cross. He was out on his own once more, and tried to speak as he struggled to control his mount, but the crowd were silent no more. A hissing as of a pit full of vipers filled the square and as it reached its loudest, a clod grazed his cheek. It was swiftly followed by another and soon after that by other, less savoury missiles. Never slow to assess a situation, he turned his horse's head and trotted out of the square towards the street down which he had ridden only minutes before. Gathering speed he raced up the street towards open country pursued by the hoots of the mob, and later by the din of renewed merry-making from the square. As he sped out of the town towards the temporary shelter of the house he already regarded as lost, he passed the drunk he had met earlier. The man had sat down by the roadside to rest; as Bracewell passed he rose, and removing his sweaty cap, bowed low, toppling forward into the ditch as he did so.

At the end of an hour, Martin Bracewell had sworn at his wife and servants; summoned his bailiff and sent a rider to fetch his attorney. He looked around him. Shipton's entitlement to all that he saw was clear enough, but he nevertheless had a legal fight on his hands and he would make him fight it every step of the way. He would impose every delay possible; there was always the hope that Shipton would give up, or run out of money. The problem was that judging by that performance in the square, money was the least of Shipton's problems, whereas, in the wake of his recent robbery he was overstretched. After this he made arrangements to move himself and his family to one of the other houses.

At the end of the same hour, the tumult in the square had died down as the crowd dispersed to their homes or to spread the news to the outlying villages and hamlets. At the same time a small procession, consisting of a coach and several riders departed the Red Lion, crossed the square and left the town in the direction of the small manor house that was, for the present, the home of Mr Martin Bracewell. At its head rode Jack with Ann at his side. He was silent as they left the town and climbed slowly up the road which Jack had last travelled in the opposite direction on a rainy night more than twelve years before. Ann wondered if his thoughts were troubled by ghosts from *his* past, but his thoughts as they approached the house that had once been, and would again be his home, were all of the future.